The
WATER
CHILD

ALSO BY MATHEW WEST

The House of Footsteps

MATHEW WEST

The
WATER
CHILD

Harper
North

HarperNorth
Windmill Green
24 Mount Street
Manchester M2 3NX

A division of
HarperCollins*Publishers*
1 London Bridge Street
London SE1 9GF

www.harpercollins.co.uk

HarperCollins*Publishers*
Macken House, 39/40 Mayor Street Upper
Dublin 1, D01 C9W8, Ireland

First published by HarperNorth in 2023
This edition published in 2024

1 3 5 7 9 10 8 6 4 2

A catalogue record for this book
is available from the British Library

HB ISBN: 978-0-00-847297-9
PB ISBN: 978-0-00-847300-6

Printed and bound in Great Britain by
CPI Group (UK) Ltd, Croydon

MIX
Paper | Supporting
responsible forestry
FSC™ C007454

For my grandparents

This book contains content which might be upsetting for some readers.
Please refer to the Acknowledgements section at the back for
a list of sensitive topics.

Part One

1.

Portugal, 1754

The largest window in the house is in the parlour and it looks out over the ocean. In fact all of the windows in the house look towards the ocean: in the parlour, in her drawing room, her bedchamber, and in John's study – all the windows in the rooms she makes regular use of, anyway. Wherever she is when she is at home, all she need do is turn her head and there it is. The vast Atlantic shifting and flashing beneath the sun, a brilliant, glittering tapestry that stretches towards the blurred haze of the horizon.

A hot slice of sun falls at a slant through the glass, shining a bright diamond shape across the parlour floor. Cecilia stands carefully positioned at its edge, her toes just clear of the burning patch. Without knowing she is doing it, she shifts her feet every fifteen minutes or so, adjusting her position to account for the sun's perpetual motion through the sky. Within the shade of the house it is cool – outside, in the full glare of the afternoon heat, it is close to unbearable.

She is staring at the water. She stands with her hands clasped before her – not in prayer, though a passing observer who happened to glance in from the outside might easily mistake her stillness for that of a churchyard statue. She watches the waves. This is where she can most usually be found: at her window, watching the bay.

Her house is located at the very pinnacle of the town, proud at the summit of the cliff, below which a tumbled confusion of dry red rooftops that zig and zag in crazed, angular patterns lie in a chaotic heap, stretching down towards the glimmering sea. Viewed from above, it appears as though the entire town must have been caught up in a landslip and the local people now live in the jumbled detritus of their former homes. But the buildings are simply very, very old, and they lie where they always have, built in centuries past when the town was nothing more than a humble fishing village, well sited beside a natural harbour.

But now, springing up all around and above this ancient town, there are new buildings, tall and grand – buildings like her house. The air smells of freshly sawed wood and new paint. At all hours of the day you can hear the knock of hammers and the toothy rasp of jagged saws slicing into timber: the sounds of construction, the sounds of expansion. The majority of these new buildings stand at the clifftop: ornate jewels upon a crown of blooming prosperity.

From her window Cecilia can see the docks: the broad, bustling port that has brought such wealth and commerce to this once-sleepy town on the westernmost coast of Europe. A conveniently located, freshly minted pin at the centre of the wheel of eighteenth-century trade. The town is built by the gaping mouth of a river where it empties gurgling into the Atlantic. A natural curve of the rocks provides it with a degree of protection from the tide, which once made it ideal for catching fish and now makes it an ideal destination for merchant ships to drop anchor. They arrive from every place, carrying anything you can think of.

Bobbing within the bay are the towering mastheads of the innumerable vessels which sail in and out from port every day, evidence of the town's place at the vanguard of civilisation. Their riggings – miles of ropes tied taut and cast black against the dazzling water – fill the bottom of Cecilia's view as she gazes from her window. They look rather like spiders' webs, she thinks. Her father once told her that a ship's ropes are made from nothing more than a hardy type of grass. Sometimes she tries to imagine how many swaying fields it would take to weave just the lengths of rope she can see from her window. Enough to cover the whole of England, she supposes.

Other vessels lurk farther out in the bay, jostling for a place in port, waiting for their turn to pull in and drop anchor and spill the treasured contents heaving within their holds: all the riches and wonders you could possibly conceive. They arrive bearing jewels and ornate stones carved or raw, metals both precious and practical, beautiful fabrics and fragrant spices, herbs and incense that perfume the stale air inside the ships' bellies.

But today Cecilia is not looking at the ships, nor the harbour, nor the new buildings built along the seafront, nor the old buildings that cling resiliently to their cliffside. She is staring past them all – past them, and towards the open ocean. Beneath the blazing sun its surface ripples with endlessly mixing swirls of blues, greens, and greys, never seeming to settle on one tone no matter how intently you screw your eyes. Relax your vision, and all you see is blue. The sea and the sky become one, a single mass, like a great sheet of lapis lazuli. All across its surface ships crawl like insects – like ants scuttling on a leaf. Any of them could be the ship that she is waiting for. But even watching from her parlour window she knows, in her veins, that none of them is.

* * *

With a sigh Cecilia turns her back upon the window and her view. The comparative darkness of the room briefly obliterates her vision until her eyes gradually adjust. When she has blinked away the blindness, she is startled to discover that she is not alone. Her maid, Rosalie, a local girl – or local woman, for Rosalie is at least the same age as her mistress, if not older – is standing patiently in the doorway. Cecilia wonders how long she has been there. She wonders how long she herself has been standing, watching the ocean, silent and unmoving.

'Y-yes? Do you need something?' Cecilia asks.

Rosalie fires off a rapid patter of syllables, rising and falling inflections that Cecilia cannot make sense of. It is English, but spoken too quickly and accented for her to follow. She asks Rosalie to repeat, which she does, patiently. Her question is only about that night's meal. Cecilia indicates her preference – or at least, she thinks she does – and then she makes to leave the room, faintly embarrassed that her maid has been watching her stare out the window so idly. But there is more. Rosalie indicates with the crook of her finger that she wishes her mistress to follow.

Cecilia allows herself to be led upstairs with the uncomfortable sense that she should not allow her staff to order her about the way that Rosalie does. She had some servants in her home when she grew up, naturally, but only to cook and clean, and never to wait upon her hand and foot the way that Rosalie is employed to do. The entire arrangement fills Cecilia with a quiet discomfort. Sometimes she thinks that Rosalie is too brash, too confrontational to be proper. *Everyone told me not to hire a local girl,* she remembers as she climbs the stairs.

In Cecilia's bedroom Rosalie presents the problem. A pair of Cecilia's shoes, pumps in burgundy cotton with neat ribbons to tie around the ankles. Or, they had been. The cotton is faded and marked by blotchy patches all around the sides. The delicate silk ribbons are curled and wrinkled and fraying at the edges. They had been nice shoes, once – fine footwear, not suited for walking down at the shore amidst the sand and the stones. But Cecilia had been wearing them by the black rocks some days ago when a large wave had caught her off her guard, surging past her feet and ankles and even touching the hem of her skirt, so that they were all soaked through entirely. She should have told Rosalie at the time, instead of kicking the shoes under her bed while they were still warm and damp. Probably there was something that could have been done to save them, before the salty teeth of the sea dried into the fabric and began to destroy it.

'They are ruined,' she interrupts whatever Rosalie is saying. 'Throw them away. There is nothing else to be done.'

Her maid objects, but Cecilia quickly turns away and departs the room, evading further questions that she does not want to answer. How did your shoes come to be soaked in seawater? What were you doing by the shore, so close to the waves? *Just throw them away*, she thinks, *and do not ask me to explain*.

When she first took Rosalie on, they had conducted the preliminary interview in English, naturally, and Cecilia is positive that Rosalie had spoken it quite well at the time. But somehow between the interview and the hiring all of that shared communication seems to have slipped away, and now the two women spend the majority of their interactions struggling to make themselves understood. Perhaps Rosalie simply expects her to be able to comprehend more Portuguese than she can, having lived here for many months now. But then Cecilia reminds herself that she is the employer, and it is not proper for her to be overly concerned about such matters.

In any case Rosalie does almost everything that is required around the house without Cecilia ever needing to understand what she is up to. There are others who help sometimes: an old man with snow-white hair and a crooked back who tends to the garden, and an old woman who helps in the kitchens. Sometimes a new girl will appear and spend the day stripping bedsheets or peeling potatoes, and then vanish. She thinks they might all be related to Rosalie in some way: uncles and aunts and cousins. Certainly she did not hire them. She allows Rosalie to keep track of it all and tell her what is required each week for wages, which is never very much. That is enough to keep the household – such as it is – running.

She is still thinking about the burgundy shoes when she wanders aimlessly into the dining room. Perhaps the fabric could be saved, or the ribbons replaced; these things are not cheap. Perhaps Rosalie is already rubbing away the encrusted salt and snipping off the tattered ribbons so that she might save the pumps for herself, or as a pretty gift for some relative. Cecilia hopes that she is.

John had been with her when she bought the shoes. Not long after their arrival in this place. Now she feels a pang of regret to think of them being tossed away. John had said something complimentary – perhaps something about the colour? – and so she had bought them. It had been foolish to wear indoor shoes down on the rocks. But then, she had not really been intending to visit the shore when she left the house on that morning. She seldom does.

2.

The house this afternoon feels too quiet, too confining. The air inside is hot and stale, despite every window being thrown wide open. Through their apertures Cecilia can hear the constant symphony of hammers and saws as the town around her audibly expands.

She spends some time wandering around, standing in doorways and staring about absently – staring at the furniture, the decorations and fixtures with which she and John had filled their new home many months earlier. Perhaps half of what she sees they shipped over with them from England. As she moves from room to room, she touches those things that they brought from home – a single touch of her hand, to make them real. Two high-backed chairs made from cherry wood; a small table beside the fireplace, still scattered with toast crumbs from her breakfast; the silver sugar tongs that were a wedding gift from her Aunt Lara. Fat flies buzz around the sugar bowl, which Rosalie has neglected to tidy away.

Their other furnishings were purchased here in town: rugs and furniture and ornaments, which they traded in the exotic and startling marketplaces during those exciting few weeks after they first arrived in port. Italian, Chinese, Indian styles sit side by side; her house is like a mongrel, a halfway proper English home cluttered with curios and artefacts from a mish-mash of other cultures.

She finds that today she does not care for any of her furnishings at all. *When John comes back, we will buy all new ones*, she tells herself.

She picks an old book that travelled with her from England off the shelf and settles down to try to read. Less than twenty minutes later she returns it to its place with a maudlin sigh.

Without thinking, she finds herself back at the large parlour window, gazing out towards the ocean once again. The day has worn on, somehow, in spite of her own inertia. Time does not wait for you to fill it with meaningful activity. The sun has already started its afternoon descent across the wide open sky. She can tell just by looking at the streets below that, by now, the edge has been taken off the shimmering heat. Sharp, jagged shadows like sharks' teeth spike and stab across the descending angles of the rooftops of the town. In the distance – from the harbour – she can hear the faint clang of a tolling bell, carried up the cliffside upon the ocean breeze. Farther out the sun is throwing long shadows off the tall ships as they glide in and out from port, so that each one looks like a sickle-curved slice of dark against the radiant blue water, as though some divine being has reached down with a celestial knife and cut a series of notches out from the surface of the ocean.

She walks out of the house just as she is, without changing a thing – without pinning a cap to her head or slipping on a light shawl. Even after all this time the dense heat hits her with a surprising force. Outside her house the streets are wide and regular, as might be found in any modern European city; but two left turns and a short, brisk walk brings her to the long road that leads down the cliff,

through the old town that has stood here since time
immemorial.

As she follows the descending road, the modern buildings abruptly give way to an aged and archaic labyrinth of
squat homes, piled haphazardly one atop the other in a
warren of skewed side streets and shadowy alleys; but her
route is a straight line through them, following the steep
cliffside path directly to the waterfront. The road has been
worn so smooth with the passage of innumerable feet over
centuries that Cecilia must slow her pace to a crawl as she
descends its treacherous incline, to avoid a slip and a nasty
fall. Even so, every time she makes this descent, she is
tempted by a perverse desire to break into a run and let the
momentum of the steep cliff carry her all the way down,
faster and faster all the way to the water and, with a single
bound flying out into the bay, past the harbour and the
ships and everything.

Today, however, she takes the descent slowly and carefully. At this time of day the only faces she sees are elderly
locals, who watch her curiously as they lean from windows
or shuffle past at a bent stoop. It is only when she begins to
draw closer to the water, and the briny scent grows sharper
in the air, and gulls wheel and flap overhead scanning the
streets for any flecks of food, and the crashing surge of the
nearing tide fills her ears even over the vibrant din of the
working harbour and streets filled with commerce – it is
only here that the town comes to life. As the cliff's steep
gradient levels out, the streets begin to buzz with vitality
and threat. Here, close to the docks, where the river water
pours forth into the great Atlantic, is where the two conflict-
ing currents of the town – the old and the new – collide
with the greatest force.

Her ears are assailed by a babble of every language known
to man – or so it seems to her. People try to proposition her:
street vendors hold out their wares and call for her atten-

tion. One man slips suddenly very close to her side and hisses something she cannot understand through his teeth; Cecilia walks on, pretending obliviousness. A short way on she is forced to step to the very edge of the street to let a trio of sailors pass by, arm in arm and drunk and singing, a veritable wall of tattooed muscle. As she watches them pass there is a tap on her arm, and she turns in fright, thinking it is the unpleasant man again. But it is a tiny old woman, wrinkled like a walnut, who mutters something in words Cecilia does not know. 'I am sorry ... I am English,' she apologizes, holding her hands out and smiling weakly, and she moves on.

She comes to the docks. Cecilia moves silently, almost invisibly, slipping and weaving her way deftly between the teeming, labouring sailors. Some wear splendid uniforms but most are clad in vagabond scraps of clothing. Some wear almost nothing at all, displaying their tattoos – vibrant and frightening images that coil up their thick arms, their chests, and even their necks and faces – tattoos that tell tall tales of who they are and where they have come from, and make wild promise of where they will go next.

Cecilia spent her entire childhood, from birth to marriage, in an English port town, and she had thought herself well accustomed to the nautical world. But the sights she recognized at home did not prepare her at all for these foreign seafolk. They had terrified her at first. But John had reassured her. He told her, whatever they might look like, these are working men. Their livelihoods – and their very lives – depend upon their labour in port, and not even a pretty girl passing by will give them much cause to break focus. It is advice that she has found by and large to be true, provided she steers clear of any sailors who are too deep into their drink.

Close to the docked ships the steaming scent of hot tar scalds her nose, stronger than the smell of the sea; stronger even than the stink of dead and gutted fish, or the musky reek of working men's sweat. The market streets smell of spices and incense and perfume, but at the docks every intake of breath is a hazard. The smells there will amaze you with their vileness. They soak into your clothes and your skin. At first she found the assault on her senses revolting; but now she finds a strange sort of comfort in its controlled, orchestrated chaos. It is amazing, the things you can get used to.

She walks the length of the wharf at an unhurried pace, trying her best not to get in anyone's way, and watching her step carefully for missing planks in the boardwalk. Where there are gaps, you can see the foaming sea right below your feet. Beside the water the air is mercifully cooler, and the towering ships standing lined in their berths cast a cooling shade. The mighty vessels rise from the waters like titans stepped out of some myth, but it is a myth of the future, not of the past. Their complicated masts and riggings pierce the sky above her head, stabbing upward into the clouds. She knows that the very highest sails bear thrilling and outlandish names like moonrakers and skyscrapers – names to make you wonder at the audacity of the men who built these machines in reckless defiance of nature's dominion. If you crane your head back and try to see to their very tops, it will make you trip over your own feet, like peering upwards at a church spire when you are standing too close. Cecilia keeps her eyes downcast and watches her footing instead.

She reads the names painted onto the prows of the ships as she passes. *La Jean Baptiste*. *The Piccadilly*. *Dona Maria*. She admires their curious figureheads, some crude, some ornate, some painted and some bare, depicting ladies in finery and wild mermaids and horses and other, fantastical creatures. *Le Cheval Marin*. *Corazon de Oro*. Names that have travelled to this place from all across Europe, or farther still. Some she could not even guess at a pronunciation. The names are strange, and the ships are strangers. None of them is John's ship. But, still she keeps looking, keeps reading. She reaches the end of the wharf, the last of the ships lined up – she has walked almost to the very edge of the town, now, when:

'Mrs Lamb? But it can't be her. Why, it is! Cecilia Lamb!' The voice cuts through the harbour din as swift as an arrow, penetrating by dint of familiarity of accent and language.

Cecilia spins sharply and immediately sees a carriage standing a short distance away, where the coastal road that leads out of the town runs almost parallel with the wharf. She recognizes the carriage at once – and, in the same instant, regrets responding so quickly to the sound of the voice. Perhaps, if she had hurried away without turning to look, she could have vanished before they could be positive that they had recognized her.

The carriage belongs to the Delahuntys. At the window, alternately pointing and waving to her, is her friend Mabel, who smiles at Cecilia with a pleasure and excitement marred by only a faint shade of confusion. It is too late to do anything but smile and wave back.

Cecilia takes a few steps towards the carriage and almost crashes into a passing sailor, who snaps at her like a dog. With her heart racing and her head down, she scurries the rest of the way more carefully.

'Why, I knew it was you, Cecilia my darling!' Mabel trills. 'Mr Delahunty and I are on our way back to the house – we have spent the day at the Moroccan quarter. Isn't it just too much of a marvel? Have you seen, they have the most fascinating market: we must take you there one day, mustn't we, dear?' This she addresses to her husband, a rather plain, paunchy, somewhat older man in his mid- to late-thirties, and not particularly handsome, Cecilia thinks.

'Get in, get in.' Samuel has clambered down from the carriage while his wife talks, and now offers Cecilia his hand to assist her up. 'We'll give you a ride back up the hill.'

'Mrs Lamb, my dear, what on earth are you doing down here beside the harbour?' Mabel asks, alarmed, as Cecilia sits down in the seat opposite.

'I expect she got turned around in these infernal alleyways, didn't you?' her husband interjects. 'Though, you should take care at the docks. It is … ah, a bit rough around here, you know.'

'Indeed, did you find yourself here by accident? Well, I can understand that – it took me simply *months* before I had a sense of the place. Even now I hate to go too far by myself.' Mabel's eyes flash as she takes in Cecilia's slipshod appearance. 'It *is* rather too warm for a bonnet, today, isn't it? I almost left the house without one, myself.'

'Yes – that's right, I must have got turned around, trying to find my way in the market,' Cecilia answers quietly, as she tries to settle herself. The atmosphere is uncomfortably cloying with all three of them inside the carriage. As they begin to trundle up the curving road that will lead them back up the cliffside – back to their homes in the new town above the bay – she cannot help but cast a glance from the window. A final, longing look at the tall ships lined up, and the labouring tattooed seamen and the screeching, scavenging gulls and the spilled fish innards coating watery planks.

'I must have got lost,' she tells them, watching from the carriage window as the road curves away from the harbour scene she knows so well. She cannot seem to take her eyes from the shore, not until it has slid from her view with the turn of the road; even then she can still smell it and taste it, and feel it stirring within her blood. She thinks that she hears a voice behind them, calling her name. A voice like John's, calling out for her amidst the chaotic burble of the harbour. But she doesn't turn her head. She used to look – perhaps the first hundred times she heard him calling to her she would turn around, look for his face in the crowd – but she would never find him. He is never there.

3.

After the road has turned them enough that the port is no longer visible from the carriage window, Cecilia sinks back into her seat; she sees Samuel Delahunty do the same, for he had also been leaning forward, peering at the bustling harbour as it passed from view.

'I believe I saw them unloading a fresh shipment of tobacco,' he says to his wife. 'Remind me to send the boy down to procure some before the first hint of sunrise tomorrow. Every last leaf shall be sold and gone by eight o'clock in the morning, mark my words.'

Mabel nods demurely. Sitting side by side with her husband, she appears a tiny, delicate thing, although she is of comparable size and build to Cecilia. Mabel is a neat, elegant woman, always dressed with style and never more than a month behind the latest fashions, and always entirely kind and thoughtful in her nature, with a heart and soul every bit as sweet as her external appearance. Her eyes move constantly, roving back and forth between her two companions in the carriage and out of the windows, a smile affixed firmly to her face even when there is no obvious cause. Whenever she catches Cecilia's eye, the smile intensifies to an almost uncomfortable degree.

'It has been an age since I saw you last – how have you been, my dear?' Mabel asks. There is a note of pity in her voice that is unmistakeable.

'Oh – you know – I have nothing to complain of, really.'

'Of course. You have been keeping busy?'

'Oh, certainly,' Cecilia answers vaguely, and then pauses, but Mabel stares at her so expectantly that she feels compelled to elaborate. 'There is so much to do about the house … You know how it is, setting up a new home – not that it is *new* any more, I suppose, but … I have been redecorating, a little, for when John comes home, you know. I just bought … the most marvellous mahogany armoire. It has little elephants carved at its feet – it's very precious.'

It is only half a lie. She was admiring the mahogany armoire in the market a few days earlier and thinking how nicely it would fit in her and John's room. Now she will have to go back to the market and buy it, so that she can show it off to Mabel the next time she comes calling.

'It *sounds* precious,' Mabel agrees enthusiastically. 'How darling. And did you get a good price?'

Before she can answer, Mabel and Samuel begin providing her with unsolicited advice about securing a fair deal in the town's mercantile bazaars, a favoured topic among all of her English friends. 'A good rule of thumb: if you paid even half of what was asked, then you've been swindled!' Samuel tells her with a snorted laugh.

The carriage rolls over an uneven stone and his leg clumps heavily against the floor. Hidden inside his long boot is a shin and a foot built from wood, the result of an old sailing injury. Hearing its lumpen thud causes Cecilia to wince with distaste as she unwillingly imagines what such a thing might look like. Samuel Delahunty is a large man in height and breadth, and it seems difficult, now, to imagine that he ever went to sea. There is a quality to both his persona and his physique which means that whenever

Cecilia looks at him, she cannot help but think that he must be a very difficult man to knock down.

By now the carriage is nearing the crest of the cliff. Mabel says, 'It is so good that you are settled here, my dear. I remember, everything seemed so foreign and frightening to me when we first arrived.' She glances furtively out of her window, as though the sun-baked streets outside still hold some lingering dread. The Delahuntys only arrived in this port some six months or so ahead of John and Cecilia, when Samuel took on some sort of nebulous, high-ranking position in the harbour bureaucracy. But they have lived overseas for many years before this, and are experienced Englanders abroad – compared to Cecilia Lamb, at least.

The carriage arrives at Cecilia's home, and she is able to say her goodbyes and thank-yous and, at last, take her leave. She still feels a squirming embarrassment inside her gut at being spotted by her friends in the rough and unbecoming environment of the dockyards, with no plausible explanation at the ready. Nevertheless she is grateful that, on this occasion at least, she has not had to make the steep climb homeward on foot.

Mabel Delahunty will not permit her to take her leave until a further meeting has been agreed to, a planned engagement this time: a dinner with Mabel and Samuel, as well as their mutual friends Captain Harding and his wife Frances, with Cecilia rounding the gathering out to an odd five. Mabel fixes a date and time there and then in the carriage – not for some weeks thankfully, after Captain Harding has returned from his own current expedition at sea – and Cecilia acquiesces politely, if reluctantly.

It is not that she doesn't want to see her friends, of course – the truth is she does not see much of anyone besides Rosalie, now – but that is precisely the reason for her reluctance. What can she possibly have to say to anyone, living the way she does? What happy news or cheerful word does she have to share? She feels drained, already, after a short carriage ride of minutes with these two. Her face aches from arranging it into a shape resembling a smile. *And besides*, she thinks, *they will all only look at me and think of John, and then they will pity me, which I cannot stand.*

Cecilia smiles, and nods, and confirms the dinner with Mabel, even as a leaden cannonball of anxiety takes form and begins to roil and roll within the pit of her stomach.

It has been fourteen months since Cecilia was married to John Lamb. It was not an especially good match for her, perhaps. As the younger of only two daughters to a relatively prosperous wool merchant, her father could offer a decent income; not to mention that she still had both youth and beauty on her side, being only just eighteen years of age at the time they were wed. She is not uncommonly handsome, she does not think, although there is nothing about her of which she is particularly ashamed, either – even if her yellow-brown hair does sometimes flash a bright shade of ginger when the sun is high. Back in England her friends had all told her she was pretty – but then again, she had called them all pretty as well, even those that she did not think really were.

Had she wished it, it is true that she might well have done better than John Lamb. Better than a ship's mate with plentiful ambition but no family name nor independent wealth to speak of, a runaway from the far-flung glens of the Scottish Highlands. But John was her choice, and she his: they had married for love.

To Cecilia's relief, and no small surprise, her father and her Aunt Lara – her father's sister who had largely raised her nieces after their mother's death when Cecilia was still very young – had not objected to the pairing at all. After waiting for Cecilia's three surviving brothers as well as her elder sister Louisa to grow to adulthood and depart the family home, she suspects that her aunt and her father were grateful just to get the last of the children out of the house. Whatever their reasons for permitting her marriage, she had been overwhelmingly happy.

Her friends back home had cautioned her not to marry a sailor. They were absent for such long periods, and you never truly knew where they went, or what they had been up to; they picked up wild and coarse habits from too much time with only other men for company – many of them foreigners, no less; they might be injured or crippled at any moment, and then you were left caring for and supporting an invalid – or, worse still, widowed! – before you were even twenty. But Cecilia had not cared to listen to any of that. She had cared only for John, known only that he was to be the one for her. Her friends had said, *He is not even a captain yet; he does not even have his own ship*. But John had plans.

Less than three months after their wedding day they had set sail from England, bound for this swelling and sweltering new harbour town on the continent, tucked along the lower half of the long and ragged Portuguese coastline. Again, her friends had counselled her not to depart too recklessly – though even the most sensible among them could not help but sigh at the romantic attraction of such a bold upheaval – but, again, her father and aunt had remained largely detached and had spoken no word of objection. John's friend on the continent, Mr Fitzgibbon, had sworn that he could secure him a captaincy among the myriad merchant companies setting up. And, just over four weeks following their arrival in port, Mr Fitzgibbon had made good on his promise. Now Captain Lamb, her husband had set sail once again with his own command, on a course bound for the West Indies. Since then, now aged just nineteen, Cecilia Lamb has lived all alone in her strange new home.

It seems so curious, now, to think of the friends she had back in England. She has not kept in touch with any of them. When she had first arrived in Portugal, she had wanted to send them letters – she had written pages of correspondence, in fact – but she had not known how to post them. John had said that he would show her, but he had gone to sea before he could do so, and so the unsent letters sat uselessly in her desk drawer. Mabel Delahunty or Frances Harding could have told her what to do easily enough, no doubt, but with all of the excitement of her new home she did not make it a priority to ask. The letters could wait, she thought. And then, with John away, and her new home still as foreign and intimidating as the day she first stepped into port, she swiftly found that she had nothing new to write. After a few months had gone by, she had put her unsent letters onto the fire. They seemed embarrassing and juvenile to her, then – full of childish expectations and stupid romantic notions.

If she were to try to write a letter now, she would have nothing to say. She has no news, no exciting dispatches from her exotic life on the continent. She could fill a page with nice-sounding platitudes, but what would be the purpose? And besides, none of her English friends have ever made any effort to write to her, either, as far as she knows. Perhaps they were never so close as she had thought.

She does wish that she could write to her sister Louisa, or even to her aunt. More than that, she longs to read a letter written by them. A letter filled with bland and unremarkable news from back home. A letter about Louisa's children, Cecilia's little nephews and nieces whom she has never met, or telling her how Louisa's husband's cows have been milking on their Devonshire farm; she would even gladly read correspondence from Aunt Lara concerning her father's gout, just to know they were all still there, still in England, and that not very much had changed without her.

But she could not write a letter full of lies to Louisa; and she would never wish to burden her sister – a new wife herself and already a busy mother – with how dull and maudlin her own married life has become. Louisa would only worry. And of course she still does not know how to send a letter to England anyway, and now she is too embarrassed and ashamed to ask. It seems like a failure, as if she has not acclimatized to her new home at all.

More even than her family in England, she wishes she could write to John, or that he would write to her – except she does not know where precisely in the world he is. Somewhere between here and the West Indies, she has to suppose, though after almost a full twelve months at sea it is anyone's guess.

She remembers the captains' wives back in England discussing the letters they had received from their husbands, deployed to some foreign port. They had passed them around and shared them quite freely with each other, as if they were periodicals about the fashions at Versailles. As a child Cecilia had listened, enraptured, whenever her aunt had entertained. It had all sounded utterly romantic to her at the time; communications that had been carried from halfway around the world, fleeting accounts of exciting lives on foreign shores and fond remembrances, written in ink and sealed tight to be borne overseas, not to be read until weeks or even months after they had been committed to paper – read, she always imagined, through eyes that brimmed with lovestruck tears. At the end of each letter the intrepid sailors would give instructions of where and when they could be contacted next, so it became a sort of race for their beloved to craft a sweet and tender response so that – God and trade winds willing – it would reach their husband's next posting before they had shipped off again. To her youthful mind the whole enterprise had seemed completely thrilling and impossibly dramatic.

Of course, when Mrs Ashdown had permitted Cecilia to read one of her husband's dispatches from overseas, it had for the most part been a matter-of-fact account of the wind speeds facilitating his journey so far, with an alarmingly detailed sidenote concerning a bout of dysentery that had swept through the crew. There had only been a single and fairly perfunctory paragraph of fond remembrances right at the end. At the time she had still supposed that paragraph must have been extremely romantic to Mrs Ashdown, having travelled so far to reach her.

She has outgrown her childish fancies of letter-writing now. But still she thinks it would be nice to be able to write to one's husband while he is overseas, or to receive a dispatch from him, no matter how abrupt and businesslike the content.

John had taken an entirely pragmatic view of the whole notion. The enterprising and uncertain nature of his voyage made matching locations and dates an inexact science at best. 'Better that we do not raise each other's hopes with the prospect of our letters reaching the other,' he had told her cheerfully. 'You know that half of what's written never makes it to wherever it's supposed to go – more than half, in all probability. And speaking for myself, I should sooner not burden another man to carry my personal correspondence.'

He had smiled kindly at her disappointment. 'In any case, this shall only be a short voyage. We'll see each other again soon enough. Six months, if the wind favours us – or perhaps so long as eight – and I'll be home again. Like as not you would see me in person before any letters I sent to you, anyway. You do understand, don't you, Cissy? We don't need any bonny words on paper to remind each other of our love, do we, lass?'

She had smiled at him, and she had nodded and told him she agreed.

John had not even wanted her to accompany him to the docks to wave goodbye as he set sail. 'No such sentimentality,' he had insisted. 'It's all uncouth labour down there, and no fine place for a wife of mine. And besides, if you come to the harbour to wave me off on my first voyage, then it shan't feel right unless we do the same for the second. And then, before you know it, we'll have ourselves a tradition to maintain; and traditions soon become superstitions that hold us under obligation.'

'But, John –'

'Now, don't think me unfeeling, Cissy,' he had said. 'Look what I have bought, here. A ring, with a compartment to hold a lock of your hair – if you will permit me to cut … Now, you see, it is fastened inside, and I shall take it with me. It shall never leave my finger. Wherever on the globe I am – whichever sea I sail in – there shall be a piece of you with me, always and forever. And now, I must away, or else they'll set sail without me, captain or not. If you'll allow a simple farewell kiss here – thank you – and I'll be back, Cissy, before you even think to miss me! Goodbye! Goodbye!'

4.

Cecilia stands at her parlour window, again. The ocean radiates blue and wondrous, as far as the eye can see. She rubs her tired eyes and pushes her fingers through the long tangles of her hair – it is growing too long, uncomfortable in the heat and difficult to maintain, and she wonders if she could ask Rosalie to trim it.

As she stares out of the window, the industrious sounds of the town filling her ears, she wonders what there is to be done with her day. She can find nothing. No purpose or goal, no practical use that she could put her time to. Her mood grows at first despondent, and then indignant. Have you really become so sluggish a wife already? A tired old madam before you are even twenty?

On the horizon ghost ships mingle, half-formed against the brilliant white haze where the sky meets the sea. Vessels that float along the very edge of the visible world, shimmering where the waters merge with the heavens, barely glimpsed over distances incalculable to her eye. These strange vessels rise from the surface of the sea, all impossible shapes and angles. Some of them coalesce and take form, and lose their fantastical proportions and become real ships – dull constructs of wood and metal and rope, crewed by weary men that surge with the tide for port. But some of the ghost ships stay on the horizon's blur, floating past for a time, until at last they simply fade from view. They vanish back into the unknowable ether where they came from, and Cecilia can only guess at whether they were ever really there or not.

She tells herself, *My home is out there, too*. Not so very far away from where she stands, these same chilly Atlantic waves roll and bash against the shores of England. *When John returns, as he surely will, then – perhaps – we might go back. Leave this lonely place that is doing me no good*. She thinks that John will understand.

She wonders: if she were to sail back to England, would she discover there, still standing on the seashore, the parts of her that she left behind? The person that she once was – whatever hopes and ambitions she once had, that she cannot now for the life of her seem to recall? The person who knew how to fill her days without staring moon-eyed and vacant at the ocean. Perhaps she is still there, waiting for the rest of herself to come back. *The person that I once was, back in England, before I was just a sea captain's wife*.

From her window lookout she can watch the weather as it rolls across the horizon. Dark armadas of storming clouds grow and swell several miles distant, spreading across the sky with a startling swiftness for all their immense bulk. They hang thick and heavy with murky rolls of rain, and then burst and dissipate far out at sea, spilling their contents in shifting columns of shadow. Sometimes thin spider-webs of lightning flicker above the water many miles away, even while sunbeams fall brightly upon the town below. On occasion a pealing downpour will make it so far as the shore, and she watches as the ships race to make it safely to port before they are overwhelmed by the tempest. Other times she sees thick banks of white fog drift in and blanket the town completely, obliterating the ancient, narrow streets and red rooftops in its vapours until all that is visible are the very pinnacles of the masts of the ships huddled in the harbour.

Most days, though, the far-off weather simply blusters and swirls meaninglessly over the ocean and never even comes close to touching land. Today the weather is fine, and the sun spears the sea with dazzling beams that dance and play across the brilliant azure surface of the water. Cecilia watches as a magnificent frigate, a giant even among its fellow ships, drifts into the bay. She can practically hear the slap of waves against its hull and the calls and cheers of its crew as they close into port after however many long weeks and months they have been at sea. She can picture them hanging recklessly over its sides, dangling from the rigging for a first glimpse of longed-for landfall – licking their lips, their stomachs rumbling with strange appetites.

The imaginary scene is inviting – she wants to go down there, walk the steep slope of the cliffside and stand close to the water's edge once again. Like all children who were raised beside the ocean, Cecilia holds the tang of saltwater in her veins. It will never leave her. Though it is true that she was not made to be a sailor – her one experience of sea travel, from England to this place, was not an enjoyable journey – nevertheless she sometimes feels a need to hear the roaring call of the ocean and stare across its seemingly infinite expanse, for no reason she can adequately explain. It has always been this way. But these days she feels the need growing like an addiction. Something she cannot do without.

She can remember a time when she had watched the sea with a hopeful anticipation of her husband's return. That had subsided after the first eight months or so. But Cecilia has not lost hope entirely. She is no fool, and she knows what happens to husbands at sea; sometimes they drown, and sometimes they find something new across the waves and they just don't come back. But John *is* coming back. She has to believe it. And somehow, even after so long with no news of her husband whatsoever, she still does believe it. There is something in the pit of her stomach, something she can hear in the whisper of the tide, that tells her that John will return. She has felt this unexplainable certainty about things before, and, in the end, she has always been proven right.

For now she just watches. The sight of the ocean is mesmerizing; it is intoxicating. Its shining, dancing surface, and its rich, abyssal depths concealed below. Its scent of decay and its echoing hollow roar. They hold a fascinating sway over her, in a way they never did when she stared at the grey and chilling waters off England. She cannot look away. The Atlantic Ocean has its hooks in her, and she is drawn back, time and time again. And so she goes.

Today Cecilia resolves to at least give her trip to the shore a purpose. She dresses and sets out for the town's sprawling markets with the vague objective of finding some new object to put about the house. Perhaps that mahogany armoire, which she had mentioned to Mrs Delahunty, if she can track it down again. And if she finds herself in the vicinity, then she may visit the offices of John's merchant company and enquire after any news. It has been some time since she has done so, after all.

She considers bringing Rosalie with her, for safety and companionship – perhaps, she thinks, if they were to spend some time together, then she and her maid might begin to grow close. But in the end she leaves her house alone.

She is determined that her route should not bring her directly to the harbour and the surging waves, like it usually does. But in this town there is no escaping the sea; it rises from the deep bay and permeates the streets with its presence. It swirls through the hot air, its scent always in your nostrils and its taste damp upon your tongue. It is in every naval uniform she sees, every mysterious foreign word she hears. It is in the clink of the coins that change hands among the market traders: shillings and peça, livres and doubloons. Coins of copper and nickel and silver and gold, metals mined all over the world and carried here for jangling commerce.

What is called the town's market is nothing that she would have recognized as such back in England. Traders set up their stalls pressed on either side of the streets wherever there is space, while shoppers jostle and browse, elbowing through the bazaars, packed tight like cattle. Here, too, among the goods and wares available for purchase, the sea is everywhere. There are sailors' things, practical tools and minor luxuries for their next voyage: quadrants and compasses, new hats and gloves, sewing kits, sticks of cheap tobacco, and hard, durable cheeses. And there are the ocean's treasures brought to land, scrubbed and scoured clean of the salt and rot and offered up for sale. Pretty shells and coral are offered as ornaments or jewellery, while fish with shocked, gaping expressions are on sale for the cooking pan. The narrow streets resemble nothing less than an Ali Baba's cave of foreign and exotic treasures: silks and spices and precious gems; silverware and china plates; and curious animals locked in cages. Lacquered furniture that would make her the envy of any of her friends back home lies piled in heaps like firewood.

Set just back from the main thoroughfares, in the shadows all around, lurking in doorways and down side-alleys, there are sleepless-looking women dressed up like silken butterflies. It had taken Cecilia some weeks before she had realized that they are prostitutes, pretending disinterest but keeping careful watch for any likely customer among the passing sailors and civil servants, all hours of the day. Also watching, also lurking, are young men dressed as sharp as stilettos in tight breeches and embroidered coats, and loitering in poses of affected, languorous boredom. These young men observe everything and everyone that passes through the markets through the tails of their heavy-lidded eyes. One of them catches Cecilia's gaze as she walks by, and his thin lips curl back into a smile. She almost expects to see pointed teeth revealed there.

Sometimes she thinks she should feel more unsafe than she does roaming the lanes and alleys alone. She must stand out: a young woman walking unaccompanied, and marked by her features and her hair and her dress as a foreigner – though that is hardly uncommon here. Over time she has practised and perfected a way of fixing her gaze at some point in the distance, some indistinct spot just beyond her immediate surroundings, while she walks. By this method she hopes to always appear to be heading somewhere with a purpose. She sets her expression as though she were looking out for someone in the crowd – a beau she is planning to meet, perhaps, and who she wonders if she has just glimpsed – as if she is right upon the cusp of breaking into a smile and a wave.

She is exploring the market streets this way – led by an imaginary acquaintance that she is always, in her mind's eye, heading towards – when she turns a corner on a whim. Immediately the soft hairs upon her neck rise, and a sharp twist of foreboding stabs into her gut; the feeling rotates into her, like a skewer through a piece of meat. She pauses mid-step and screws her eyes. There is nothing untoward visible in the street ahead, not yet, but she knows – she *knows* – that something is coming. To her side a mother walking hand in hand with a young child brushes past, but Cecilia snatches out impulsively and catches the mother's arm, pulling her back. The mother turns to look at her full of shock and indignation, but Cecilia shakes her head in mute warning.

One second later and it comes. Raised voices audible from the far end of the street – yelps of alarm, and then a full-blooded scream. The crowd seems to part like water, and then something small and dark and misshapen lurches into view. An ugly little troglodyte creature in the approximate shape of a man, naked save for some sort of primitive hair shirt, comes careening around the corner, scampering on stubby legs and waving its long arms in the air, its gruesome face twisted into a wild grin of riotous energy. Cecilia recognizes then that it is no type of man at all, but a largish ape, running loose through the market streets. Men come running behind it, shouting and carrying ropes and sticks – but when the ape halts its rampage in the middle of the street and reels around to peer at them, they freeze in place, too, apparently afraid to get too close.

The ape stops, and sits, and rocks on its haunches and looks around. The street has fallen so silent that Cecilia can hear the creature burbling to itself, like a baby. Then, with a sudden shriek, it reaches out a long, hairy limb and lifts a nearby market stall from the ground with a single, mighty jerk of its arm, flipping it and sending an array of fine china crockery flying and shattering all around. The vendor cries out in dismay but remains pressed as tightly as he can against the building behind; the ape shrieks with a savage, childish delight at its destruction.

A sailor steps forward from the crowd then, with a pistol drawn. He holds it at arm's length and brings it to aim upon the oblivious beast. Time seems to freeze, just for a second; Cecilia's heart skips a beat in anticipation of the roar of the shot and the vision of senseless bloodshed. But, mercifully, the sailor's decisive action seems to spur life into the men chasing the ape. One of them immediately steps in front of the sailor, blocking his aim and crying out in protest. Three others move swiftly to surround the primate, which has not moved; now it spins about, looking from one man to the next and shrieking, its powerful arms flailing around threateningly.

In an instant all four men have fallen upon it, and there is a great tumult of cries and screams – man or beast, she cannot tell – and then, finally, they have it tied up, arms lashed to its sides and a rope around its neck. The ape lies on its side, writhing and screeching pitifully. One of the men staggers back from the melee with his hands upon his face, ruby blood streaming from between his fingers. Both the injured man and the bound ape are led away with no further word of explanation nor apology, hobbling and limping hurriedly back to wherever it was they all came from. The entire spectacle lasts for barely a minute, and then the street is quiet again.

At length, the involuntary audience to this bizarre scene seems to exhale a collective sigh of relief. The breath that they had all – man, woman, and child – been holding on to is released. Voices resume, laughing nervously and exclaiming in various tongues: *What a curious sight that was to behold!* The young mother beside Cecilia turns to her, one hand upon her heart and the other still protectively clutched around her little boy as if the villainous ape might yet return to snatch him away with a shriek. The mother expresses her thanks in breathless French. If Cecilia had not stopped them, then mother and child would surely have walked directly into the wild beast's path. With the little of the language she can remember, Cecilia modestly dismisses her role as nothing but fortunate timing.

'But, how did you know that anything was coming?' the mother asks, wide-eyed.

'I just did.' Cecilia smiles and lifts her shoulders in a shrug, and she continues down the street.

5.

Two days later and Cecilia is back at the harbour. Its pull is irresistible, despite the potential for prying eyes to observe her out of her element. She is still cautious after her previous surprise encounter with Mabel and Samuel Delahunty. Even though her friends had not pressed her for an explanation of her business on that occasion, she is nonetheless embarrassed that they witnessed her roaming the docks alone. If they only knew how often she has walked that same, aimless route past the lined-up ships, for no reason that she can really explain ... Most likely they would confine her to her bed and summon a doctor. But she tells herself: *It cannot be a morbid obsession, to simply wish to hear the sound of the waves.*

Today, to give her walk through the sun-washed streets some sense of pragmatism, she makes an overdue visit to the offices of the merchant company that chartered John's ship, in one of the grandiose new buildings that stand tall and shining along the waterfront. There was a time when she called upon them almost weekly hoping for news, but her attentiveness has waned with time. As usual she does not make it past the sparkling, oak-lined foyer. The pleasant young man waiting in the reception tells her there is still no word from John's vessel.

'Who is it that plotted their course? May I speak with him? Perhaps he has some notion of where they might have ended up,' she asks.

'The voyage was bound for the West Indies, and thereafter to follow its own course along the coast of the Americas seeking trade and profits at the captain's discretion.'

'I know that,' she replies with strained patience. 'But who decided the course across the Atlantic? Perhaps they were taken off their intended route and decided not to aim for the West Indies at all.'

'Captain Lamb himself decided the route, naturally, in consultation with Mr Emmerich.'

'Mr Emmerich? And may I speak with him?'

'Mr Emmerich is the ship's master,' the young man tells her. When she does not appear satisfied with that explanation, he adds, 'He is also on the voyage. On board your husband's ship. So I am afraid that it is impossible to speak to him. We anticipate word from them any day now. We will send a boy for you the very second that we have news, Mrs Lamb.'

Back in the streets, everywhere she goes she sees John's face. Perhaps it is because she is always pretending to recognize faces in the crowd – walking around imagining she is on her way to meet someone – that means she ends up thinking she *does* see him, on every street and around every corner. She spots him paused at a market stall, touching his finger to pair of Spanish boots and asking the merchant for a price. She has seen John shuffling cards and laying bets with seamen in squalid alleyways. She has seen him hauling crates and heaving ropes on the waterfront. She has seen him, many times, walking directly towards her, and she has smiled and almost raised her hand to wave at him with relief and delight: *Imagine, that we should find each other again, after so long, and here, of all places!*

But time after time, when she looks again, the face is no longer his. Usually it was never even like her husband's at all, save for some small detail: in the colour of the hair or the way it drops in curls over his forehead, or the squashed shape of the nose, or a paunchy slant of the jowls. On second glance the faces inevitably belong to some other man she does not know, and her momentary flight of surprise and happiness is brought crashing down into disappointment. Other times it is his voice that she hears, calling out her name above the general hubbub of the crowd. But whenever she looks around for him, he is never there.

No one pays her any mind at all if she just stops and stands on the dock. She is as good as invisible, a lone Englishwoman taking up a single square foot of space on a teeming foreign wharf. She is standing in this way, watching the ships as they come and go, and blissfully minding her own business, when:

'Excuse me, madam?'

The voice surprises her out of her daydream. She turns sharply and sees that a young man, dressed like some sort of petty official with a smart coat and cap, has approached. He lingers a short distance away, as if uncertain whether it would be proper to step any closer.

When Cecilia doesn't reply, he repeats, 'Madam, excuse me?'

'Yes?'

'I am sorry to intrude upon you, but I do believe that I have some correspondence for your attention.' The youth's accent is foreign but his English is clear. His tidy appearance and polite manner stand him a mile apart from most of the wild and swaggering sailors and dockhands.

Cecilia blinks. 'Correspondence? For my attention?'

'I believe so, yes. I apologize for intruding upon your peace just now. I was to deliver it up to your home, you see' – he points up the cliff – 'but, well, by good fortune I have found you here …'

'A letter for me? Are you sure?' she asks, bewildered. The young clerk begins to flick through a thick sheaf of papers he is carrying, scanning what she presumes is a list of names written there. 'Mrs John Lamb?' she prompts, with a hopeful skip in her heartbeat.

'Yes – yes, right here. Mrs John Lamb. There is a bundle of letters for you, actually. Perhaps you have been expecting them? There was a delay in their delivery, I fear. If you would just follow me, I can explain everything.'

Her head swims for a moment, and although the young man half-turns to move away, she cannot take a step after him. Letters from home? Letters from John? Could it be possible? The clerk watches her expectantly, waiting for her signal that he might lead her wherever it is they must go. With an effort of self-control she nods, and they both begin to walk.

Hurrying after the young man's brisk stride she asks, her voice high and shrill: 'You mean to say that you have letters for me? From whom – from my husband?'

'That's right, ma'am. Mr John Lamb.'

'But – but I am afraid I don't understand. How did you know who I was when you saw me?'

He does not seem to hear her over the harbour's din. They arrive abruptly at a small desk that has been set up right there upon the pier, in the shadow of a docked brigantine. Behind the desk a fat, dirty man wearing a battered tricorn hat looks up at them – first at the boy with a derisive sneer, and then at Cecilia. His eyes widen slightly and his features soften.

'Mrs John Lamb,' the young man declares crisply. 'I believe there is a parcel of letters, from Mr Lamb – there was some sort of delay,' he reports, tapping the papers in his hand.

'*Captain* John Lamb,' Cecilia corrects him.

'Right, right, right.' The older man yawns, sniffs, and straightens his posture. 'Lamb … Lamb …' He has his own excess of papers to sort through, which lie stacked in some disarray across the desk; Cecilia watches on, her mind spinning.

'I am afraid that you have me most confused,' she ventures to say, after several seconds. 'Do you mean to say … Do you mean to tell me that my husband has written to me, several times? From where? And how – how did you come by these letters?'

'That is our business,' the older man tells her, squinting up from his documents. 'People write letters, they pass them to us. We deliver 'em where they need to go. Pretty name, Lamb. You wear it better than your husband, I'd wager.' He winks. 'Ah – here it is, Omar.' He hands one of his papers to his young colleague, who reads it quickly and then runs up the gangplank of the docked ship.

'Omar shall return with your letters forthwith, my good lady. Now – as to the fee, let me see … it shall come to the sum of two pounds and ten shillings. The price is quoted in English pounds, naturally, but I can accept the local currency – or most others, at your convenience.'

'Two pounds and ten shillings! I do not have so much on me. But – surely my husband has already paid you, when he sent his letters?'

'The fee is only payable upon delivery, dear lady. Our assurance to the customer, you see. Should we fail to deliver, they do not pay.'

'But I didn't know anything about this,' Cecilia exclaims. 'How can you ask me to pay so much when I was not informed beforehand?'

'I expect that your husband likely mentions it in his

letters.' The man smirks and passes a grubby sleeve across his lips.

Cecilia looks up at the ship. She can hear its boards groaning and grumbling with the sway of the tide. High above where she stands a sailor is leaning idly over the helm, his great, sunburned arms dangling downward, watching the proceedings below dispassionately. The sailor looks back at her, and then leans forward and spits a jet of brown tobacco that lands noiselessly in the water below.

John could have written letters to me from wherever he is, she thinks. To explain his long absence, perhaps. It would make sense that he should write. *Isn't this what I have been hoping and longing for?*

'I do not have so much money upon my person,' she tells the man behind the desk. 'Perhaps you should deliver the letters to my house, as commissioned, and I can pay in full then.'

He jabs a finger underneath his tricorn and scratches at his scalp. 'What do you have? I should be more than happy to hand the letters over now, for a sum smaller than the full amount. I can send Omar to collect the remainder later, at your convenience. I should hate for you to leave the dock today, madam, without seeing what your husband has written. How much can you pay me, right now?'

Doubt is tapping out a rhythm at the back of her head, quiet at first but now louder and faster. She looks up at the ship again – there is no sign of the younger man returning. 'If what you tell me is true,' Cecilia says slowly, 'then you should let me at least see the letters first. Then I shall pay you what is owed.'

'Omar shall return with them forthwith. You might have sent a gentleman aboard with him, but, ah – you seem to be here alone, no?' He leans back in his creaking chair. 'I am happy to take whatever you have on your person, at this time. Better that we complete the financial aspect, now, if you please. You see … I have known ladies to become so entirely overcome by emotion at the merest sight of their husband's handwriting – well, best get the business side of things out of the way first, hmm?'

Cecilia takes a step back from the table. She shakes her head. She is positive, now; she can feel it inside, her every nerve on edge and telling her to walk away.

'How could your man have recognized me,' she asks, 'as I was standing upon the wharf? No … No, I do not believe that you know who I am, after all, or who my husband is. I am sure there has been a mistake. Any letters that you have are undoubtedly not addressed to me. John would not entrust such things to … There has been a mistake.'

The man raises his bushy eyebrows in astonishment. 'Mrs Lamb. You do not wish to receive the letters that your husband has written for you?'

She shakes her head, and with a trembling voice declares, 'There are no such letters, I believe. I cannot imagine where the confusion is, or … or what your business is about here. But I *am* certain that I should not become involved. And … I expect that any of the British officers to be found hereabouts on the dock would agree with me, were I to find one and ask him to take an interest.'

The man leans back in his chair, turns his head slightly and regards her wryly under the brow of his battered hat. 'Well, then,' he grunts, 'in that case you can kindly fuck off.'

6.

When Cecilia tells Mrs Harding about her encounter with the two villains at the docks, her friend immediately puffs with the comfortable outrage of someone who was neither involved nor injured in the offending act.

'My goodness! How terrible! I am entirely shocked, Mrs Lamb. But it does not surprise me in the slightest. I do fear that such confidence tricks are all the rage these days among the dregs of society. These charlatans seek to prey upon a wife's instinctive concern for her husband when he is at sea – her natural weakness and suggestibility, you understand, at a time when her poor mind is otherwise overwhelmed. It is unconscionable, and scarcely creditable, but I have heard similar stories before.'

Frances Harding takes a long sip of her tea before continuing. Cecilia sits beside her on one of Mrs Harding's wide, oriental settees. 'Such men are truly capable of anything,' she goes on, repeating ominously, '*anything*. You did well to see through the ruse, my dear – you are to be commended. I can only imagine that the entire experience was most distressing for a person of your sensitive character.'

Cecilia does not argue with this; there does not seem to be any point in disputing that her character must indeed appear rather sensitive to the eyes of a woman like Frances Harding.

'I sometimes have a feeling for such things,' Cecilia tells her instead. 'A feeling inside – in my stomach – that tells me when something is wrong.'

'Feminine intuition,' Mrs Harding agrees.

'No – no, I don't think it is that, precisely. Oftentimes I just feel as if I know that I am about to hear bad news or see something awful. Sometimes I can do something to stop it, or at least stop myself from seeing or hearing it. Though not always.'

Frances clicks her tongue. 'In any case, we must tell Captain Harding, when he comes home. And Mr Delahunty as well. I am sure that the port authorities will be able to do something about your case.'

Mrs Harding has been, after Mabel Delahunty, Cecilia's closest companion since she and John arrived here from England. Their husbands, Captain Harding and Mr Delahunty, are her friends as well, of course, in as much as their company signifies. If Cecilia had ever needed to know the going rate for West Indian tobacco, or when the next Dutch schooner was due to arrive in port, she knew who she could turn to. They are all of them travellers from Britain, self-imposed exiles who have arrived in this place for their own, private, reasons. Being born upon an island off the northern edge of Europe is where the similarities between Mabel Delahunty and Frances Harding end, however. Where Mabel is entirely soft and sweet in nature, with a gentle and pliant – if sometimes overbearing – concern for her friends, Frances is all sharp and abrasive edges, though no less kind, in her own way.

'Thank you,' says Cecilia, 'but I really don't see what the authorities could do now. And I am no worse for the experience, truly.'

'Just so. In any case, the villains are probably halfway to Calcutta already, now that you have exposed their ruse. If only I had been there, too!' Frances adds with gusto, though she does not elaborate as to why. She stands up and begins to fuss impatiently around the room, punching silken cushions and brushing her fingers across surfaces that are entirely devoid of dust.

She stops her fussing and turns to Cecilia with a look of real concern. 'Oh my, it has only just struck me how your poor hopes must have been raised and then dashed at the prospect of correspondence from Captain Lamb. There is still no word from him, or indication of where he might be? No, of course not,' she says without waiting for Cecilia to respond, and then she sighs and shakes her head. 'No, you must not dwell on such unhappy thoughts.' A sudden inspiration appears to strike Frances. 'Now, come with me, my dear. I have just the thing to divert your mind. I have some new specimens to show you.'

With some reluctance Cecilia abandons her comfortable seat and still-steaming cup of tea to follow Mrs Harding towards the rear of the house, where her large conservatory is located – an extension, built to Frances's own design, latched on to the side of the property, with one long wall and the semi-domed ceiling consisting entirely of glass, which allows the space to soak and marinade in the blazing afternoon sun. Inside the atmosphere is intolerably muggy, and scented with a sweet and acrid odour which makes Cecilia think of poison; she takes a deep, involuntary breath as she steps into the oppressive heat, and almost chokes. The glass walls are fogged and dripping with streaks of condensation. Inside the conservatory are rows and rows of cast-iron shelves, filled with cluttered arrangements of potted plants in all shapes and sizes. Some with beautiful and exotic flowers in bloom, others with leaves that are wide and sharp as daggers, or small and budding on thin stems, or creeping ivies which dangle trailing from their perches, wilting in the heat. Not one of the plants looks particularly healthy – their leaves are more yellow than green, and some are curling and browned at the edges.

This is Frances Harding's hobby: botany. More specifically, collecting and cataloguing samples of plant life from all across the globe in her treasured herbarium. Some flowers she sources from the town's markets and traders, and some are brought to her by her husband, collected on his travels; Mabel has told her that Mrs Harding also has discreet arrangements with the captain of an American clipper, as well as the first mate upon a Spanish ship, both of whom provide her with a steady stream of exotic flora.

In the centre of the conservatory a large table is set up with even more plants, still with some greenness to their colour and resilience in their upright postures. Lying open upon the table is the herbarium itself: an immense scrapbook filled with pressed flower specimens and Frances's painstaking notes and drawings.

With a scraping noise like a peal of thunder Frances drags two hefty pots across the table and briskly strokes the small, pinkish petals growing within. 'Hydrangeas, from the Far East – bought as seeds, all the way from the Korean peninsula,' she explains. 'Really marvellous specimens. They are growing nicely, don't you think?'

'How lovely,' Cecilia tells her politely. She looks around. 'Some of your plants don't seem to be taking to the climate particularly well.'

Frances follows Cecilia's gaze, towards the walls of limp vegetation that stand around them. 'Oh, but you see, Mrs Lamb, those ones are supposed to be wilting like that. You must allow them to die, just a little, before they are pressed.'

Now she grabs her large book, her herbarium, and turns it around so that it lies open before them. Frances gives a little hum of pleasure as she begins to turn the wide, crinkling pages slowly, proceeding backwards through her treasured collection. On each page the desiccated remains of a single plant lies spread out and flattened – leaves, roots, and all – decorated by a series of precise, scientific annotations and observations written by Frances. It is an undeniably impressive compendium, though the sight of the squashed remains of the flowers, and the plants all around her helplessly awaiting a similar fate in this tropical heat, strikes Cecilia as unaccountably sad and unfair.

'What are those shapes?' Cecilia asks, pointing towards the page which appears to have been left blank save for a series of precise patterns sketched in thick pencil.

'That is cross-section of the plant's stem,' Frances explains. 'As viewed through my microscope. I am not much of an artist, and try as I might, I cannot draw the plants themselves to my satisfaction, as some ladies are able to. But their internal structures I find quite fascinating. Some are entirely unique, and I find them beautiful, in their own way. Others follow similar patterns – recurring forms that occur in plants native to almost opposite corners of the globe. It is most fascinating.'

'Fascinating,' Cecilia repeats dutifully.

After perhaps a dozen more pages and plants have passed before them, Frances stops turning the pages and announces, 'I do find my herbarium a most rewarding pastime. It is so important to maintain improving pastimes and hobbies, as a married lady. To keep one's mind occupied, you understand, and to engage one's curiosity during the long days and weeks. Captain Harding is overseas right now, of course. Though I expect his return within the week.' She clears her throat, gently. 'Mrs Lamb, do you maintain any hobbies, my dear?'

'Honestly, I am not sure that I do,' Cecilia admits. 'I like to walk, I suppose.'

Frances shakes her head. 'We must find you something more productive. Idleness and lethargy can be quite fatal, you know. They are deadly to the spirit. Any competent doctor will tell you. Do you draw? Sing?'

'I played piano a little when I was younger, though I was not accomplished.'

'Take it up again. Do you have a pianoforte? I have no doubt one can be acquired for a ready price at the markets. Stimulate your interests, and keep your moods bright. It is too bad that botany does not hold much fascination for you. I understand that some ladies like to make a collection out of some little thing: postage stamps, for example. I cannot see it myself, but it holds an appeal for some.'

Frances sighs. 'It is so important to distract oneself. I know ... I do understand: the long solitudes ... and the uncertainty. Ever the prospect of tragedy, waiting at the end of it all.' Her small eyes dart away from Cecilia's, and she blinks rapidly. 'Fill your time with small, rewarding pursuits, like my herbarium, and you will be too busy to think of the future. Distract yourself from any negative prospect and you will find that everything turns out for the best.'

Cecilia frowns. 'Are you sure?'

'Of course. I have known sailors' wives to be driven half from their wits – and aged by years – when their husbands are ... absent.'

'Do you mean ... I should distract myself to stop my mind from playing tricks on me?' Cecilia asks, guardedly.

Frances's eyebrow raises a fraction.

'When Captain Harding is at sea,' Cecilia attempts to explain, 'do you ever find yourself ... imagining things? So you might think that you see his face in the crowd, even though you know he is not there? Because he cannot be, it is impossible; he is overseas.'

'Mistaken identity is quite natural,' Frances tells her, doubtfully.

'Or you see things, like ships in the distance, that are not real,' Cecilia goes on. 'Or – at times, at night, when you are alone and the house is dark, you find yourself doubting that he ever sailed away at all. You think that he is still here, with you, even as you lie in bed. You can feel his presence … in a way. As if … you had just heard his voice call out, except you didn't – you're just left with the memory of something that did not happen. I do not know how to say it. Or, when you turn over in your sleep, and you can smell the scent of his hair upon the pillow where his head never lay …'

Frances is looking at her very strangely, now. Cecilia wishes she had not said anything. 'We must find you a pastime, Mrs Lamb.'

'Yes. I shall think on it. Though, of course, I do expect Captain Lamb to return any day now, and then I shall be too busy for hobbies,' she adds, dutifully.

Frances nods. 'We all pray to see him again. And you are quite right, of course – after Captain Lamb makes his celebrated return, when next he sets sail, no doubt you shall be left with a child to take care of. Those make for an excellent distraction, I hear.' She reaches out and twists a withered, brown branch away from a nearby stem with a dry crack.

'Oh! Well, John and I have not really discussed such plans, yet –'

'Plans!' Frances laughs. 'Plans – I like that. My dear, it is only natural and inevitable. For you I am sure it will be a great relief.'

Cecilia shifts uncomfortably, unsure of what to say. The atmosphere within the conservatory feels suddenly choking. At last she says: 'We shall see.'

'I have no doubt that motherhood shall fit you like a glove, just like dear Mrs Delahunty. Of course, James and I were never so blessed. Until that day comes, find small uses for your time. Make yourself too busy to worry. Do you keep a journal? You will find that it helps.'

'Yes, I suppose that you must be right,' Cecilia says. She can feel the skin on her neck and down her back beginning to turn red and sweaty, and a nauseating spiral beginning to turn inside her guts. The heat in the room feels filthy and she has an intense desire to leave. 'I shall try to do as you say, Mrs Harding.'

7.

Cecilia considers Frances Harding's advice and decides there is wisdom in some of her friend's words. She needs a hobby, or more than one: activities to occupy her festering mind, and to hold her from slipping any farther into a deep malaise.

Drawing, painting, and music she was never very good at, and they seem immature and pointless now. But keeping a journal – writing down her thoughts and maintaining some sort of diary of these interminable days – that might be a beneficial diversion?

She locates an empty notebook, which she brought with her from England, and sits at the desk in her drawing room to begin. The blank page stares back at her like a closed window. She strains her memory: how does one begin a journal? She has done so before – many times over, she is sure. What did she write about when she was young? Was it nothing more than a simple list of her day's pursuits?

She writes:

Today I –

And then she hesitates.

Today, I what? What is there to write about her day? Today I woke late, and I stayed in bed, just listening to the sound of distant waves. Today I watched a spider as it crawled a slow progress across the parlour wall. I stood and just watched it, for perhaps a full half an hour.

Recording such bleak fascinations can lead to no good. She tears out that page, marred by its two-word false start, and on a fresh sheet she writes, quickly and almost desperately:

John is at sea. Things all came about just the way that he said they would. His friend Mr Fitzgibbon was as good as his word and secured him his own command. It was only two months after we arrived, I did not think that it would happen so fast. Now John is at sea. A ship's captain with an entire crew of men and a great galleon all under his command. I am so proud of him. The company have put great faith in him. He is due back any day now.

She stops, sits back in her chair and sighs. She reads back the banal record she has just put down. Her brow tightens, an impatient irritation flickering and sparking through her nerves.

She strains her memory. When she was a child, her journal was for her hopes and dreams – and her innermost secret thoughts. She sets her pen against the paper.

Mrs Harding tells me that John shall want for children as soon as he returns. I do not know if she is right. At first I thought, no she is not, but now I am not so certain. We have been married for a year, after all. What else do wives do for their husbands? I cannot recall John ever speaking of children. I cannot guess what he thinks of it. I wish that I could talk to Louisa. Or John, to know what he really wants.

The chair creaks as she leans forward, her pen scribbling more urgently.

Sometimes I can still feel his fingers mingling in my hair. Like when he cut away a lock that he could take away with him. He still has a piece of me, sealed inside the compartment of his ring. I take some comfort in that. Knowing that I am with him, in a way, and he with me. I can still feel the scissors snip but when I spin around there is no one there.

Another pause. Then she leans forward and writes again, her pen marking the paper in a series of aggressive stabs and slashes.

John has been gone for too long. Too long by three or four months at least. There is no word from him, no one has seen his ship, and no one can explain. My friends all believe that he is gone. That he is dead and drowned in the ocean or else fled to some other port never to return. Gone. They will not say it to my face but I know it is what they think. I see it in their eyes and I hear it in what they will not say aloud. They pity me. They think, 'She is a poor widow already.' But they do not know what I know. I cannot make them understand it, but I know that John is alive. I know that he will come back to me. I feel it in my stomach, deep inside. I feel certainty in my soul. Like the time I was certain that Aunt Lara's lost kidskin gloves would be found beneath the stone at the bottom of the garden even though there was no reason for them to be there, and when I convinced Father to lift the stone there they were just as I knew, and everyone thought that it must have been me who took them for how else could I have known, even though I did no such thing.

He will return I know it. He will return. Until then there is nothing I can do. I have nothing to do. I do nothing. I count the cracks in the ceiling plaster, in the parlour, and in my bedchamber. Every day I measure them by eye and I am convinced that they are growing longer and deeper, but the house is brand new or near enough and I think that it should not have cracks in it already. But I do not know. John would know. I fancy that it is the sea. That the water has soaked into the very foundations of the town, into my house, and into every house here, trickling and oozing up and up through the stone and timber. Sometimes I expect the cracks above my bed shall begin to dribble and pour with water, and drown me here at the very top of this cliff. As if the sea wants to take me as it wishes it could take my husband –

The legs of her chair scrape roughly against the floor as she pushes herself away from her desk. She stands and walks quickly away, leaving the page half-filled.

She knows she has been spending too much time at the harbour recently, and that she must be pushing at the limits of her luck. It cannot be long before Samuel Delahunty or someone else spots her meandering aimlessly around the port again. She might pretend she is there to visit John's company offices, or his legal advisor Signor Capello – she can even pretend to herself that this is the true intention of her walks – but the excuse will not hold up to scrutiny. She pictures the small Italian clerk, holding out his hands, baffled: 'Captain Lamb's wife? No, she has not visited my office for a great many weeks.'

Capello handles most of John's business on land, and Cecilia dislikes his awkward, officious manner – not to mention she resents that he knows more about her husband's business interests than she does herself. On occasion she has heard Mrs Harding describe running her own husband's affairs while he is at sea, and it bothers her that she is not able – or permitted – to do the same for John.

But the real reason she has not visited Capello is that the last time she set out for his offices, with a mind to enquire into the state of her household's remaining finances, she was struck by a dizzying, spinning helix of foreboding in the core of her being so intense that it made her turn around and walk straight home again. In that moment she had known two things with certainty: that Capello has no news of John's fate or whereabouts; and that the next time she speaks to him he will tell her nothing that she wants to hear. It will be an unpleasant conversation she would rather avoid – and so she has, though she does not yet know why.

That afternoon she instead walks the longer route down the cliffside and makes her way to a quiet spot along the waterfront, some way past the harbour proper, where the bay is too shallow and stony for the great merchant ships to draw close. A jagged line of blackened rock stands out from the shore like a single fang. At its end is a lighthouse: a squat, solid tower built many centuries ago to guide small fishing boats home. There is a simple jetty where the elderly locals who still fish in the bay tie up their boats; dotted along the quiet jetty and out upon the rocks, old men with skin as bronze as Greek statues and thick beards of white and grey curls sit or stand with their lines cast into the waters. As long as there is any light left in the sky, there are men here fishing. None of them ever seem to pay her any mind.

Cecilia walks past the disinterested fishermen like a phantom, picking her way over sodden coils of rope and dried-out starfish, spilled fish heads and splattered crimson stains on the boards where guts have fallen and been scooped up almost immediately by the ravenous beaks of the ever-watchful gulls. She has become accustomed to the appalling sight and smell, although today it makes her so nauseous that she almost gags. But she is reluctant to step down to the white sands and dark rocks of the seashore proper, where the tide sloshes and surges and the sand bubbles beneath your feet with every step – that is where she ruined her burgundy shoes the last time she was here. Today she has worn a rough calico skirt that will withstand the spit and spray of the waves, at least.

She stares at the beach with a sort of longing as she walks. Small seabirds with long, bright-orange beaks and legs stalk the sand, pausing from time to time to tilt their tiny heads and peck their quaint, elongated beaks, probing for tasty morsels. Rusty-red crabs scuttle past, vicious pincers held high like tiny prizefighters waggling their fists in warning. She has heard that crabs may only move sideways. Back and forth in a single line for their entire lives, the sad things.

A large wave crashes in, engulfing the crabs and sloshing white foam over the jetty and over her skirt, and sending the tattered fish scraps slipping and sliding everywhere. Behind her the town shrinks from view as she makes her way steadily and unhurriedly towards the jagged outcrop of rock where the lighthouse stands. Where the sand ends, the shore is piled high with pearly-white boulders, huge and calcified, and shards of driftwood baked white beneath the hot sun. She wonders how they all came to be gathered there, stone and wood, white like bones, heaped on the seafront like some giant's ossuary. When the tide slips back far enough, you can see the undersides of the bleached white stones and wood, all green and claggy with the sea's touch, hidden below the waterline.

She stops just short of the rocky peninsula where the lighthouse stands. From here the ships drifting in and out of port look like children's models made in miniature, or neat drawings upon the page of a book. Any of them could be John's ship. She wonders if she would feel an uncanny twist of recognition in her stomach if she were to glimpse it over such a distance.

Another spray of water dashed across the rocks alerts her that the tide is coming in, fast. Looking down into the water close to her feet, she can see small black fish swarming there: quick, writhing things, like squirming tentacles flashing in the brackish shallows. They pick and peck at the rocks and wood for whatever they can scavenge. Where the tide is deeper, she can see rubbery fronds of seagrass that sway with the currents. Here and there she spies something larger – something moving, deeper down still: glistening scales on a long, powerful body, coiling like a serpent through the water.

A whisper of breeze floats across the rocks and cools the droplets of saltwater that fleck her cheeks. She lifts a hand and wipes them away. The tide hisses in her ears, a pulse that she can feel in her bones. The sound of the tide is like breathing. Inhaling, exhaling. Like the roaring lungs of some great, unfathomable monstrosity that dwells deep beneath the lapping waters. A wave crashes and almost touches her shoes, bubbling greedily on the glistening rock around her feet. She closes her eyes. *Carry him back to me*, she thinks. *It is long past time that you gave him back*.

She feels a sigh escape her lips, but its sound is drowned by the deafening crash of the waves.

8.

As dusk begins to burn across the sky, Cecilia leaves behind the few fishermen who remain on the black rocks and makes her way unhurriedly back towards the town. Even while the clouds glow red and orange like embers with the coming sunset, she can see a sea mist crawling in from across the horizon that will soon envelop the town entirely in its white vapours.

Her heart is still heavy with longing, and her stomach is still discontented with the same unpleasant nausea that has not subsided since morning. It is in her head, too: an ache, behind her eyes, as if they were strained in their sockets. Too much bright sun and too little sleep, she self-diagnoses.

Only walking the waterfront with the waves in her ears seems to bring any measure of relief. As she returns to the harbour, she watches as a ship eases slowly away and glides out to sea, commencing its voyage. Before it has even made it clear of the bay, a new vessel is moored and anchored in its place. *La Anabella* departs; the *Neptune* replaces it. The heated evening air carries a tropical scent of spices, incense, and strong liquors.

She has been on her feet for the entire afternoon now, and her legs are aching and her ankles swollen; so she pauses to stand for a while, resting with her back leaned lightly against an unattended stack of crates. She faces away from the water, allows her eyelids to droop, and just listens to the world as it carries on around her. The maritime clamour that continues as long as there is light to work by: the men and the ships and the seabirds, and below it all, the constant, hissing build and release of the waves. It is peaceful, to stand passive amongst such industry. It is as if she has become invisible, somehow, simply by closing her own eyes.

She has not been standing long when a sudden and bilious wave of nausea rises within her, surging upwards and through her innards with the press of the tide; it seems to brim with the crash of the waves, and then washes away again. She clenches her jaw against the gagging impulse to retch and places a hand to her stomach in alarm. The feeling of sickness passes, mostly, but something else is left behind in its place. Inside her belly – a not quite familiar sense of foreboding which squirms and writhes inside.

Cecilia opens her eyes and looks about, startled, but the scene is unchanged. Everywhere is motion, heaving ropes and hauling crates, men waving and pointing and shouting, hands curled around their mouths to be heard. But none of the noise seems to reach her ears. The world is muted, as though she were submerged beneath the waves, suspended in salt water. Her insides continue to churn uncomfortably. She feels an impulse to keep moving, to keep walking: an instinct tells her this unpleasant sensation will only go away if she keeps walking along the shore, even though her feet are tired and aching.

She resists. Something is not right. This is like her uncomfortable premonitions – that heavy lump twisting inside her – only the sensation she feels now is not quite the same. It is something she has never felt before.

A jab of pain – or, not pain, but *something* that she has no words to describe – shifts, somewhere inside her. Inside her belly. Very gradually, a creeping prickle of realization begins to press its way forward from the back of her mind. It is not *she* who wants to keep walking. It is something inside her. Some *thing*, inside – but not a part of her. It doesn't like that she stopped moving, and that is why she feels ill, why she is so unsettled. Her stomach is churning now, brimming and bubbling like the slosh beneath the wharf. It feels as though the fish she ate for dinner last night has somehow reconstituted itself and is now swimming discontented circles inside her gut.

Beads of sweat break all over her body. *It is just that and nothing more*, she tells herself. *It is only last night's supper disagreeing with you. Or harmless bubbles of air caught between your ribs. This is your imagination playing tricks – again.* But the sensation does not go away. It remains, writhing inside of her, around and around. She lifts a shaking hand and presses it flat against her stomach, gently at first, afraid of what she might feel – suspicious of her own body. Then she presses with more force. She pushes down against her insides, and her blood turns to ice as she feels something push back. Something squirms and lashes against the pressure of her palm. Like a kick.

'It is not possible,' she murmurs aloud. Her senses are consumed by the blood spinning a typhoon through her head: it is all she can hear, or smell, or taste. She snatches her hand away from her stomach, terrified now, and touches it to her forehead, which is damp with perspiration. Her entire body is drenched, as if she were some bedraggled thing pulled from the sea on a hook. She glances to her left and to her right, but no one around seems to have noticed her distress. She turns slowly upon the spot, feeling like an outsider caught up in a play she does not recognize or understand, an unwilling participant in some grotesque melodrama. It is then that she spots him, watching her. High upon the stern of the ship docked directly opposite where she is standing, is John.

Not a face like John's – not a stranger who only resembles her husband for a passing glance, no – this *is* John. He is staring directly at her, and she sees his eyes flash as they meet with her own. She calls out his name, or she thinks she does, but his face betrays no emotion. No surprise nor joy to see her. No concern at her unfolding distress. He is just watching. The ship beneath him begins to move, heaving and shifting, pulling away from the harbour – away from her.

With a cry Cecilia stumbles across the boardwalk, chasing the enormous vessel even as the watery gap between it and the dock stretches wider and wider. John stands and watches without moving a muscle. Something catches at her foot, some uneven board or a loose coil of rope, she doesn't see, and it brings her at once down onto her knees – one of her hands flies up to arrest her fall, the other moves with immediate instinct to cradle her midriff, which continues to writhe and wriggle beneath her touch like a thing alive; a thing that is rearranging her insides and making a space for itself. She lies there, a vision of pathetic distress, her head dropped low and her eyes downcast. Through the gaps in the boardwalk she can see the green water foaming, and the slippery black fish twisting and turning just beneath the surface.

Next Cecilia feels hands upon her, large, rough hands, patting her back and pinching her arms, pulling and trying to hoist her back upright. She is aware of bodies, men swarming into a huddled group around the spot where the poor senhora has fallen.

One voice, which speaks first in Portuguese and then in English, cuts through the rest. 'Stand back! Stand back and leave her be! Let her lie, now.'

Still hunched over and foetal, she lifts her head and attempts to peer through the forest of legs that has gathered, trying to catch another glimpse of her husband drifting away from her, but her view is blocked. She asks, 'That ship – what ship is that?' but no one seems to hear her.

The same voice – it is a man's voice, but not one she can recognize – is still appealing for calm, urging the sailors and dockhands to step back and give the lady some room to breathe. He appears kneeling by her side – by his voice and dress she expects to see an Englishman, but when she looks at him, his complexion is dark and he appears Moorish, or perhaps Middle Eastern. When he speaks, however, he is English once again: 'Good lady, are you all right?'

'Yes, thank you,' she answers automatically. 'I only tripped. But – there was a ship, there. Can you see it?'

She points and the crowd parts, but John and his ship have both vanished. The sea mist is almost touching the shore now, and they must have vanished into its concealing cloud – if they were ever truly there at all.

'A ship?' The young man looks puzzled. 'Please, senhora – please do not try to move. I am a doctor. *O médico.* Do you understand me? Remain still a moment or two longer, if you please. You say that you tripped?'

Her hand is still touched to her belly, but now she can feel nothing. No movement, no discontented writhing, and no stabbing premonition. Her heart is gradually slowing its frenetic beat.

'Senhora? Do you understand me?'

'I am English,' she tells him. 'I can understand you. You are English, too? Who are you?'

'I am a doctor,' he tells her again. She can feel her blood cooling now, and her faculties returning. Already the gathered crowd is starting to dissipate, seeing that there is little more distraction to be found here. Cecilia exhales slowly and tries to take in the stranger's appearance. He is young

– younger than she would have thought possible for a doctor – but, indeed, he is dressed the part in a simple, deep-blue coat and pristine white shirt and stockings. There is nothing sombre or clinical in his expression, though, which strikes her as quite genuine in its concern.

'A doctor? Well, thank you, doctor, but I am quite all right now. I am not hurt, I am positive. I only tripped over a loose plank, there, or some such thing – I do not know what it was. I … I thought I saw a ship, and was distracted …'

'What manner of ship?' His soft brown eyes are studying her own very carefully, so that she begins to feel uncomfortable.

'I don't know – it was nothing,' she stammers. 'I was just trying to get a better look, and I tripped and fell. That is all, thank you. Can I stand up now?'

He frowns doubtfully, but nods and assists her to her feet. 'I should not fancy that many ships would dare navigate the port through this mist. But – you are English, you say? A curious coincidence: I am only newly arrived here and have not yet made the acquaintance of many of my countrymen.'

Once Cecilia is upright, he presents her with a handkerchief, which she dabs self-consciously against her dripping forehead and upper lip. Now they are both standing, she can see that the doctor is very tall, taller even than John. 'Now, my good lady, you are quite certain you are unharmed? It appeared to be quite a bad fall.'

She is only half-listening. 'Yes, yes, thank you, doctor. Really, I am fine. I … I should be going now. Thank you for your assistance.'

His hand darts into his jacket and produces a card. 'Please, should you happen to discover any lingering aches or pains, or … should you need anything at all, do not hesitate to call.'

She takes his card without looking at it. 'I … I shall. But I should have to talk to my husband first. You understand.'

He smiles, and bows.

'Thank you again, doctor,' she tells him, and hurries away from the scene. As her unsteady legs carry her as fast as they can up the steep, slippery cobbles that lead back up the cliff towards her home, she tells herself over and over: *It could not have been John that I saw. It is impossible. John is still at sea. It was my imagination and nothing more – another mistaken identity, some man who looked only fleetingly like him, just like all of the other times.*

And the thing that she felt moving inside her – that was impossible, too. Most certainly. Over and over she repeats: *You felt nothing, you saw nothing,* as she hurries up the hill, and farther and farther away from the deep, rich, blue waters of the bay.

9.

The misty evening pursues Cecilia all the way home. She opens her front door just enough to slip herself inside and then she shuts it tightly behind her, sealing out the creeping fog – as if she could shut out the memories of her long and troubling day so easily.

She is still standing at the door with her fingertips laid upon the handle and her forehead resting against the cool wood of the frame when Rosalie surprises her.

'The man, Signor Capello, he calls for you again today,' her maid informs her. 'I did not know how to say where you had gone.'

'Again?' Cecilia asks impatiently, without removing her head from the doorframe. 'He has come here before?'

'*Sim*. Yes. You don't remember I told you this?'

She tries to recall. Perhaps Rosalie did tell her that Capello visited, a week or two ago. She wonders what he could want. She cannot avoid John's lawyer forever, she knows. Whatever he has to tell her may be important. Perhaps the money John left behind has finally dried up – after so many months she feels sure that their funds must be dwindling. But at this moment she does not want to think about any of these things. She tells Rosalie, 'If he calls again and I am not here, tell him I will visit his offices as soon as I can. I have been … occupied, recently.'

'Yes, Senhora. Do you want something to eat?' Rosalie asks. She sounds worried.

'No,' Cecilia answers quickly. 'No, I am not hungry. I am going to bed.'

It is the truth. Despite her long day walking the shore with nothing to eat since breakfast, she does not feel hungry at all. The nausea that had plagued her all day is gone now, but it has not left behind a hollow in her stomach to be filled. She feels filled up with … something.

In the sanctuary of her drawing room Cecilia at last has time to think about what happened on the dock. What she felt – *inside* her. The vision of John standing at the stern of the departing ship is easy to dismiss as nothing but her confused imagination, even though it seemed entirely real at the time. But, though her innards are at peace now, the feeling had been unmistakeable. Something was moving – and a kick, something lashing out that she could feel through her skin and her clothes. That was not her imagination, she is positive.

But could it really be *that*? Her mind reels. Even in the privacy of her own chambers she blushes as she is forced to reflect upon her entirely incomplete understanding of the subject: how a baby is made; well, she is a married woman and understands that well enough. But everything that comes after she feels less certain about.

She stands in front of her mirror and turns this way and that, but her body, her shape, looks much as it ever did. When she places her hand to her stomach, there is no maternal swell that she can detect. *Is this how it happens?* She asks herself: *Can this really be how a woman comes to know of her condition?* One moment, nothing, and then, all of a sudden – a child wriggling and turning, announcing its presence with undeniable physicality. She had no idea. It is not at all what she expected.

She casts her mind back and struggles to recall the little that her governess told her, the small signs which a lady must watch out for. She wishes she had paid more attention to the old woman's cryptic hints and euphemisms, but it had not seemed terribly important at the time. When she puts her mind to it, she believes that she *has* been late in her cycle for some time now – but in the endless haze of days it is difficult to be certain by how long. Time has become a fluid thing, something that oozes past at its own rate and does not stand to be sliced and measured by neat divisions of weeks and months.

She tries to remember. Does the blood stop before or after you feel the baby shift and kick? When will her stomach begin to grow, like her sister Louisa's did? How soon will Rosalie be able to notice, or Mabel? Her heart begins to race as she wonders how, precisely, it is that a baby is supposed to find its way out of the mother. Surely it cannot be a similar method to how it gets in? Questions come to her, questions that she wishes she had asked long ago, when she had a chance. *Perhaps*, she thinks, *if I had a mother growing up and not an aunt, I might have been told more about what to expect. Then again, perhaps not.*

Cecilia crawls into her bed long before it is fully dark, but even after midnight she is still wide awake. She lies on her back and squeezes her eyes closed, but the entire room seems to shift and sway around her, as if her house were rocking like a ship knocked and buffeted upon a stormy sea. Her ears fill with the sound – the crash of the waves and the spray lashing against her bedroom walls, the unsteady creak and groan of the timbers of her home. But when she opens her eyes and sits upright, everything is still and silent.

She gets out of bed and looks from her window across the town enshrouded in mist, lit by a sliver of silvery moonlight. The fog is so thick it seems as if a person could walk across the top of it, like it is a beautiful field of untouched snow.

After rising and returning to her bed three times, and still as wide awake as she has ever felt in her life, Cecilia moves to her drawing room, sits at her desk, and begins to write.

Dear Louisa

How I wish that you were here with me. The most remarkable thing has happened. I think that I am to be a mama. I think so, but I cannot be sure. If you were here now, then I could ask you – wasn't it about a year after you were married that it happened for you? It is the same for me. Perhaps it is in our blood.

Do not think me wicked, Louisa, but I am not filled with joy. I know that it is a blessing, and the duty of every wife. It is just that I do not want it. Not at this time and not in this place. Not when John is still at sea. It seems a terrible thing to be carrying John's child when I do not even know where in the world he is. It feels like a cruel joke. Poor John shall be the very last to find out. What a thing, to sail away from a wife and return to a family! Well, he shall not be the first sailor it has happened to, I suppose.

The more I think upon it the more positive of my condition I become. It muddles a woman's senses, does it not, Louisa? A baby inside you will make you think and feel differently. Perhaps that would explain some things.

I wish I could speak to you. I wish that I could send this letter, but of course I probably will not. I wonder if you could even recognize that it is your sister writing, if you were to read this. I do not think I am the same person who left England.

I shall have to tell Mrs Delahunty and Mrs Harding
soon, won't I, Louisa? They are my friends here and they
will help me, I am sure. It is just that, if I tell them, then
they shall pity me all the more. They already think me half
a widow – and now with a child on the way, perhaps. They
will say nothing to my face of course, but it will be plain
in their eyes. They must think me a fool if they imagine I
can't see it – see what they really think. They will think
'the poor lamb', and they will regard me with such
pathetic kindness and concern in their eyes that I could
just scratch them out I could –

She stops. A blot of ink mars her sheet; where her next
frantic words would go, there is only a growing black stain.
She watches its dark tendrils spread, slow and insidious,
seeping light into dark. A cankerous malady infecting her
pristine page.

With both hands she crumples the sheet into a ball
between her fists. Then she uncurls it, smooths it out again
and tears it into strips, rending the paper to shreds with her
fingernails, and lets the dog-eared scraps scatter across the
surface of the writing desk, where she mixes them up with
the tips of her fingers so that the ragged remnants of words
mingle into a chaotic and meaningless jumble. Finally she
rises, walks away from her desk, and drops back into her
bed with a hopeless, desperate sigh.

No sooner has her head touched the pillow than the
room begins to lurch and sway again, her entire house
borne away upon an illusory, nocturnal tide – just like the
ship that first carried her to this place, carried her away
from her family and her friends and all of the life she had
ever known. Carried her to this solitude and confusion, all
those many long months ago.

10.

Cecilia dreams of her voyage from England. Despite growing up right upon the sea's shore, she has only ever set foot on one real ship in her life, and that was the one that carried her and John to this new, foreign home.

That ship had been named the *Wildflower*, a name which had pleased Cecilia and which she had quickly decided to accept as an auspicious sign for her and John's voyage. When she first approached its gangway, she had happened to glance upwards and the sheer, dizzying verticality of the construct looming gargantuan over her head had, for a moment, overwhelmed her. She had been around ships all her life, but, until that moment – or so it seemed – she had never stood quite so near to one, nor fully appreciated their daunting scale. Its dark hull seemed to rise impossibly out of the lapping waters, its very flotation an apparent defiance of all natural law; the thing was the size of a house and yet balanced upon nothing but the bobbing tide. Until she had seen it close up, Cecilia had never considered that the buoyancy of a ship could be such an affront to her senses.

She had tried to reassure her nerves by concentrating on the clever construction of the thing. Whenever she saw them sailing past at great distances, Cecilia liked to imagine ships as being carved neatly out of a single hulk of wood, great ornate sculptures gliding through the water. But she could see every plank that the *Wildflower* was made from, straining and groaning against their fixings, many overlapping and cobbled together through a process of makeshift repairs. She could observe each jagged nail and the thick, dripping applications of black tar that streaked its sides.

When she dared to raise her eyes skywards again, she saw rising from the leviathan's back its three masts, lashed into place by innumerable ropes pulled taut and forming a chaotic crosshatch against the grey and overcast sky. Slowly she craned her neck farther and farther, until she could glimpse the British flag fluttering in the stiff breeze high above – good weather for sailing, John had told her that morning.

Gawping upwards like that, she quickly became dizzy again and stumbled, but John had caught her with one arm around her waist and given her a reassuring squeeze. Cecilia glanced about sheepishly, but no one was looking at them.

'Easy there, lass,' he said, his voice close to her ear. 'Mind your step on the wharf. If you were to fall in, I should have to dive after to fish you out – and I'd hate to wet my clothes before a long voyage.' His voice was soft and low, and careless. His teasing words were a comfort. John was not afraid. He had set sail dozens of times, on journeys far longer than theirs would be. As long as he was with her, she knew that nothing could go seriously wrong.

'The ship is so … huge, when you stand beside it,' she told her husband in wonder. John had chuckled fondly – at her, and at the ship.

'Aye, it's a beauty,' he agreed.

'Where was this ship built?' she asked, casting a wary eye over the lopsided carpentry and the damp, porous gaps in the spongy-looking woodwork.

'I told you that already. Bristol. It's a fine vessel, don't you worry. Come on now, Cissy, we'd best follow our belongings on board, lest they cast off and make the crossing without us.'

She linked her arm in his, and they had proceeded together up the gangplank. John took the steps slowly and held her arm tight, considerate to her nervousness. Trepidation fluttered in circles around Cecilia's chest and prickled like pins around her collar; she wondered if everyone felt so anxious before their first sea voyage. Perhaps even John had felt this way, once. Though somehow she thinks not.

Even though he had never even laid eyes upon the sea until he was fifteen years of age, when he had fled his family and a crofter's future in the distant highlands of Scotland, John had taken immediately to a life before the mast. He was fond of saying that, although he never glimpsed the ocean as a boy, the glens and vales he grew up with had churned and rolled just as mysterious and wild; so that when he did, at last, arrive at the coast, he knew he had found his way home.

John's sea legs did not trip or falter for a moment as the two of them stepped onto the deck of the *Wildflower*, and Cecilia had felt for the first time the alarming lurch of the swaying ship beneath her feet. *We are still at dock*, she had thought, with a rising panic – *How much worse will it be once we are untethered, adrift upon the tempestuous sea?*

'John,' she had said suddenly, gripping his arm with both of her hands. He looked down at her, his eyebrows raised mildly. 'You *are* sure, aren't you … that this is the best thing for us, I mean? You're certain that we should go …'

John had taken her hands in his, enveloping her fingers in his own. He swallowed, and nodded. 'I am certain. This is the best thing we can possibly do, you'll see. I know you're nervous – the truth is, I am too, a little. But, you see, Cissy, that's how I *know* this is the right thing to do. That nervousness you feel – that's the venture, lass.' And he had smiled at her then, a little awkwardly.

His voice dropped to a hush, not to be heard by the strangers all around on the ship's busy deck. 'There will be opportunity for me, over there. For both of us. I can make a name for myself at last. This place, here ... England, it's no good any more. A man like me – a man born as I was – he can only make it so far. The game here's rigged, by Parliament and the King; they're all corrupt as you like. All they want is to see the money go back into the pot, back into their own pockets. There was a time, once, when *any* man could make his name at sea, no matter where he came from or who his father was. But now ... If there was a war on, perhaps it might be different.'

'I would not be glad if you were at war,' she had objected.

John winked at her. 'Cissy, whether the hold is filled with spices from India or cannonballs from Birmingham, there is danger enough at sea. But as it is now, with the laws they pass, if you haven't got the connections, if you haven't the background ... Oh, but over there, Fitzgibbon already has everything arranged. My own command, Cissy. Imagine – my own ship, at last. And the Portuguese, they've had their setbacks in the last few years to be sure, but they're on their way back up. Now there's gold in Brazil, and diamonds, they dig them from the earth by handfuls. Yes ... I know this is the best thing for me. I'll make my fortune. I'll make you proud of me, lass, you'll see.'

A troupe of sailors pushed past, forcing husband and wife to press together to allow them by. 'We'll be weighing anchor soon. Let's find our quarters,' John had said, and he let go of her hands and looked away. Cecilia watched her husband as he scanned the ship's deck, taking in the crew's movements and actions, glancing to the rigging and the clouds above with an able seaman's eye. The fingers of her right hand nervously twisted the wedding band she wore upon her left, where it still itched sometimes – unfamiliar, and tight against her skin.

In spite of his own urging, John had dragged his heels, seemingly reluctant to leave the deck as the ship was made ready for launch. Once they had descended below deck, out of the sunlight and – Cecilia realized with alarm – closer to or even below the waterline, John had confided in her: 'It feels all wrong to be on deck and not start barking orders. I had to bite my tongue not to tell those men to attend to loose knots and straighten their shirts. Though it seems a fine wee craft and a competent crew, all told.'

Her husband is a tall man with strapping shoulders and a strong jaw that he juts out stubbornly when he wants to make a point, and Cecilia has little difficulty in imagining him ordering seamen about with a commanding authority. But she also knows that her husband is fair and kind-hearted, in spite of his sometimes domineering physical presence. When she first met him, she had not cared too much for his face, it being rather box-shaped, and marked by a pox he had survived as a child – that, and she had thought his ears were too prominently placed upon either side of his head. But with time it is those features that she has somehow come to love the most. Funny how your understanding of a person can change, she had mused as she watched her husband shove open the door to their quarters.

'Well, here we are. It's not much – I fear you'll be a touch uncomfortable, Cecilia. Though you can trust me that most of the men on board have it worse. We can bear this out for a mere few days, can't we, lass?'

He had smiled his easy smile, but Cecilia could see the anxiousness in his eye as he watched for her reaction to the cramped, stifling space they would be forced to call their marital suite for the short duration of the voyage. With an effort she had forced some enthusiasm into her voice: 'Oh, it's much larger than I had imagined it would be!' she exclaimed. 'And we're close to the deck, so that I might take a walk and enjoy the sea air. This will be wonderful, John; we shall be most comfortable.' It was only a temporary home, after all, and nothing she couldn't endure for the handful of days that would bring them to their new home on the continent.

Above their heads the sailors were shouting. Bells clanged and the ship around them began to creak and heave into motion – a creature rousing itself from a deep slumber. Their voyage from England was underway.

As it had transpired, Cecilia ventured above deck to take in the sea air only once, and on that occasion fleetingly. She had spent the majority of their journey to Portugal violently ill, her stomach roiled into angry protest by the merciless rocking and swaying of the *Wildflower* as it sailed. John had promised her that a walk and the fresh ocean breeze would do her some good, but when she had first emerged from the ship's bowels and into the blinding sunlight, the vision of the salt spray crashing high over the side, and the line of the horizon rising and dipping in wild vertical swoops as the boat lurched back and forth, had made an immediate and unhealthy impact upon her. She had turned back at once and cried, 'I don't like it, John, let me go below.'

'Wait, wait, just give it a moment to settle. The trick is to find your own balance – the sea will rock you whether you like it or not. Relax, and move with its motion. It is almost like a dance. You see?'

He stood for a moment, holding her and swaying with the veering wave of the vessel. It hadn't made her feel very much better.

'Listen to that, Cissy,' John whispered. 'Can you hear it?'

Cecilia listened. She could hear men shouting, boots stamping, boards creaking, waves crashing, and gulls squawking. 'Listen to what?' she grumbled.

'The sea. The open sea. It's got a voice all of its own. Don't you hear it? Never mind the din all around – look out there, and really listen.'

She had looked up at him, forgetting her queasiness for a moment as she wondered at the curious tone that had entered his voice. John had raised his arm and pointed out towards the blue expanse that stretched in every direction, his eyes round and wide and his lips curved into the faintest trace of a smile. She had looked to where he pointed, but the dazzling brightness of the sun flashing off the water, and the churning motion of the waves, only brought back her seasickness. She screwed her eyes tight shut and tried to listen.

A minute passed. 'I can't hear anything,' she said. 'Just the waves.'

John had laughed cheerfully. 'The sea doesn't sing to you like it does to me. I suppose we should be grateful – two born wanderers would make for no kind of family at all. It's a difficult thing to explain, Cecilia. I don't know what it is that makes a man hear it, but you could ask every man jack on this crew and they'd all recognize what I speak of. There's no resisting.'

He inhaled deeply and smiled. 'Ah, just look at it. I remember when I was a boy, I'd climb to the tallest point I could find, whatever rock or tree that was, and I'd look out, squint my eyes as hard as I could over the hills, the purple heather and the drab yellow fields, as far as I could see. I told myself then: wherever the horizon is, that's where I want to be. And out here … out here, there's nothing but horizon.'

He had fallen silent then, for a long moment, until finally he had laughed his big laugh and said, 'But it's not a life for everyone – my poor Cissy!' and he had squeezed her tighter still, so that she felt a wave of illness inside and she had been forced to break free and scurry back below decks there and then, before the assorted sailors could witness her divulging herself of her queasiness in a most unladylike manner.

John had stayed by her side for almost the entire trip, the good man that he was, bringing her food and water and watching over her with apprehensive concern – concern that had turned instantly to a show of cheer and positivity whenever he knew she was watching him.

'Not much longer now, lass,' he would soothe her. 'We shall have arrived before you know it, and this will all have been worth it – you'll see.'

The voyage from England had been a miserable experience for her, though she had discovered a new respect and sympathy for her husband's calling. That crossing had lasted less than a week, but when she finally touched her foot to solid ground again, she felt she had travelled across a thousand years and miles; and she had wondered how John – how anyone – could ever get used to such a terrible and unnatural way to travel.

11.

The appointed date for dinner with the Delahuntys and the Hardings, fixed when Cecilia had run into the former unexpectedly at the docks, arrives. Cecilia had hoped, but not expected, that Mabel might have forgotten about the plan, but a note arrived two days before to confirm that there is no such easy escape. It also breezily mentions that Captain Harding has returned to shore on schedule and will round out the company to five. *Good for Frances*, Cecilia thinks, uncharitably.

Cecilia's very first thought that morning is to anticipate the evening's engagement with a sense of dread in her guts. And that is not all; the child is in there too, squirming and churning.

Her child. Any doubt about her condition that she had entertained after she first felt it moving has now passed. Every morning it is there, stirring before she does, waking her with its uncomfortable motion. Slithering wetly through her innards. Shed of the blinders of her initial shock down at the waterfront, the sensation is unmistakeable: there is a life growing inside her. This has gone on for almost two weeks.

At least she is still not showing. Even though Cecilia feels like she must be bloated like a filled waterskin, the flesh across her belly rippling and undulating for all the world to see – until she has stared at the ocean for an hour or more and the baby lies calm again at last – when she looks at herself in the mirror, her physique remains unchanged. The only part of her that is growing are the rings under her eyes. She watches Rosalie carefully, but her maid appears to have noticed nothing.

Cecilia's second thought that morning is to consider what possible and plausible excuses she might employ to get herself out of Mabel's dinner. She does not want to go. The expectation of sitting around a table with those people – her only friends in this place, she has to keep reminding herself – and making polite small talk all evening drives her to queasy distraction.

She tells herself she is being foolish, as she always is when any such social engagement is required, ever since she was a little child. Mabel Delahunty has been nothing but kind and considerate, as has Mrs Harding, and their husbands, ever since she arrived here and John departed. Any concern they feel is genuine and heartfelt. *It is not their fault that they do not know John will return, in the way that you do. They are not sensitive to such things. And as for what's inside you … they know nothing about that, either.*

Her reflection stares back blankly in the looking glass while her internal monologue trundles on: *What is more,* she reminds herself, *these are important people to know. Mr Delahunty and Captain Harding have connections and influence that may be important to John's career, and you must represent him here on land while he is absent. Surely you can face some small discomfort for one evening. Smile and be polite. You have done it before. Think what John must be going through as he battles his way home.*

'What's this now, Cissy? Why go at all if you really don't want to? Why not just call it off?' John's voice comes to her from some place behind where she stands, speaking over her shoulder from the far side of the room, out of view of the mirror's reflection.

She answers him without turning to look. 'How can I? What can I say at such short notice that would not cause a scandal?'

He laughs. 'A scandal! I hardly think so.'

'Even so. What excuse could I offer them?' She waits, but there is no reply. John's voice has no answers for her that she does not already know.

'If I pleaded some prior engagement,' she says, 'then they will wonder what it could be – and what should I tell them then? What engagement could I possibly have? And if I claimed I was ill, Mrs Delahunty or Mrs Harding might come to look after me, and then they might –'

'Aye, aye – just imagine Frances Harding as your tender nurse. No ... best you go after all, lass.'

She smiles but does not laugh, while John's low chuckle fills the space between them. 'Don't be cruel,' she says. 'Mrs Harding has been kind to take me under her wing. They all have. And besides, you know that Captain Harding and Mr Delahunty are connections we can hardly afford to lose. No, I must go and play my part, and then when you are back –' but she stops. In talking to her husband she had absent-mind-edly turned away from the mirror to face where he should have been – the empty place where his voice had emerged from – and seen that, of course, there is no one there. She sighs, and finishes getting ready to go out.

In her imagination – in her dreams – this is how he comes back to her, time and time again. She is at her mirror, or standing at the window looking towards the ocean, and suddenly he is just there, behind her, his voice calling to her from the open doorway, his return unexpected and unde-clared. *That would be just like him*, she thinks.

*   *   *

Ultimately the pressure of social obligation outweighs the clinging anxiety that Cecilia has struggled with all day, and come the evening she finds herself seated at the Delahuntys' dining table. Sitting beside her is James Harding – Frances's husband, newly ashore. Captain Harding is a bright, cheerful man, quick with a smile and a laugh, and Cecilia is glad of his company – though even when on land he talks and thinks about the sea even more often than John does. Next to Captain Harding is Mabel, opposite him sits his wife Frances, and the final place opposite Mabel is taken by her husband Samuel. The chair opposite Cecilia is conspicuously, unavoidably vacant, the unset place a lacuna in the table's careful symmetry.

Before they could sit down to eat, the party had witnessed a short display of Mr and Mrs Delahunty's two young children, Charles and David. They were led out by a maid and played for a while as the assembled company sat and observed. At first Cecilia had watched passively and felt their innocent and uncomplicated games lighten her spirit somewhat. But then she became strangely aware of how still and stagnant the thing inside her was lying that evening – she could hardly feel its presence at all, in fact – and she began to wonder whether watching Mabel's children shouldn't be awakening more maternal feeling within her.

She and Frances had paid Mabel some usual, polite compliments towards the quality of her offspring, but it quickly became apparent that Mabel wished to hear some more, and Cecilia had found herself at an awkward loss of anything to say. And then one of the children – the younger one, though she could not remember whether that was Charles or David – had seemed to take a liking to her and kept asking its mother, 'Does Miss Lamb see what I do, Mama? Does she see?'

Mabel corrected him each time: '*Mrs* Lamb, darling,' and then she looked at Cecilia with a sort of expectant eye, but again Cecilia had found herself unsure of how to respond, so she had only offered the small child a sort of serene and – she hoped – encouraging smile.

After the children have finally been led away and the group repaired to the dining room, Frances turns to Mabel. 'Your nursemaid, she is new?' she asks.

'Why, yes. A Dutch girl. The children like her. That reminds me – Mrs Lamb, have you had any luck yet in finding a new cook?'

'Oh, no, not yet.'

'Go French or, failing that, Belgian, if you can,' Frances advises. 'They make the best cooks. But – my goodness, Mrs Lamb, tell me that you're not still relying on that shiftless-looking local girl to do everything around your home?'

'I am,' she confesses. 'Though she is quite a good cook, actually. And she has been improving her manner, I think,' says Cecilia, remembering guiltily how Rosalie had audibly tutted at her when she had sent her breakfast away again that morning without taking a bite.

'Oh, but the locals can't make anything right,' Mabel cries. 'You shall want to replace that as soon as you are able, believe you me. They never cook anything for half as long as it needs. And their cakes – those nutty, flaky things, I can't stand them. Where's the point? No, you should find French, or Belgian – or German in a pinch – for the kitchen. And for your household maid you simply cannot do better than English, of course; or Scotch or Irish if you must.'

'My Scotch girl was stealing from me,' Frances declares ominously.

Dinner begins and Cecilia is swiftly reminded that she never needs to worry what she has to say for herself when she is with her friends; they are far too busy talking about themselves to allow conversation to lapse long enough that she might be required to provide an update from her own life. Mabel talks about her children, Frances about her plants. They all complain about the weather and boast about what they have bought in the markets. Whenever there is a sufficiently robust dialogue between the ladies, Captain Harding and Mr Delahunty lean towards each other and discuss maritime business in low tones until they are called back to society by their wives. Conversation around the table is general; they are too long acquainted to stick to the stilted English formality of addressing only those seated to one's left or right.

Frances and Mabel are discussing a decorated Chinese hand fan that Mabel has been conspicuously opening and wafting all evening, waiting for someone to mention it, when Cecilia's curiosity is piqued by a conversation she overhears their husbands engaged in.

'The boys swim down, you know, with nothing but a rock lashed to their foot for a dive-weight and hog fat smeared across them for warmth,' James Harding is saying, with no small wonder in his voice. 'And yet by such methods they are able to harvest what remains out of reach of more civilized men. The most accomplished may spend hours at a time deep beneath the waves, searching and harvesting, having trained themselves to breathe like a fish. It is quite remarkable.'

'Are you talking about the islanders who dive for pearls?' Cecilia asks, turning in her chair. 'I read about them once; I was most fascinated.'

'Fascinating indeed,' Captain Harding concurs. 'It is an ancient practice for them, almost like a ritual. And now it's making them bally rich.'

'It would, if they only understood the true value of what they fish up,' Samuel Delahunty comments wryly. 'They trade them away for cloth. And now they have discovered what they can get in return, they dredge as many as they can from the ocean floor, as if they were barnacles. The pearls shall not sustain their value.'

'It must be a wondrous thing, to swim so deep,' says Cecilia. 'I cannot imagine what it must look like. John told me once that, as distant as the horizon appears, to drop to the very deepest parts of the ocean would be farther still.'

'Oh, by a long way, yes,' Samuel smiles and nods. 'The pearl divers work in shallower parts, of course, but even so it is an impressive feat.'

Frances appears mildly agitated by the discussion. 'Certainly though, a civilized diver with the aid of a bell could submerge to still greater depths than those islanders – could they not, James?' she asks.

Her husband's eyes light up suddenly with a strange enthusiasm. 'You know, I spoke to a man not so long ago who made his living as a diver,' Captain Harding tells them. 'His trade was to walk the seabed in a sealed suit and helmet of his own design and salvage the debris he found there. He worked on contract for the merchant companies bringing things up, lost cargo and the like, but he said that most of his money he made by laying claim to the wealth of forgotten salvage that lies upon the sea floor. It was his observation that the Mediterranean Sea constitutes the world's largest graveyard. Surely, it lies littered with wrecks and treasures, the bodies of the drowned dead and sunken ships, forgotten for decades or even centuries.'

Cecilia keeps her gaze on Captain Harding, but, in the corners of her vision she sees both Frances and Mabel glance at her.

Frances tuts. 'My dear, please. I am sure that we do not wish to hear about such things … shipwrecks, or anything so morbid.'

Mabel gives an uncomfortable little cough.

'I am very interested,' Cecilia says quickly. 'Please, Captain Harding – what treasures did the man find?'

James Harding seems only faintly aware of what they are all saying, in any case. A faraway sheen glazes his eyes as he goes on. 'The diver told me,' he says, slowly, 'that it is an extraordinary world that lies beneath the waves. There is an undiscovered landscape at the ocean's bed: a country yet to be colonized, and not yet described or understood by the scientific minds who have done so much to trim away the mystery of the world on land. This diver, he spoke of fish with bodies that are clear as glass, near invisible to the naked eye, which flicker like flames through the water. Eels that have grown long, with forms like that of a gigantic tropical snake, and a gruesome head to be found at either end. Fish that have learned to walk along the seabed upon their fins, as if God had granted them legs like a land mammal. He claimed to have once come upon an ancient Greek trireme, a ship almost entirely hidden beneath a blooming field of algae grown over a thousand years or more. Within its frame he witnessed a phalanx of skeletons, still sealed inside their armour – bone and metal fused together over countless lifetimes.'

Frances gives a performative shudder. 'Please, dear.'

'Go on,' Cecilia insists. James turns and locks eyes with her as he continues.

'Stranger still – the diver said he had seen things beneath the waves that should not be there, things which he could not account for. Rocks and corals that resemble architecture – where the geology of the seabed itself has formed into deep, structured crevices, like the corridors of some Byzantine faculty; or rising in vast temples and ziggurats. He spoke of statues, sculpted images in the close likenesses of men and women, far down upon the sea floor where they have no place or reason to be, frozen in time beneath the waves –'

Frances interrupts again with a derisive scoff. 'Really dear, this is too much – the man surely spoke only to vex you.'

'How could he see so far beneath the waves?' Mabel asks. 'When you look into the ocean you see only shadows, the sun does not penetrate … So what light had he to see by?'

Captain Harding sits back in his chair. 'You know, I am not entirely sure,' he admits. 'Perhaps some manner of lantern?'

Samuel Delahunty stirs. 'I have no doubt that the world below the waves would appear full of marvels to our eyes. But buildings and statues … no, I think not. Why, surely what the diver saw was only the contents of some classical galley that was tossed overboard or sunk, just like his Greek trireme. A ship's hold filled with sculpted marbles, scattered across the ocean floor and left a score of centuries, would make for a wondrous sight, I am certain.'

Captain Harding frowns. 'I trust myself as good a judge of character as any, and I did not doubt this fellow's sincerity … No, nor the awed tremble in his eye as he described to me these visions. I allow that we had enjoyed a drink or two. But I say, why shouldn't it be as he described? We sailors only skim across the surface of the ocean with barely a second thought to what lies fathoms below.'

Now Mabel comes to his defence: 'I suppose that old legends of Atlantis and the like must have some basis in fact, surely? And the world as it was before the deluge – perhaps there is some trace of it still, at the sea's floor? Could it not be so?'

'I claim no authority on such subjects,' her husband Samuel replies haughtily, 'but what I *do* know is that ships go down all the time. They are marked in my ledger, with a red line through them. I expect the diver only saw their valuable cargoes scattered across the seabed and was deceived in the darkness. One thing he told you was true enough – the sea is a graveyard. Almost every day there is a vessel that does not make it to this port. The waters off this coast alone must be the final resting place for hundreds, if not thousands of such ships, and their crews – God rest their souls. No wonder it should appear a strange and inexplicable place to the eye of some crackpot with a diving contraption, who does not know the harsh realities of maritime venture.'

Samuel settles back in his chair, his piece said. Cecilia is aware that Frances, Mabel, and Captain Harding are all looking at her, now, from the corners of their eyes. After a short delay Mr Delahunty's satisfied smile freezes and he too catches her eye, and his complexion turns a quite ghoulish, bloodless shade of grey. He opens his mouth as if thinking to say something more, but a sharp glance from his wife silences him.

'I am sure that we can think of a happier subject to speak of, now,' Mabel says, her voice high and strained. 'I for one have heard quite enough of salvage and … and graveyards, and I am quite positive –'

'It is all right,' Cecilia says. The clear sound of her voice surprises even herself. 'It is all right, everyone. I realize what you all must be thinking. You are embarrassed, and sorry for me, I imagine, to think that I should hear you speak of such things. Because you suppose that, when I hear about ships lost and sunk at sea, I cannot help but picture my John at the bottom of the ocean, too. That his ship has joined those poor others upon the seabed … soon to be scored through with a red mark in Mr Delahunty's ledger.' She sees Samuel flush and reach for the brandy decanter.

'Perhaps you even imagine that I urged Captain Harding to speak on the subject due to some sort of morbid fascination. That I long to picture the ocean floor, littered with wrecks and skeletons, where my husband now rests. But it is not so. There is no need to be embarrassed, or to worry for my sake. I am not anxious for John. I know that he remains above the tide, in the sun's glory and breathing the fresh sea air.'

She swallows. 'I know … I *do* know, what it looks like. His return is overdue – long overdue. And until he stands before us and tells us with his own breath just where he has been, there can be no explanation for that. But I am positive that he *shall* return and explain it. He is speeding back to me even now, as we sit here and talk and eat so pleasantly. I am certain. And so, you need not worry. And that is that.'

Just a fraction of an instant too late – after the very merest of pauses that lays bare their want of sincerity – her friends around the table call out their agreement. They raise their glasses and salute John's hasty return, and commend Cecilia's loyal, faithful resolve. They nod and smile, and toast absent friends; and then they toast England and the King, and then they move on to other toasts, one after the other, boisterous and happy, and meaningless.

Cecilia stops listening to them. She closes her eyes, and in the clinking of their glasses, over and over, she hears the crash and the crescendo of the distant tide as it rolls on, immutable.

12.

The remainder of the meal passes unremarkably and, before Cecilia knows it, the Hardings are calling for their carriage and it is time to go home again. Frances and her husband offer her a seat for the journey back, but Cecilia politely declines. 'It is not far to walk, and it is still light – I shall enjoy the stroll through the evening, thank you,' she tells them.

Once the Hardings are gone, Samuel also offers his farewells and disappears to another room. Mabel lingers with Cecilia a while longer. It seems she has more to say.

'I must tell you, Mrs Lamb, it raised my spirits more than I can say to hear you speak with such passion of Captain Lamb's return,' Mabel says, looking very earnest and holding Cecilia's gloved hands in her own.

'I am humbled by your patience and your resolve, truly,' she goes on. 'When Mr Delahunty used to go to sea, before his injury … well, I would just make myself sick with worry for his safety; and if his return were even a week or two overdue, then –' She catches herself. 'Oh, but such concerns were quite silly and unfounded, of course. Mrs Lamb … you must know that John is in our prayers, every night – mine and my husband's, and our children's too.'

'Thank you. But I know that worrying about John will do him no good at all,' Cecilia replies simply. 'John is a great sailor, and he shall be home soon.'

'Of course. And, you know, next time it shall be easier for you.'

'Next time?'

'The next time Captain Lamb goes to sea, of course. What I mean to say is, you shall not be left all on your own, will you?'

'I am not sure I follow ...'

Mabel laughs, as if it were a joke that they are both in on. 'La, you mean to make me say it, do you? What I mean is that after Captain Lamb returns – as surely he shall – the next time he goes to sea, he will undoubtedly leave you with a family! A little baby does make things easier, you shall see. There is precious little time to feel lonesome or sorry for yourself when you have a child to dote over. There is little time for anything at all!' She laughs and claps her hands. 'Oh yes, once you are a mother, you shall find that you hardly notice *where* your husband is any more.'

Cecilia is glad that Mrs Delahunty let go of her hands while she spoke, for if she had still been clasping them, then she surely would have felt the jolt that ran through Cecilia's entire body at her mention of motherhood. The budding life inside her remains still, as it has all through the evening with her friends. *Mabel does not know*, she tells herself. *There is no way that she can know, yet.*

'Oh, I see,' Cecilia murmurs. 'It is quite strange – Mrs Harding said the same thing to me only a few weeks ago.'

'Of course – it is only natural, isn't it, my dear?' Mabel beams at her. She looks for all the world as if Cecilia had already shared the news that a baby is expected. Cecilia's mind races; she is sure she displays no outward signs that Mabel might have perceived. Or does she? Could there be some signal that only those who are already mothers themselves know about?

'If anything, I might wonder that you have waited so long – but then, you are only recently wed, aren't you, and Captain Lamb did set sail so quickly, and – oh, and it is none of my business, besides! Samuel is forever telling me that I let my thoughts get entirely carried away by themselves. I suppose that he is right, isn't he? I haven't caused offence, have I?'

'No, not at all. I … I expect that you may be right, and John may wish to start a family, when he returns,' Cecilia says carefully.

'But of course he shall – you may hold me to it! Oh, but you mustn't frown, my dear! I am here, and Mrs Harding too, of course, to help you with everything. You are still so young, and far from home, after all.'

It is not Cecilia's habit to speak impulsively, without carefully weighing her words beforehand – perhaps, then, it is the two glasses of strong wine that she drank to fortify herself through dinner that make her suddenly say, 'Indeed, I have no doubt I should welcome your advice. In fact, I might have questions for you even sooner than you expect.'

Mabel's smile remains fixed, but she screws up her eyes, puzzled. 'Yes, well … After your husband returns home, no doubt.'

Why not just tell her now, Cecilia thinks. *Why not tell Mabel what I have felt … stirring?* She opens her mouth, but it is at that moment that the child awakens. Something turns and writhes inside her belly, flexing viscerally against her inner walls. Her jaw clamps shut in surprise and fear.

The pause hangs awkwardly in the air between the two women for several long seconds. Finally Cecilia manages to say weakly, 'You are too kind, Mrs Delahunty. We shall talk soon.'

Mabel beams, and they say their goodnights. But before she turns to go, Cecilia asks one more question.

'Mrs Delahunty … I wonder … What if it is not what *I* want?'

Mabel blinks. 'Whatever do you mean, my dear?'

'I mean, what if I do not want to be a mother, not yet? What if now is not the right time?'

Mabel laughs, uncertainly. 'Oh, you mustn't worry about that. You might not know it yet, but you *do* want it. It is what every woman wants, is it not? You shall see. But, my goodness – I have got ahead of myself again, haven't I? First things first, you must get that husband of yours back from wherever he has gone – or failing that, we shall find you a new one!' And she laughs again; gaily, at first, and then a little nervously, and then she bites her lip.

Cecilia forces herself to smile and laugh, too. 'Of course. Any day now, I pray. Goodnight to you, Mrs Delahunty.'

13.

A soft indigo twilight hangs in the sky, and the air swirls with dusky heat and salted ocean breeze as Cecilia walks the short distance to her empty, waiting house. She encounters no one as she walks.

Soothed by the pleasant evening climate, Cecilia takes a longer, rather more circuitous route home from the Delahuntys so she can enjoy the best views of the bay as it blooms with the beautiful and eerie colours of the lingering sunset. Far below her the waves slither through the mounting darkness like serpents. Silhouettes of distant ships drift silently past, still coming and going, like phantoms. Inside her belly the baby lies gurgling and contented, as it always does when her eyes drink in a view of the ocean.

Her mind wanders to Mabel's two children, Charles and David. They are sweet enough to look at, she supposes, for a short time at least. And it is abundantly clear that for Mabel their appeal holds no limit. It has been the same for every mother she has known: their own children hold a fascination for them that is difficult to comprehend. Even her sister Louisa … They had been so close growing up. Then Louisa had moved to Devonshire where her new husband's family lived. A year later her first child arrived. When Louisa had first moved away, they had written to each other every week; but after Cecilia's niece arrived, the spaces between her sister's letters had become longer, and longer, and the contents less interesting. She finds it difficult to understand how that can happen. For the first seventeen years of her life she had been her elder sister's shadow; now, she can scarcely seem to bring the details of her face to mind.

She stands watching the bay until the last of the light is all but gone, and then finally she turns for home. A small noise reaches her ear: a soft, plaintive cry, very faint but still plainly audible against the distant murmur of the ocean waves. At first she thinks it is the whimper of a small baby, and the hairs on her neck rise, electrified by some primitive instinct. For a moment she even imagines that it is the thing inside her, crying out audibly when she removed her gaze from the sea.

She stands for a moment, ears straining. Just as she is about to tell herself that it was only her imagination playing tricks, she hears it again: the meekest of sounds, almost pathetic. This time the sound comes from a distinct direction, and when she turns to look she sees a lumpish, dark-furred cat sitting not ten feet away from her.

The creature lurks down a side lane, sitting at an angle but with its head turned to stare directly at Cecilia through misty-green eyes. Her first thought is that it may well be the largest cat she has ever seen. It sits very neatly, with its paws nestled tightly together and its ragged tail tucked around it forming a tight ring. In the fading light its fur appears almost black, but even through the gloom Cecilia sees with distaste that it appears to be greasy and unclean. The cat's face is battered and scarred, with nicks visible in both ears, and one eye drooping half-closed either through injury or indolence. The cat is, in short, hideous.

Without breaking its gaze, it opens its mouth to reveal pointed, yellowing teeth, and gives voice to a third cry, small and mournful. It seems too small a sound to come from such a singularly large thug of a feline.

'What do you want?' Cecilia asks it.

The cat stares at her and licks its lips.

'Why are you lurking in that lane?'

It does not react. She takes a step towards it, and the cat stands up in a single, fluid movement, its tail uncurling and flicking bolt upright. Then the cat looks away, and stares abstractedly towards the blank wall opposite.

Cecilia looks around, wondering where such a half-feral-looking stray might have come from. This is a nice neighbourhood.

'If you are looking for food, you might have better luck at the docks,' she tells it. 'That way. They throw away all manner of fish scraps there, ready for the taking.'

The cat looks at her again and blinks slowly. 'You shall have to fight the gulls for it, but I imagine that should present no trouble for a brute like you,' she adds, wrinkling her nose slightly. She can't help but imagine what the creature's dark, dank fur must smell like; she can almost taste it at the back of her throat.

She and the cat both look away at the same moment. Their encounter, it seems, is concluded, and Cecilia resumes her walk homeward.

When she looks back after a minute or so, the cat is following her.

'No – the docks are that way,' she tells it, and points. The cat stares through her, with eyes as green and as deep as the ocean.

'You can't follow me,' she says. 'That is … I suppose you *can*, but there's nothing in it for you.'

Then she sighs. *What are you doing, Cissy, talking to a stray cat in the night?*

She walks on. When she looks over her shoulder again, the dark cat is gone.

The weather becomes increasingly intolerable, each day hotter than the last. It has been weeks since any rain fell out of the stunning blue sky. The nights are short and sickly, and too hot to ever get a good night's sleep. Under the twinkling dark of the cloudless night sky the town falls silent, like a held breath. In her room Cecilia lies on her bed and listens to the tide, its sound sloshing back and forth to fill the four walls. Every night she lies like that until her breath falls into rhythm with the tempo of the waves, her chest rising with the ebb and exhaling with the flow; until she is one with the distant roar, one with the ocean. As though she were breathing in its drowning waters. Only then does sleep come, and when she opens her eyes, the sun shines hot and bright upon another day.

A noise wakes her in the night. She had been dreaming of storms far out at sea, and at first she thinks it is just that – a squall blown in, at last, to rattle at the windows and disrupt the soporific haze that has fallen over the coast. Half-asleep she rises from her bed, thinking she must close the window before the rain gets in. She takes a groggy step towards the opened shutters, and with a start sees two green eyes staring back at her from right there upon the window ledge.

Jolted awake, Cecilia gasps, and the eyes vanish in a blink. Against the shadowy backdrop of the night she makes out a form, furry and sleek, as it turns and drops away from the window in a smudge of oily grey. She runs to the window and looks down, but the cat – for she is sure it was a cat that she saw, watching her sleep and then dropping from her window ledge – is nowhere to be seen.

She stands there for some time, staring into the moonlit view and wondering how and why a cat should have climbed up to her first-floor window; and, whether it could have made it back down so swiftly without injury. Not just any cat, either: she had seen those green eyes before.

She is wide awake now, and even after she is positive that the street below is deserted, she lingers at the window for some time, staring into the night. Finally a yawn strains at her throat, and her bed calls to her again. It is not raining but she pulls the window closed anyway, the room having grown somewhat chilly in the night – and, as a precaution, in case the strange cat should come prowling back.

As the glass closes across the aperture, she gives a cry; reflected in its surface, inches from her face, she can see the mirror of the room behind her. In the glass she sees plainly that the door to her bedchamber stands wide open, with a figure filling it. Her first, hopeful thought is that it is John at the door, arrived home in the middle of the night, as she has long dreamed he might. But even in the dark and distorted reflection she can recognize that the silhouette does not belong to him. It is more like a woman's physique, small and slender, closer to her own than her husband's. The figure stands with one hand upon the door handle, the other raised, as if it is just as shocked as she. Cecilia cannot make out an expression nor any features at all, but she can see that the person in the reflection is facing her, directly towards where she is standing at the window with her back turned. A tremble shakes her from head to toe, and Cecilia spins upon her heel to face the doorway and confront the intruder. But the door is closed, and the figure is already gone. She is alone in her room once more.

All too late, she feels the familiar twist of apprehension screwing into her stomach – her clairvoyant intuition warning her that something is not right, that she must be cautious. Except … usually, she feels that way *before* the fright comes.

*   *   *

Cecilia does not have to ponder for too long about at least one of her nocturnal visitors. The cat reappears later that same morning.

First she hears the raised voice of her maid echoing from somewhere at the back of the house. For a while, Cecilia continues to sit, lazily listening to Rosalie's angry, remonstrative cries, until finally she ventures downstairs, curious.

She finds Rosalie in the kitchen, standing at the back door, which she holds half-open. One of her hands is clasped firmly around the door, while her body is positioned to prevent any ingress through the space already available. She is ranting and raving and gesticulating towards something in the hot glare of the street outside.

'What on earth is going on?' Cecilia asks. Rosalie twists in surprise, not moving her body an inch from where it is blocking the doorway.

'The cat,' she replies, in English, as though the answer were obvious.

'The what? There is a cat? Let me see.'

But Rosalie gives no ground. 'He wants to come inside,' she explains, exasperated. 'All day, whenever I open the door, there he is, waiting to sneak past.'

Cecilia presses closer until her maid has to give some ground. Over Rosalie's shoulder she can see the same ugly cat that she met a few days earlier, and again last night looking in through her bedroom window. In the bright of the morning its fur appears a lighter shade of grey, like smoke, and if anything, even dirtier and less appealing.

Rosalie hisses and gestures angrily, but the beast gives no indication of even noticing. It stares up at the two women and meows plaintively.

'Every time I open the door, there he is! He try to come inside house, like … like a thief!' Rosalie explains in halting English, followed by a word of Portuguese that Cecilia is fairly certain must be obscene.

She looks at the cat. The cat looks back. Its long, white, twisted whiskers twitch, but the rest of its body remains perfectly still, and it shows no sign of intending to make any effort to move past them.

'Well, why don't you let him in?'

Rosalie is aghast. 'Let it in? It is dirty, look. It is a … a wild animal!'

'I hardly think it's dangerous. Just give it some food. He's probably hungry. I believe I saw the same cat prowling around here a few days ago, too.'

'Give him food! Then he always come back. Every day, he will expect more. Senhora, this is not a good cat.'

'Just find some leftovers,' Cecilia says, and then, looking around the kitchen, starts to tear a little cooked meat onto a plate herself. 'I suppose he must have followed me here, though I can't imagine why. Once he's eaten something, I expect he'll just … wander off again.'

She does not mention seeing the cat at her window; somehow she thinks it would not help matters.

She brushes the crumbs from her fingers onto the plate, then gently but firmly pushes Rosalie to one side and places the dish of meat scraps onto the kitchen floor, just inside the doorway and out of the sun's searing rays. The cat stands up immediately, trots through the doorway to the plate and begins to eat.

Rosalie clicks her tongue in disapproval. 'It comes back tomorrow for more, you shall see,' she says. 'Every day. Now we have a cat to feed.'

Cecilia smiles. 'Perhaps,' she says. And she leaves them, the cat eating contentedly and Rosalie staring down at it with arms crossed, her face folded into a deep frown.

14.

Weeks pass. Every day is the same: hot and too long. She wakes from not enough sleep to another dry and stale morning. She watches the bay from her window until the afternoon heat has smoothed off its edges, by which time the infant inside her will permit her no peace unless she leaves the house and walks right down to the water's edge. So she makes her way down the cliff to the harbour, or sometimes farther out to the black rocks.

The day of John's return is getting closer. She can feel it. The child grows – she can feel that, too, though it still does not show on her outwardly. She wonders which will arrive first: John or the child. She asks herself, *How long does a baby take to be born, anyway?*

She supposes that she should call for a doctor or a midwife. It is what ladies in her condition do, after all. But then there doesn't seem to be much need, not yet. She does not feel ill. One day soon she shall speak to Mrs Delahunty about it, she promises herself, day after day, but she never does.

She writes letters to Louisa, but she doesn't send them. Even if she knew how to get a letter to England – it cannot be that difficult, surely – the words that she writes never seem to come out right. She cannot explain what is happening to her, how she feels. Not even to her own sister. A heap of unsent correspondence begins to amass in her desk drawer, sheet upon sheet, like a soft bed built for an animal, or a nest.

One day, as she is trying to write, a creak at her drawing room door disrupts her thoughts. She thinks it is Rosalie and turns sharply in her chair, annoyed, but when she looks there is no one there at all. The door stands only slightly ajar. Then, after a moment's pause, the large, dark cat slips into the room through the gap. It flits across the floor with surprising speed and stealth for its great bulk and vanishes beneath a small settee. A moment later Rosalie does appear, bursting through the doorway with a vengeance.

'Yes, I saw it come in. It's under the settee, there,' Cecilia tells her calmly, and points.

'All day he sits and waits outside, waiting by the door. Waiting to get in, you see,' Rosalie fumes. She storms to the settee, hissing and bristling, not unlike a cat herself. 'Ay! *Sumir*!' she exclaims – a word Cecilia has heard her maid use not infrequently when chasing away children that play too loudly in the street outside. She claps her hands, but no dark or furry shapes emerge.

'I don't mind,' Cecilia says. 'Just leave it be. It probably wants to get out of the sun, that is all.'

Rosalie stares at her.

'The cat can stay. Thank you,' Cecilia tells her, firmly, and her maid nods and withdraws from the room, with only a minimal amount of eye rolling and head shaking.

Alone again – or almost alone – Cecilia gets up and walks over to the settee. There is still no movement, no sound, from below. After a moment's hesitation she drops to her hands and knees, and puts her head close enough to the cool wooden floor to peer underneath. Two green eyes, one half-closed, peer back at her from out of the darkness.

She abandons her half-formed letter and walks to the window to stare out across the rich blue sea. After several minutes have passed, something stirs in the corner of her eye. A grey shape, hopping into view. It is the cat, alighting upon the windowsill beside her. It does not look at Cecilia, and Cecilia does not look at it. It just sits down beside her, silently joining her vigil over the inscrutable comings and goings of the port below.

More and more the child places a constant demand on her attention. She feels it moving, pressing against her organs and her ribs from the inside; a sensation that is neither pleasant nor unpleasant, though it is certainly not comfortable. Sometimes it lies heavy and motionless, but still *present*. Other times it flits and twists, swimming circles inside her. Her senses seem to dull; food becomes flavourless and bland on her tongue, when she can stomach swallowing anything at all. She had thought that you have to eat for two when you are with child.

Only staring at the ocean, or walking by the shore with the waves in her ears, seems to bring any measure of peace. Only then does the child seem to be content to slumber inside her belly, waiting and growing. She imagines it watching the waves through her eyes, like a sailor with a telescope. *Perhaps it listens to the tide through my ears and is lulled to sleep by the sound*, she thinks. Surely it is its father's son.

Had she been left to set her own pace, Cecilia would likely have put off sharing her secret with Mabel Delahunty for many weeks longer – but, in the event, it is Mabel who comes to her, dropping by unexpectedly one afternoon.

'I do hope you don't mind my calling without notice,' she trills. 'I shall not stay. I only wished to look in, my dear, to see you and ease my mind that all is well. We were all so worried, you see – we thought perhaps you were ill, or that you might have heard about … Well, we thought that something might be wrong. So of course I had to call. There is a terrible malady going around, you know. Precious little David turned as hot and red as the tip of a poker with it, even in this heat. Oh, I have been beside myself with worry, you can imagine. Samuel said that I worried myself into a worse condition than the child – he said that of our own child! But he can be horribly unfeeling sometimes. Don't worry, little David pulled through of course. He takes after Samuel in that respect, you know, so does Charles; all three of them just bounce back from whatever contagion they pick up, not like me at all. But … but, well, in any case, the fact of the matter is that I thought I should just call and check whether you were perhaps ill or suchlike, my dear?'

Even by Mabel's standards she is speaking too much and too quickly, her head bobbing back and forth like a bird's. Something clearly has her worried.

'I am quite well, thank you,' Cecilia tells her, 'but I am afraid you have me at a loss, Mrs Delahunty: why should you imagine that I was ill?'

'Well, you know, dear, we were all so worried when you missed Mrs Harding's event.'

Cecilia hesitates. 'Mrs Harding's event?'

'She called it an event! I call it a little cards and some drinks with friends. But that is beside the point; we had all expected to see you there.'

Cecilia has a vague recollection of Frances proposing such a gathering – but has the date really come and gone already? Her memory of the recent past unspools loosely in her mind like a dropped ball of wool.

'My goodness,' she says, without much conviction. 'I must have forgotten completely. How rude of me – was she terribly upset?'

'Oh my, no. I imagine you should have to leave a murder victim in her drawing room to cause Frances any *real* offence. No, my dear, we were all just worried. We thought that perhaps you were ill, or had received some news?'

Mabel's eyes are wide with expectation. Cecilia feels her heart leap in her chest; or perhaps it is the child, swimming spirals in her belly. Mabel cannot know about her condition, can she?

'News?' she asks with a tremble in her voice.

Mabel looks away. 'News of Captain Lamb ... I did wonder if perhaps you could not come because – oh, good heavens, is that your cat?'

The creature has strutted haughtily into the room. 'No ... he is no one's cat, I think. He just sort of comes and goes,' Cecilia says. She holds out her hand to stroke its back as it slinks past, entirely ignoring both ladies. Its fur, she has discovered, is soft and not unpleasant to touch at all, despite its greasy appearance. 'I don't know where he came from. He has sort of moved in here, some of the time.'

'How darling,' Mabel says, wrinkling her nose.

As Mabel watches the cat, Cecilia steels her nerve. She knows that this is her opportunity to tell Mabel – to tell *someone* – about the baby. It cannot remain her secret forever, and she has already waited too long. The child, which had been stirring restlessly only moments before, is now still; if it has any objections, then it keeps them to itself.

'I am sorry to have caused you all any concern,' she says. 'The truth is ... I have been out of sorts lately. Not myself, I mean. You see, something *has* happened –'

'News of Captain Lamb?' Mabel cuts in, raising her hand to her heart. 'I knew it.'

'No – no, there is no word from John, still. No, it is news of an entirely different character ... You remember, when last we spoke, you told me that it should not be too long before John and I were to start a family. Well, I do believe that your predictions shall come true sooner than you could have realized.'

Mabel's eyes grow wide as saucers. 'Mrs Lamb, forgive me – before I say something indiscreet –'

'You have understood my meaning, I believe. I am expecting a child.'

Mabel has moved to sit beside her in an instant and taken grasp of both of her hands. 'Oh, how wonderful! I cannot describe how delighted I am. It is a blessing, a blessing for you and … and –'

She pauses, cutting her sentence short, her eyes flickering with doubt and confusion.

Cecilia is too buoyed by a floating sense of relief to notice. 'I must admit, I felt quite afraid to tell you.' She laughs. 'I cannot imagine why, now. It's so silly. I feel much relieved, just to have shared the news.'

'But … but my dear, forgive my confusion … I must ask, Captain Lamb has been absent for well over a twelvemonth by this time, has he not?'

'He has.'

'But, you see – you see …'

'I imagine the baby shall already be here when he returns. The poor man can have no inkling what he is coming home to!' Cecilia giggles.

But Mrs Delahunty is not smiling now. The two women stare at each other for a span of seconds, each uncomprehending of the other's confusion. Finally Mabel swallows, and speaks, seeming to choose her words very carefully. 'You see, my dear – it takes no more than nine months for a baby to be born, never so long as twelve. I have never heard of such a thing … No, it is simply not possible. So you see … for it to be Captain Lamb's child … Well, it cannot be so.'

'Oh,' Cecilia says, feeling blood rush to her face as if she had been slapped. 'I … I did not know that,' she admits. 'I … Perhaps I have become confused of the dates, or –'

'But certainly, Captain Lamb has been absent for such a length of time. And so, my dear, are you quite positive of your condition?'

'Yes. At least, I thought I was. I have felt it moving, you see, moving around inside me. Every day, and sometimes without respite. There is no mistaking it.'

'Felt it?' Mrs Delahunty's frown deepens. She seems entirely bewildered by what she is hearing. 'But there is nothing to be seen on you; it cannot be of such a size, yet … What you felt – was it a fluttering inside your stomach, like butterflies?'

'No. No, not like that at all. It feels like … Do you know the little black fish that swim in the shallow waters of the harbour?'

Mabel shakes her head. She looks almost frightened now. 'And the other signs by which a woman might know – Mrs Lamb, do you know what they are? Did your mother, or anyone, ever explain to you?'

Cecilia feels like a little girl with her legs dangling over the edge of her seat. 'My governess explained it to me, and my older sister … though they did not always speak as plainly as they might have. I know some signs, and I have observed them, I think. I have no appetite, and I feel a sickness in the morning, and … well, my monthly courses have been stopped for some time. You know. But I suppose the truth is, there is very much that I do not know about the woman's part …'

Mabel nods patiently. 'Not to worry. I shall find you a doctor – a good doctor – and then we shall know the truth of the matter. Leave it to me.' She leans forward conspiratorially. 'Naturally, Mr Delahunty need know nothing about it; do not worry about that.'

Cecilia looks away, dazed. 'Thank you. I thought … I was positive. I know I have felt it; felt something. Something moving. I did not know what it was. And then, I thought, it could only be …'

Mabel clears her throat. 'Forgive me, Mrs Lamb, but I must ask – if you are correct, and there *is* a child, and it cannot be Captain Lamb's … then might you be able to hazard a guess as to whom else it could belong?'

There is another embarrassing pause as it slowly dawns on Cecilia just what is being asked. 'No one! There has been no one else, I swear it. I could never do that to John.'

'Of course you couldn't, my darling. None of us could; but then, there it is. You are entirely positive? Well, then, there is nothing to worry about. And no one else knows, do they? Not even your little housemaid? Good, that is for the best. Yes, a doctor first, and then we shall know for certain.'

Mabel's manner is all steely, non-judgemental pragmatism. She nods, her mind made up. Then her eyes screw up with a sudden suspicion. 'And Captain Lamb – there is still no word, you say? Poor dear, it must be trying. You must be so worried.'

'No, no word … It is a long and arduous wait. But, as you know, I remain convinced that he will be back soon.'

'Indeed. And I do so admire you for it. But Samuel … My dear, I must tell you that in private my husband grows increasingly concerned that you are not entirely accepting of your situation. When a man is absent for so long at sea, we must be prepared –'

'I am aware of what *may* have happened,' Cecilia says, a little sharply. 'But that does not change how I feel … I do not know how to explain it. Mrs Delahunty, don't you ever just know a thing with an absolute certainty? As if you can imagine a scene playing out, and then it all happens precisely as you had envisioned it? Or, if you misplace a thing, you know for sure whether or not you shall see it again one day?'

'A husband is quite a thing to misplace,' Mabel says, her eyebrow rising. 'I cannot say that I follow you completely, Mrs Lamb. I pray that you are right, but … Remember, my dear, that we may well *hope* for miracles, but we must never *expect* them.'

In the next instant her manner has changed again, her forthright tone concealed once more beneath the layers of good-natured sweetness and cheer that is Mrs Delahunty's familiar costume. A rainstorm that had been haunting the horizon that morning begins to tap against the window-pane, and Mabel must say her goodbyes.

At the door she pauses to stare into Cecilia's eyes for a moment, her own misting over with a sudden emotion. 'Poor child! Remember that in me, and in Mr Delahunty as well, you have firm friends who may be relied upon, whatever happens. Oh, and la! Will you look at this rain, did you ever see the like! Well, it is a relief, though, and the grass needs it, too. But I shall be entirely drenched!' She laughs with delight, then pounces forward for a swift kiss, and runs for her carriage with a final wave goodbye.

15.

Despite what Mrs Delahunty has told her, Cecilia continues to feel the thing inside her moving, twisting, and turning as if it were trying to prove a point. She cannot believe that there is nothing there. She presses both hands to her stomach and feels her skin pulsing softly beneath her fingertips. She wants to find Rosalie, to take her maid's hand and push it against her belly and demand to know – you feel it too, don't you? But she is afraid. Because what answer could Rosalie give that would bring her any measure of comfort? No, I feel nothing, Senhora. Why don't you lie down, and I will fetch the doctor for you, now. Or, yes, I feel it too – but what it can possibly be, I have no idea.

Mabel returns the very next day bearing a gift and a proposition. She and Frances have planned a walk for the five of them along the continental coastline. They will take their carriages some distance out of the town and then follow a cliff path on foot – a little uneven but quite manageable for the ladies, she is assured – towards an old, ruined, coastal fortress that Captain Harding has heard tell of as a local point of interest.

To her own surprise Cecilia readily agrees to the outing. The prospect of a bracing walk along the cliffs is enough to quiet her usual hesitance towards social gatherings. 'That sounds quite wonderful; exactly what I need,' she says, and it is the truth.

'And are you quite certain you are up to it? Your health – your constitution – will allow it?' Mabel asks, her voice dropping to a hush though there is no one to eavesdrop except the cat.

'Yes, I feel quite capable, thank you. I am sure I can keep up with you all.' Cecilia makes no mention of how much she walks, each and every day, up and down the town and along the waterfront, back and forth. 'Unless you suppose I should wait until I speak to the doctor?'

'Not to worry – I have that in hand, also,' Mabel says with a subtle grin.

She announces that she cannot stay; but before she leaves, she has something else to give.

'You are altogether too kind to me, Mrs Delahunty,' Cecilia tells her with a smile, and Mabel's cheeks positively glow with pleasure. She presents Cecilia with a smallish, somewhat gaudy pendant, dangling from a thin chain. The jewellery is heart-shaped, around the size of an apricot, and made from a thin layer of what might be real gold. Mabel takes some time to show off the amulet first, turning it this way and that to show off its oriental-styled decoration. Then she turns a clasp, opening the heart like a locket and revealing what is inside: an odd little ball of what looks like dirt, about the same size and shape as the end of her thumb.

'What is it?' Cecilia asks, trying and failing to hide her disappointment.

'Have you heard of a Goa stone?' says Mabel. Cecilia shakes her head. She leans closer to inspect the curious lump and is met by a faint odour, sweet like dead flowers. The small ball is a sickly olive-green in colour, flecked through with droplets of silvers and reds on its smooth, shining surface.

'It is a kind of bezoar: a medicine. From … someplace in the Far East, I don't know where. Their kings and sultans and who-knows-what use these Goa stones to ward off poisons. But *this* one is made by European Jesuits, who have entirely perfected the formula. They are quite rare and valuable. Samuel went to some lengths to procure this one for me, to soothe my illnesses when I was carrying David.'

She snaps the amulet closed again and holds it out towards Cecilia, the flashing heart charm dangling on its chain from her balled fist. 'I want you to take it, my dear.'

Cecilia hesitates. 'I am not sure I understand. It is a medicine? For what?'

'Why, for whatever ails you! It is a remedy for just about anything, I find. Headaches, stomach upsets, low moods, or anxieties …' Cecilia looks from the amulet to Mabel, who glances away.

She holds out her hands and Mabel drops the object into her cupped fingers. It is weightier than she expects. 'Do I wear it?'

'No, no. That is, I suppose one could – but I never did. No, you shave a little – just a little – off its surface, into a cup of water, or tea if you prefer, and drink it down whenever you feel the need.'

'You want me to drink this?'

Mabel nods enthusiastically. 'It draws out the poison. And you know, Mrs Lamb, there are many things that may infect us so. An imbalance of humours – too much melancholy, or phlegmatism … or an excess of sensibility, such as at times of great stress. These are all types of poisons, too,' she explains with a slow emphasis.

The implication is hardly subtle: *She believes that I am mad*, Cecilia thinks. And yet she finds that she is touched, all the same. Even though Mabel supposes I have invented this thing growing inside me, she still thinks to bring me medicine.

'Thank you, Mrs Delahunty, you really are too kind,' Cecilia says, with feeling.

'Trust me – trust me, my dear. And – do be sure to keep it shut inside its case, there, to retain the potency.'

After Mrs Delahunty has left, Cecilia walks upstairs to her drawing room and to her desk. She pulls open a drawer and drops the gaudy heart charm and its unappealing contents onto the soft pile of unsent letters inside; then she shuts and locks the drawer and walks away, dangling the key care-lessly from her fingertips.

16.

Cecilia stands at her window for the rest of the afternoon, staring out to sea with the cat sitting beside her. But although her gaze is fixed on the wide Atlantic, in her mind's eye she is looking back through time, thinking over scenes from her past. Mabel's proposal of a walk along the sea-battered cliffs has caused her to reminisce; to remember happier times, when she and John had walked such routes, before they were husband and wife.

John had still been in the King's Navy when first they met, a master's mate newly stationed in Cecilia's home town. The naval officers in their smart uniforms had always been a familiar sight for Cecilia growing up; but it happened to be the same summer John and his shipmates had arrived that she had discovered within herself a new and quite startling fascination for these young men in their dashing royal blues.

John was older, closer in years to her brothers than to her. Cecilia was just of an age to be introduced at various social functions, and John was always there, too; in fact, her first impression of him was merely one of ubiquity, rather than being drawn by any particularly remarkable or attractive features. On the edge of every function room that she had stared around with wide and innocent eyes that summer, there he was, in her eyeline. It hadn't occurred to her until much later that this might in fact have been his design all along.

A group of them had started to take walks through the local countryside: Louisa – who was then unmarried – Cecilia and a set of their friends, and whichever naval officer Louisa was attached to at the time along with a number of his male companions. They all went together for the sake of decency, though on their walks girls and boys (for they were just girls and boys, children playing at adulthood, it seems to her now) would inevitably split into distinct pairings with long distances lagging between them: a loose chain of hopeful, potential couples following the same route.

Somehow Cecilia always found herself walking with John. For a long time the pair had said almost nothing at all; the entirety of their first two rambles she spent watching her own feet, while John had gazed away with half-squinted eyes, only once or twice commenting on some feature of the landscape.

It was only on the third walk that she had begun to suspect he was waiting for her to introduce a topic of conversation. On the fourth walk she did, tentatively. 'I hope that Louisa does not lead us too far today. I do find these walks overlong and quite tiresome,' were the first substantial words she had spoken to her future husband.

She cannot now remember what he said back, but it was something funny, some light-hearted comment that had put her more at ease. She had quickly realized that in contrast to his quite severe and serious appearance John had a good-natured and easy-going soul, always quick with a small joke or a private, sideways smile. He was not the man she had first taken him for.

After Louisa ultimately married a clergyman who had inherited land in the South-East, the others fell away, until it was only Cecilia and John left on their walks. Left to decide their own path, they followed the coastal trails, rough and wild, hiking up and down vaguely picked tracks banked with tall, thick beach grass and dense briars dotted with yellow flowers, high atop the rugged English cliffs where the trees all grow sideways with the wind. Her memories of those happy days seem weighty and solid: the powerful waves pounding against the cliffs, the thick quilt of white cloud hanging overhead with a misty sun just swirling through, the cold grey rock of the cliffside streaked and columned with age; everything about that place and that time seems heavy, even her recollection of it.

But it was not a restricting weight – on the contrary, she had felt a greater sense of freedom, then, than she thinks she ever has before or since. A freedom to roam without fear. They could walk for miles and not see another soul. And with John by her side there was nothing to be afraid of.

Everyone at that time must already have known that they were to be married, she supposes, otherwise surely her family would not have allowed her to roam so far without a chaperone. Only she had been surprised when John had proposed; not even her occasional gift of premonition had prepared her for that.

It has been the same all my life, she thinks. *When it comes to the twists and turns of life, everyone else always seems to know just what route I shall take. Everyone except myself.*

When the tide was low and the weather fair, she and John used to venture down from the rugged clifftop trails, descending rough slopes hidden in the thick yellow grass towards hidden coves scooped out along the edges of the coast. Tiny hidden beaches secreted away just for the two of them to discover, though these beaches were littered with hard pebbles and stones, slippery and cold underfoot and uncomfortable to walk on.

'They look like little eggs – hundreds of little eggs!' Cecilia had exclaimed the first time they descended to one of these secret beaches and she had heard the stones rattle beneath her shoes.

'Like no eggs I've ever seen,' John had chuckled, bending and scooping up a particularly chunky specimen in his hand. Every stone seemed to have been worn to the same smooth, oval shape, the only variance coming in their size; some were as tiny as a thimble, some so large Cecilia could hardly have lifted them with both hands.

Cecilia had stood in the centre of the cove and stared around. 'But doesn't it look like a nest, of sorts, John?' she asked.

'Aye, it's a fanciful thought, but I can see the likeness. And all of these, eggs laid by a dragon; or – no, I've got it – by a griffin, I'd wager.' He looked at her then with a smile upon his lips. 'You've heard of griffins, haven't you, Cissy?'

'Of course. Half a lion and half an eagle is the general idea. Only – I'm afraid to tell you – they're not real, you see. They exist only in story books.'

'Is that so? And I had thought …' He pretended to be perplexed. 'Well, it must be, if you say so. Only – if that's the case, how could they have laid all of these eggs?'

John laughed then, and stooped to place the egg he had picked up back onto the ground with mock tenderness.

They returned to those hidden griffins' nests – after John had conjured the idea, Cecilia could not help but think of them as such – frequently during their walks. It had been on one of those pebble-strewn beaches that he had finally asked for her hand. The tide had been coming in and the wind blowing hard, howling mournfully against the cliff walls, but John had been unusually insistent that they should go down.

When they reached the shore, the waves were surging hard and quick, bubbling and fizzing white foam across the heaped stones and slimy clumps of dark green seaweed. Beneath the cliff there was no sun and Cecilia had found herself shivering in the shade, buffeted from all sides by the stiff sea wind.

'Well, here we are,' she had told him moodily, and she wrapped her arms about herself and turned to stare over the churning water. Her memory of the entire scene is remarkably vivid.

After a moment John had appeared by her side. 'Here now, don't be sour, Cissy,' he said gently. 'Take a look at this,' and he had quickly pushed a stone into her hands. It was small – slightly smaller than a hen's egg – and coloured charcoal-black with a curious hoop of silver-grey banded around its middle.

'What is it?'

'It's a curious one, wouldn't you say? I've never seen a pebble that looks like that.'

'It's quite unusual, I suppose,' she said, and she had almost dropped it carelessly back onto the beach there and then – she wasn't in the mood.

But something in John's voice and manner had made her take notice. 'That one's a real griffin's egg, I think,' he told her with a kind of nervous earnestness. She could see his throat shift as he swallowed beneath his collar. 'It's a real rare find. A true treasure. Just like you are, Cissy.'

She had looked down at the small, cool lump sitting in the palm of her hand. 'You should – try and open it up,' John went on.

'I beg your pardon?'

'See what's inside. Just try. Try and open it.'

She hesitated, for a moment, but it was clear he was up to something, and so she took the stone between her fingers and tried to crack it open, split its shell as you would a real egg. Nothing happened.

'It's as hard as rock, of course.'

'Try twisting at it.' John was watching her closely. His cheeks were flushed scarlet by the buffeting wind, but the rest of his complexion was quite pale.

She looked at the stone, turned it around in her hands, and then gripped it between her fingertips and twisted along the edge of its silver banding. To her amazement the egg split and broke apart in an instant; it crumbled away to nothing in her fingers, leaving her holding nothing but a handful of black, powdery dust in the middle of which sat a small, silver ring.

'What is this?' she had asked, shocked.

John laughed. 'Can't you see it's a ring, Cissy. For you. For us to be married. It's all been arranged, you see. I spoke to your father, and he's already agreed to everything; I only asked him to keep it a secret until I could tell you, my own way. I think he actually liked that.'

Although the timing – and most certainly the method – of the proposal had caught her off-guard, it had nonetheless been what Cecilia had been hoping for. But she supposes that she must have stood there dumbfounded, and not provided the immediate happy acceptance John had been hoping for; for he had turned away from her then to hide his rising emotion.

'I know,' he said, over his shoulder, 'I know I'm not rich, though I've a small inheritance to come from my uncle. But we won't need that anyway, because I'll make my own fortune, out there.' He thrust his arm out towards the sea.

'There's an entire world of riches across the sea, Cissy. A globe ready for the taking. Far beyond old Europe, there are lands that haven't even been discovered yet. New maps are being drawn up every day. And I'll see them all. If there are griffins out there, lass, then I'll find them. I'll bring one back for you – I'll tether the beastie with a golden chain. Britain … this small island … it's never been enough for me. There are a thousand fortunes out there, and I mean to have my share! I'll be a man they write about in the papers, you'll see. I'll do it for us, Cissy. And I'll always come back to you, I swear it.

'So – what do you say? You'll be my first treasure, Cecilia. My greatest treasure of all – my wife – if only you'll accept me?'

Still, Cecilia had said nothing. She was only half-listening. She was staring down at the black and silver powder in her gloved hands. The wind was snatching it away, fast, but flecks still stuck clinging to her fingers, and to the glinting ring sitting in her palm. The stone – the egg – it had been a fake, some sort of clever construct. Solid as a rock, and then not there at all. She never did understand how he had pulled off that trick.

17.

The appointed day arrives for Cecilia's cliffside walk with the Delahuntys and the Hardings. The weather looks as pleasing as might be hoped, even if the temperature remains exhaustingly high. Cecilia's mood is similarly bright – she has been looking forward to escaping the city: breathing fresh air that is not ripe with fish guts and exotic perfumes, and admiring the shifting ocean from some different perspectives to the views that she has become so accustomed to.

The Hardings call early in the afternoon to collect her in their carriage, and they trundle out of town into the hot and dusty countryside. As the road leads them inland, the roar of the sea is replaced by a constant and deafening drone of thousands of insects that swarm in the fields of yellowing crops, which now surround them on all sides. A short distance behind, the Delahuntys follow in their own carriage.

The heat inside the stifling compartment and the drone of the insects outside conspire to make Cecilia sleepy. She tries to listen to Frances talk, smiling and nodding whenever the occasion seems to call for it. The baby grows tired as well and lies lethargically in her belly, twitching occasionally as if in impatient anticipation of the coastal trails and sea air, the wild waves and frothing surge that await them at the end of the ride.

She wonders if Mabel has mentioned anything to Frances about their last conversation – if so, Frances is giving nothing away. Cecilia remembers with some guilt Mabel's medicine, the Goa stone, still locked untouched in her desk drawer.

At last the thrum of insects subsides and the welcome crash of waves returns as they near the starting point of the walk. They will leave the carriages behind and follow the cliff on foot, hugging the coastline until they arrive at the promised castle where, all being well, the carriages will be waiting to collect them again for the homeward journey.

The carriages halt, and Cecilia steps blinking into the sunlight and inhales deeply of the fresh, open air; she rolls the stiffness from her shoulders and stretches out her legs as she takes a few steps towards the foaming blue expanse of the ocean. The infant stirs as well, invigorated; she can feel it, behind her eyes, looking out. She feels a rush of blood to her head as her pulse quickens with her child's excitement.

When she turns back to the carriages, she is surprised to see not just Mabel and Mr Delahunty, but a third individual climbing down from their carriage. And it is not just any individual; with a plummeting sense of realization she recognizes his face, his dark coat. Cecilia has met this unexpected interloper once before, and not in the most opportune circumstance.

It is the same young English doctor who had rushed to her aid the day she fell at the docks. When she tripped on the boardwalk; the first time she had felt the thing – the child – shifting and moving inside her. The day that she thought she saw John, standing upon the stern of a departing ship, staring at her with a callous indifference in his eyes.

The doctor remains beside the carriage, engaging Samuel Delahunty in small talk. As he looks around admiring the view, his gaze meets with hers, and he smiles politely. She cannot guess whether he has recognized her as well. But she is positive it is the same man. It doesn't take her long to surmise that this must be the promised doctor whom Mabel has procured for her – only, for some reason, Mabel has decided to invite him to join them all on this excursion instead of setting Cecilia up with a regular appointment.

Mabel waves to her in greeting; Cecilia marches over and, taking her by the arm, leads her politely but firmly out of earshot of the others.

'That is the doctor you found for me?'

'Yes indeed! I thought it was lucky enough when Samuel happened to mention that an English doctor had arrived in port. I had no idea that he should be so young and handsome, as well –'

'But what is he doing here? You invited him on our walk?'

'Of course. It seemed the perfect plan. The poor soul is a stranger in town and hardly knows anyone at all, I gather. What better way for you to be introduced?'

'But … but what do you even know about him? Who *is* he?'

'Doctor Clement Mayberry; he arrived in Portugal a mere matter of weeks ago, I believe. I don't know much about his family, but his father is also a doctor, with diverse business interests across the world that bring in a considerable income. And Doctor Mayberry has absolutely no brothers or sisters, you know.'

Cecilia is only half-listening. There is a fiery panic rising inside her. She can feel her two worlds colliding like bubbles about to pop: the respectable life she pretends to lead with her friends, and her secret existence spent roam-

ing the wharfs and the seafront, aimlessly and beyond
explanation. She narrows her eyes and imagines this
Doctor Mayberry telling Samuel Delahunty: Why, that
young lady – I have seen her once before, you know, in a
state of no small distress, flustered with emotion and
rambling about a man on a boat. She had been loitering
among the dockyards all by herself and proved quite unable
to explain her reasons …

'Can I trust him?' she hears herself ask out loud.

Mabel seems surprised. 'Of course, my dear. He comes
highly recommended, I imagine.'

As soon as the party sets off, Cecilia finds herself forced into
walking with Doctor Mayberry. Mabel has quickly returned
to her husband, and the Hardings remain similarly paired-
off, leaving the two awkwardly unattached members of the
group compelled to be each other's company. The doctor
approaches and bows politely. 'Good morning – may I
presume that you must be Miss Lamb?' he says.

'*Mrs* Lamb. Good morning, Doctor Mayberry.' When her
eyes dare to meet with his, she can discern no hint of recognition. *Perhaps he really doesn't remember me*, she thinks with
relief.

They walk following an indistinct and winding path
along the coastline. Cecilia is quickly disappointed to
discover that the promised clifftop trail falls some way short
of her expectation; to her right the countryside is spread out
like a flat wasteland, fields of crops in wan greens and
yellows like overcooked peas, and here and there a copse of
squat, dark trees. To their left the land slopes gradually
down towards the sea, matted thick with hardy yellow grass
until the ground crumbles away into coarse sand the colour
of eggshells, where a placid ocean laps. It is nothing like the
dramatic cliffs and hidden coves of home. She feels cheated
somehow.

Cecilia and the doctor begin at the rear of the group, but they overtake first the Hardings and then the Delahuntys until they are far out in front. Even then Cecilia does not realize just how fast she is walking until she hears a voice from behind: 'I had not realized that today should be a foot race – I daresay you shall beat the carriages to the fort at this rate'.

She looks around and sees the doctor trailing some two dozen yards behind. Cecilia forces herself to slow and fall in step with her companion. 'I am sorry, doctor. I did not realize how fast I was going. I most often walk alone, these days.'

'Don't hold back on my account,' he replies cheerfully. 'I also enjoy a brisk pace. Although, I own that I am not so acclimatized to this heat as you clearly are.'

'Yes … the heat is tremendous,' Cecilia agrees dully. She watches the doctor wipe a handkerchief across his slick brow, and it occurs to her that she doesn't even know what, if anything, Mabel has told him about her condition, or if he even knows she is in need of medical consultation. Nothing the doctor has said or done so far suggests that he knows anything about her except her name. She wonders just what Mabel's game is with all of this.

They walk on side by side for a while, in an easy silence. It is Cecilia who eventually breaks it. 'I must admit,' she says, 'to being a little disappointed with the countryside here. I had been rather hoping for scenery more like home.'

'More like England, you mean? It's funny, I was just finding enjoyment in a similar thought. The land here is so similar and so different in the same instant. The colours of the grass and the trees, and the sky and the sea; they all seem a shade which I am not yet familiar with. Like a painter who has drawn from a palette I have never before come across.' He catches her eye and laughs. 'Ah – I fear I sound like a novice traveller, taking his first faltering steps away from home and marvelling in every trivial detail. It is true, I am afraid. You must think I sound terribly dull and naive.'

'I don't think anything,' she says. 'You had never left England before you came here?'

'Never.'

'Neither had I. You know, doctor,' Cecilia says suddenly, seized by an impetuous instinct to take the bull by the horns, to own and, perhaps, direct the lingering tension which she still feels, 'we have met once before, you and I. You may not remember –'

A voice interrupts her from behind:

'Doctor Mayberry! Excuse me, doctor!' It is Frances Harding. Cecilia and the doctor must have slowed their pace, or else the married couples had picked theirs up, for the gap between them all has closed considerably. The doctor stops and turns to her politely.

'I wonder if you can help us,' Frances smiles. 'James and I have been discussing you. We are trying to discern what you *are*, you see: are you a mulatto?'

The doctor smiles blandly, and lets the question hang for just a second before answering. 'My father comes from Norwich. My mother comes originally from the west coast of Africa. Father was conducting business in her homeland when they met. They fell in love and were married – and so they remain, as happily married as any match that I know of. As for me, I am as you see before you.' The words trip off his tongue, an automatic reply that seems well rehearsed, though there is a flicker of irritation behind his mild mask that seems unmistakeable to Cecilia.

Frances appears not to notice, however. She looks pleased with the information. 'Yes – yes indeed. As I thought. I *told* you, James.'

They move off, Cecilia and the doctor taking a smart pace until there is a good-sized gap between them and the others once again. When she is sure the Hardings are out of earshot, she says softly: 'The Hardings and the Delahuntys have been very kind to me. They are not as … judgemental as Frances's blunt manner might suggest. It is just that … as travelled as they are, I believe they still view the world through a very narrow pinhole.'

'But you do not?'

'Well, I suppose that –' she flounders, but the doctor continues quickly.

'Forgive me, I meant nothing by it. It is just … I have been answering Mrs Harding's question all of my life. I suppose I shall never stop answering it. I had hoped that after I achieved my qualifications, perhaps … And then, here in this foreign place, I liked to hope that I might be less worthy of attention. But it is no matter,' he sighs.

'Is that why you came here, doctor? To get away from England?'

'In part, perhaps. I don't know – I don't think I had any single reason, is the truth of it. I had heard there is work here for doctors. Back home I was at the top of my class, but since I completed my training, the opportunities have been – well …' he lets the sentence drift off, snagged on the ocean wind.

She remembers the card that he gave to her, his earnest entreaty that she should call on him. 'We have met before, you know,' she tells him for a second time; this time the doctor hears, and he looks at her curiously.

'Indeed? Then I believe I must owe you an apology, for I do not –'

'Frankly, I am glad if you can't remember me,' Cecilia laughs. 'It was a fleeting introduction, and in a rather unfortunate circumstance. I was … You came to my aid when I fell down – near the harbour.'

'Aha! So that was you? What serendipity that we should meet again. I wondered where you had vanished to, you know. You did not call as I asked.'

'I'm sorry. There did not seem to be any need; I am quite recovered, as you can see.'

The doctor stops abruptly in his tracks. 'Perhaps I should be the judge of that,' he says – he is smiling, but it does not seem to be a joke.

Cecilia has stopped a few paces ahead of him, and he waits patiently until she has walked back to where he stands. Her forehead burns even hotter beneath the afternoon sun as he puts his hand to her chin and gently turns her head back and forth, studying her eyes with a steady, professional curiosity. Then he takes her arm and places his fingers against her wrist.

Something slithers in her abdomen, and she wonders if the doctor's fingertips can detect her pulse skipping a beat. Her heart taps rapidly in her chest as she waits for him to finish; she wonders just how many secrets a medical man might uncover from so cursory an examination.

'I concede, you do appear to be in good health,' the doctor says at last. 'No long-term damage done. Even so, I do wish that you had called.'

It is on her lips to say something there and then – to tell the doctor about how she has been feeling, about *what* she has felt; what she can feel even now, moving wetly around in the pit of her stomach. But Doctor Mayberry speaks first. 'Mrs Lamb,' he asks with a frown, 'might I enquire as to what you were doing at the harbour that day –'

A voice – Samuel Delahunty's – cuts in. 'Come along, you pair, no idling. Not very much farther to the fort, I shouldn't think,' he calls out, a little breathlessly, and then he laughs as if he has made a joke. The married couples have closed the gap between them again while Cecilia and the doctor were standing.

'We were only admiring the view – waiting for the rest of you to catch up,' the doctor smiles back. They let the Delahuntys and then the Hardings pass, each nodding hello to the others as if they all happened to be passing in the street. As Mabel passes close to Cecilia, she winks at her and then breaks into a wide smile and whispers something into her husband's ear as they move away.

By the time they start walking again, the doctor seems to have forgotten his question, and Cecilia has swallowed her sudden impulse to tell him about the child. They walk on in silence. Cecilia turns her head towards the ocean and the distant white haze of the horizon. The ghostly outline of a ship is crawling past. It passes directly beneath the sun, and the ocean flashes, bright and white-hot; and then the ship is gone, vanished like vapour, and the long line of the horizon is blank and empty.

18.

The trail dips and then rises, and from the next summit, the party's destination – the coastal fortress – becomes visible, sitting upon a rocky bluff set against the crashing tide. Cecilia's heart lifts as, at last, the scenery develops into something closer to her memories of home: high rocky cliff walls, and a cauldron of churning waves below.

They all pause for just long enough to admire the view and recover their breaths, and then the six press on. This time Cecilia walks with Mabel, the latter having made a deliberate move to partner with her, linking their arms with a gentle determination and waiting for the rest of the party to set off so that the two ladies might trail behind.

'What a marvellous day! Look at how blue that sky is. Even the sun seems not so unbearable when paired with a good sea breeze; though don't the birds make an awful racket?' Mrs Delahunty says brightly. 'Now –' her tone changes, suddenly, and she pats Cecilia's arm with her free hand, 'I saw you speaking with Doctor Mayberry, my dear. He is a fine young gentleman, isn't he?'

'He certainly seems like a decent man, and has made for a pleasant enough companion.' This time it is Cecilia's turn to become suddenly serious. 'Mrs Delahunty, what does the doctor know about me? Did you tell him anything about John, or … my condition?'

'Oh, I told him nothing about *that* – about your … unwellness, I mean. Of course, you must discuss it with him, and seek his counsel and so forth – but all in good time. I believe I did mention a thing or two about poor Captain Lamb. Only that he is at sea, and … Well, yes, that is all. I told him only what I thought he should know in advance.'

'In advance of what?'

'Of meeting *you*, my dear, naturally! You really needn't worry; I only touched upon a few points here and there.'

'But, Mrs Delahunty, wasn't the whole purpose of seeking a doctor so that I could consult him about my condition? About the … the child?' As Cecilia says the word, Mabel turns to glance at her sharply.

'You remain convinced, do you?' she says with something like disapproval. 'Well, naturally, you must speak to the doctor. But … you didn't mention that to him yet, did you?'

'No, I haven't.'

'Good.' They follow the trail in silence for a while, the red castle inching closer and closer. After a minute or two Mabel speaks again: 'He likes you well enough, I daresay. I could see. The way he walked with you, and the way that he talked. The doctor thinks very well of you.'

'Indeed!' Cecilia scoffs. 'What else were we to do but walk and talk?'

'Even so. I know what I saw, and I saw that he admires you.'

'Well, if you are correct, then he is wasting his admiration. I am a married woman.'

'Of course, of course. And yet … it does no harm to keep your options open, does it? We women must be pragmatic, after all. Think of the future.'

She turns to look at her companion. 'Mrs Delahunty, what do you –'

'Think of the future,' Mabel insists. 'The doctor is newly arrived; he shall be thinking to put down roots here. A busy young man like that can never make do on his own – he will need a wife. Now, do not misunderstand me. We all pray for Captain Lamb's safe return. But there can be absolutely no harm at all in making your appeal plain to the good doctor, and holding his attention for now, so that you shall not want for it later. You understand, don't you? Think about what is practical, here and now, and what might come in the months ahead. It would be good for you, Mrs Lamb, I think, to maintain your focus on what is real.'

Her bright eyes are as hard as diamonds. For the second time, Cecilia is caught off-guard by Mabel's flinty, determined pragmatism, and in that moment she can only nod mutely in reply.

She has a feeling that she should be angry at Mabel for saying such things. But she cannot be – for the fact is that her advice is sound, and Cecilia knows it. She wonders if she should be angry instead with Doctor Mayberry – if his friendly candour had truly concealed an ulterior motive – but again, there is no wrath inside her. Somewhere in the darkened labyrinth of her mind a crack of light appears, as if a door has been opened by a fraction. A door that promises to lead somewhere new, located where she had believed there to be nothing but a dead end.

At long last the group arrives at the fortress. Up close it stands squat, rugged, and weather-beaten; reddish stone worn into softly jagged edges, like the milk teeth of some colossus lying indolent against the shore. The place seems entirely abandoned, and most of it lies in a state of disrepair; it is rather less poetic than it had appeared from a distance.

They enter the ruin through the gaping mouth of an empty archway and stand inside the hollow walls, staring around at the bare stone. It is not clear what any of it had been, once upon a time.

'We should have bought some sort of guidebook,' Frances declares impatiently, her voice echoing.

'Look, this was a fireplace, once,' James says, standing under an arched alcove. Then he looks up and adds, disappointedly, 'Oh – there's no chimney, above, though.'

Spying a narrow doorway almost hidden in the corner of the room, Cecilia breaks off to investigate what lies beyond. Enclosed within the shade of the stone walls the air is cool and crisp, if a little musty, and reverberates with the muttering voices of the wind and the waves outside. It is like standing inside a seashell.

Another voice – a human voice – speaks over the swirling din. Doctor Mayberry has followed her. 'I suppose that castles the world over must all look largely the same, from the inside,' he observes.

'I expect so,' Cecilia agrees, and looks around for another exit from the room they are in, but there isn't one – the doctor is now blocking the only doorway, his head angled to one side so that he can fit his tall form into the ancient frame.

She hesitates, looks around in the half-light once more and then says, 'Excuse me,' and moves to leave. Doctor Mayberry steps aside, and bows as she passes.

She wants to be alone with her thoughts. She hurries away, past the married couples in the next room, following the wordless moan of the waves and the harsh screech of seagulls until she emerges once more into the sunlight. Now Cecilia finds herself in some manner of courtyard – the inner sanctum of the castle, now overgrown with thick, flaxen grass. Three sides are bound by the high castle walls, while on the fourth there is nothing but the wide open ocean. She walks across the grass to the middle of the court-yard, where the ground before her simply falls away into a treacherous drop, all the way down to the sea and rocks below. She glances over her shoulder expectantly, but no one seems to have followed her outside.

She ponders whether the castle might once have had a fourth wall, standing tall against the Atlantic, that one day simply collapsed with the cliffside and gave way to the devouring waves. Or perhaps it always stood open to the sea, with enormous wooden cranes like those she sees at the city's harbour to lower goods to vessels below. There is no way to tell. Turning her back on the ocean, she can see where the fortress once rose into two towers at the points where its three surviving walls intersect. What remains of the tower on her right is in a poor state, but the tower to her left stands intact. Her eyes follow its irregular brickwork upwards, higher and higher, until the brightness of the sky blinds her. She squints until her eyes adjust and she can make out the jagged battlements at the tower's pinnacle, high above the spot where she is standing.

Cecilia is struck, then, by the curious realization that she is looking *for* something. She did not happen to wander into this courtyard by chance; her eyes are not scanning those high battlements out of mere admiration for their historic architecture and engineering. No ... consciously or not, she came out here in search of something specific. Something she expects to find, even though she does not yet know what it is.

Next there comes the creeping itch at the back of her skull, and the spiralling tension through the core of her body: her intuition, her premonition – call it what you will. A voice inside her head whispers: *He is here*.

Then she sees. Almost indistinguishable from the high battlement walls, set against the stunning blue of the midday sky, she can see the shape of a figure. A person, standing at the top of the tower, their head and shoulders emerging distinctly above its crenellated edge. They might be looking out towards the ocean – or, they might be looking down towards her, staring back; they are too distant, too small, too obscured beneath the glare of the hot sun for her to tell.

Almost as soon as she can be positive of what she has seen, the figure in the tower is gone: vanished from view. They might have taken a step back from the battlement's edge. They might never have been there at all – but an uncomfortable coil stabbing at her insides tells her that her eyes were not deceived.

The whipping sea breeze turns cold in an instant. She clutches her arms around herself and heads back inside, following the reedy echo of her friends' voices until she locates them again. Mabel watches her approach with a frown. 'Mrs Lamb, are you quite all right?' she asks.

'I'm just feeling a little chill. The sea – the wind, it is cold here … The tower, how do you suppose you get up there?'

All five look puzzled. 'I believe I saw some stairs back that way,' Captain Harding offers, uncertainly. 'They didn't look in a very serviceable shape, though – collapsed, like half of this old ruin. I'd be careful if I were you.'

Cecilia moves to follow his directions, but then she hesitates. 'There is no one else here, is there? In this castle … There can be no one else here, can there?'

More confusion. 'I did not see anyone when we arrived,' Doctor Mayberry says softly.

'Are you quite sure that you are well?' asks Mabel.

'Perhaps I should come with you,' the doctor offers, but Cecilia holds up her palm in a flat rejection.

'No. No, thank you. I think that … I just want to admire the view from the top of the tower, by myself. If I can find my way up. If there is a way. I … I do not mean to be rude; I just want to be by myself, for a time.'

As Cecilia hurries away, she expects Mabel or the doctor to follow, but they do not. She locates the stairs that James had mentioned; they curve upwards narrowly, a tight, vertiginous spiral, the rough-hewn steps spaced with such irregularity that her feet never seem to land quite when she expects. She follows the spiral up and up – soon she is wheezing for breath, but she does not slow her ascent. Doors open onto other parts of the castle: blank and shadowed rooms, which she passes with barely a glance.

The tower is even taller than it had appeared from below, and her lungs are burning with ragged gasps of breath by the time she finally she bursts into daylight at the top. For a moment she is struck blind by the sun, again; at the same instant a gust of wind buffets her with such unexpected force that she grabs the edges of the doorway to steady herself. The sea wind is blowing a gale at the tower's pinnacle. She squints her eyes against the sun and peers around. There is no one else there.

She steps out tentatively, walks to the battlement, and looks down towards the courtyard. A dark shade upon the grass seems to mark the very spot where she had been standing only moments before; and she herself is now precisely where the figure had been. As if they had swapped places. The wind whispers in her ears and whips her hair about her head where it has fallen loose from her cap. The wind and the sun seem to scatter her thoughts; she cannot think rationally. Her heart is still pounding, her lungs smouldering from climbing the staircase – and inside, that anxious turning sensation. *He is here, he is here*.

She spins on the spot, suddenly, as if a hand had landed upon her shoulder and turned her by force. In the doorway which she has just emerged from – the door leading back down the tower's spiral stair – there stands the shape of a man. He is almost hidden in the shadowed doorframe, but a pale face, sombre as a skeleton's, emerges from the gloom, watching her. Bright buttons down his uniformed front flash momentarily as the figure turns and disappears down the stairs.

She follows. Perhaps she calls out after him, but the wind snatches away the sound. She follows through the doorway, back into the muted darkness and echoes of the castle walls, and down the staircase, taking the steep and winding descent as fast as her feet will allow, almost slipping and falling more than once. She spies him again through the first doorway she comes to, standing at the far end of a long, empty room, some medieval dining hall or audience chamber that now lies bare. The figure seems to linger for just long enough so she can spy him through the tail of her eye as she passes – then he disappears, slipping through another door and to another part of the castle.

Cecilia pursues, her heart clamped so tightly in her mouth she can almost taste its sanguine tang. The long room stretches before her and her legs won't seem to move quickly enough – it is as though she is dragging them through slopping tar, as if she were in a dream. The sound of waves fills her ears, the ocean's roar amplified through the conch shell of the hollow ruin. Those shining yellow buttons, that dashing blue uniform. She had known them so well, once. But that was a long time ago.

With agonizing slowness she reaches the next doorway, but there is no sign of him now; multiple doors open off from the next room, multiple paths to choose from, and not a clue which way to turn. She follows her ears and her nose, follows the sound of the waves and the faintest scent of fresh air, turning this way and that through the ruined castle until she is entirely lost. She feels as though she is running in circles, yet never enters the same room twice. At one point she thinks that she hears her name being called – Captain Harding or Mr Delahunty, calling out to her from somewhere far below – but she scarcely acknowledges it.

At last the echo of the ocean leads her to a flash of daylight and a door which leads outside. She emerges to find that she is standing on a section of the castle ramparts, at the top of its crumbling walls. She must be on the western edge: behind her is the tall tower, and in front of her the ramparts lead towards nothing but the open ocean.

John is there. He stands at the farthest end of the wall, facing her with his back to the sea. It glitters like crystals against the darker shade of his Navy frock coat. Now that she can see his face plainly, there is no doubt that it is her husband. Except, it is impossible.

John is standing entirely still, at ease, arms hanging by his sides. His face shows no emotion – no surprise, no joy, no mischief – nothing.

She finds her voice. 'John – come away from there. The wall is old; it might collapse at any moment.' It is the only thing that she can think to say.

He does not move a muscle.

'What are you doing here? How – how … You cannot be here.'

Now his head tilts, slightly. 'I cannot?' John replies. His voice comes to her faintly but clearly, like a distant bell chiming.

'It makes no sense. How can it be?'

'Does my wife not want to see me again? Am I not the one you wished for?'

'You are, but … but, that is all that you are. A wish. Or something worse …'

'Indeed?'

The air rings with the mocking screech of gulls, like laughter. She says, 'What is it that you want from me?'

'A man may check on his wife, may he not? Such a cold reception you give me, Cecilia. Is this what I have to look forward to? Not long to wait now, lass. Not long 'til I come home.'

She looks away. 'Yes, but … the man I welcome home shall not be you. Whoever you are.'

When she looks back, John has taken a step closer – or, he *is* closer, suddenly, though she did not see him move. He holds out his hand, palm outward, slowly extending his fingers away from himself so that he might admire their adornments. 'Do you recognize this ring, Cecilia? Our wedding band. Or did you forget it? And what about this one – it carries a lock of your hair, remember? A little piece of you that travelled away with me. A strand of hair to tether us together across a thousand miles and more. Be sure to remember that one, you hear?'

She shrugs. 'That you wear his rings proves nothing.'

But then her skin prickles. This cannot last for much longer, she knows. This moment, this visitation; whatever it is, it is almost over. She has to ask him, now. 'John,' she says, her voice softening, 'John – this thing … inside me. This child I am carrying. Can it truly be yours?'

'Naturally. Who else's?' His expression has remained impassive all this time, but now his lips peel back into something like a smile, though not a smile that she can recognize.

'Mrs Delahunty said that it could not be. That it has been too long for such a thing to be possible. And how it feels within me … I do not think it should feel this way. I am afraid, John.'

The smile is replaced by a grimace of sudden hostility. 'Mabel Delahunty? Why do you listen to that blethering wench – what does she know?' His eyes narrow suspiciously. 'If you say it is not mine, then … then the question must be, whose is it? Whose bed have you been sharing while I'm away, wife?'

'John, how can you ask me that –'

She stops. John's hand has dropped back to his side, and a band of red is spreading starkly around the cuff, a glistening crimson stain that begins to drip wetly onto the stone below.

'John … there is blood, on your cuff.' She points. 'Whose blood is that?'

John frowns. He looks annoyed, shakes his head, and moves his arm behind his back and out of her sight, but the fallen droplets remain spattered like tiny red flowers by his feet. 'Pay it no heed. It is no matter to you.' Then, more gently – almost sounding like the John she knows – 'That is mine alone to worry about.'

A moment of silence passes between them then, broken when the wind rises to a wail against the old stone edges of the ruined fortification. John's eyes meet with hers. 'Time for me to go now, lass,' he says.

'John, wait –' she gasps, but he has already turned on his heel and is striding away – long steps across the ruined ramparts, away from where she stands. Cecilia hesitates, and then she begins after him, navigating the cracked and crumbling stonework on trembling legs. When she looks up again, John is almost at the far end of the wall, where it falls away to the sea; he does not break his stride – he simply steps off the edge, seeming to pause for a moment before he drops out of view, as if he is caught floating on the currents of the ocean wind for the briefest of seconds before he drops, plummeting down the cliff face. She screams his name, breaks into a run, but the wall is old and unstable. It breaks apart beneath her feet, and she is standing on nothing, and then she is falling. She is falling from the wall, and there is nowhere to land except the crashing white waves below, and the jagged rocks like teeth, waiting to catch her, catch her and devour her at last.

* * *

'Look! Look, she is stirring. She's coming around. It's all right, darling; she is all right.'

A man's voice. John's voice, she thinks at first with a confused rush of hope, in spite of all that she has just witnessed.

'Oh, Mrs Lamb – my dear, can you hear me? Are you all right?'

Her head twitches. She is lying on her back against something cold and hard, and it feels as though her head is being cradled in someone's hands – she can feel their fingers pressed against the back of her scalp.

'Please don't try to get up. Just lie still, now. Mrs Lamb, do you hear me?' She recognizes the third voice immediately – it is Doctor Mayberry.

'What happened?' she manages to say. Her own voice sounds very faint and very distant.

'Just lie still,' the doctor says firmly. Her vision washes into focus, the fuzzy greyness recedes, and she can make out four faces peering down at her, as if she were an infant lying in its crib. Closest is Doctor Mayberry, his youthful features serious and reassuringly professional. Just behind him Mabel Delahunty is hovering and twitching with worry.

'Tell me that you are not hurt, my dear?' Mabel asks. 'No – no, say nothing, just lie there and let the doctor take care of you.'

'I *thought* she was acting most peculiar,' she hears Captain Harding murmur at the back of the group. Frances shushes him.

The young doctor checks her pulse, then he places his palm gently against her forehead.

'Did I fall?' Cecilia asks, afraid of the answer. 'Did I fall from the battlements? Am I injured?' She is frightened to attempt to move her arms or her legs, in case she cannot. Then a feeling like cobwebs tingles over her body as she remembers the child inside her – the life that she is responsible for. Her hands fold instinctively over her belly, which at that moment feels entirely empty and still.

The doctor raises an eyebrow. 'The battlements? Nothing so dramatic, I am glad to say. I believe you had a fainting spell, that is all. We found you here.'

'I found you,' Frances points out.

'I was … I was up on the wall. I wanted to see … the tower. And then I thought that I fell. Where am I?' She shifts and tries to sit upright. The fingers holding her head flex and, with a surge of embarrassment, she realizes that it must be Samuel Delahunty crouched behind her.

'Mrs Lamb, just lie still a moment longer, if you please,' commands the doctor. Even lying where she is, Cecilia can see that she is inside the castle, laid upon its hard stone floor, and not below its high, crenellated walls at all.

'Too much sun and exertion with the walk this morning, I fancy,' the doctor explains. 'Nothing to be overly concerned about, I expect. But, Mrs Lamb, what's all this about the battlements?'

'Perhaps she hit her head when she fell?' Mabel says, raising her hand to her mouth with worry.

'I … I wanted to go up and admire the view, that's all. But I didn't. I must have got lost, and fallen.' Even in a half-conscious haze the silky lies come to her effortlessly. What she thought she saw, she cannot attempt to explain to her friends.

At length the doctor permits her to sit upright, and then helps her stand. 'Thank you. Thank you, everyone. My goodness, I feel so ashamed,' Cecilia says, blushing.

'I should say we have all had enough adventure for one day,' the young doctor orders. 'The carriages are outside. But first, lunch – I don't know about the rest of you, but I for one am famished.'

He offers her his arm as they make their way out from the cool, echoing ruin, towards where their carriages wait to bear them back to town.

'Yes – I think I want to go home now,' Cecilia whispers, so that no one else can hear.

19.

She sits by the window; she feels too tired to stand. Her fall at the castle has left no lasting damage save for a draining fatigue that saps her in the days that follow. Either that or it is the thing wriggling and writhing within her that is using up her reserves of energy. It has been unceasingly active since she returned from the clifftops. Sleep is impossible. She is too tired to even walk down through the town to the sea's edge, though her inability to leave the house seems to only aggravate the infant further: it is a vicious cycle. The child flits and shifts, squirms and coils, and there is nothing left over for her. Her body is not her own now. It is a commodity in service to them both.

She settles back in her chair and closes her eyes. For what could be the hundredth time she tells herself: *John could not have been at the castle because he is still out upon the sea.* What she saw and heard – the man and the things he said – that was not truly John, only his likeness, serving some purpose which she cannot guess at. The real John, her John, he is still out there, set against the vicious and vindictive ocean on his homeward odyssey. *Not long to wait, now.*

Her eyes open as slits, and through the glass of the window she scowls in silent loathing at her ineffable rival;

at that cruel and fickle entity, the ocean itself, that holds her husband as its hostage. The pulse of her heart sounds words in her ears: *He is not yours to keep. He is my husband. Give him back to me. Give him back.*

'Who are you talking to?'

The unexpected voice startles her from the depth of her thoughts. Rosalie is standing at the door, watching with her mouth half-open in wonder.

'No one. Only the cat,' Cecilia replies with a sigh, and reaches down to stroke the grey beast that sits hunkered close to her chair. She runs her fingers through its fur, down the length of its back, which arches to press into the cup of her hand, and then shivers with pleasure beneath her fingertips. Then it moves unhurriedly away from her reach, stepping sideways in an almost drunken lurch before skittering towards the open door. Rosalie steps aside and glares at the creature with mistrust as it passes.

Rosalie has come to tell her that a visitor is here. But it is not the doctor, nor even Mabel Delahunty, either of whom Cecilia has been expecting ever since their day on the clifftops.

Her visitor is Signor Capello, John's agent and lawyer who handles most of his business on land, and whom Cecilia has spent the last several months avoiding. She has several reasons: she does not like his officious, obsequious manner, nor does she appreciate how closely John and he guard their dealings together. But most of all, she knows in her gut that there is nothing whatsoever that Signor Capello can tell her which she would wish to hear.

But he has caught her at home at last, and this meeting seems unavoidable. She finds him downstairs. Capello is a small man, standing roughly level with Cecilia and shorter than Rosalie, with thick black hair slicked back upon his scalp and dark, severe eyebrows, both of which seem designed to draw attention to a forehead so voluminous it must surely be a credit to his profession. His every motion seems swift and deliberate, made with a surgeon's precision. There is something about him which always makes Cecilia think of the sharp young men who lurk in shadowy doorways close to the docks, eyeing up potential victims like barracudas.

'I apologize for intruding without prior appointment, Signora Lamb,' Capello begins in fluent English. 'I have tried to visit on previous occasions but found you otherwise engaged – perhaps your maid neglected to pass on my messages?' He glances at Rosalie, who crosses her arms; she has remained lingering in the doorway, watching over proceedings with an icy, protective gaze. Cecilia smiles at her and nods, signalling that she may leave.

'No matter,' Capello goes on, once they are alone. 'I have come here direct from the company office – by which I mean to say, the merchant company which owns Captain Lamb's ship, yes?'

'Yes, I follow.'

'Just so. As I say, I come from the company office, who have this morning been considering the matter of Captain Lamb's expedition. You are undoubtedly aware that there has been no contact from Captain Lamb's vessel since they embarked from this port some months previously. Delays in communications are not uncommon – they might be expected. But no word whatsoever, for so long a time, it is – ah, it is decidedly a cause for concern.'

'Indeed,' Cecilia agrees. She grits her teeth – the child is lashing like a tempest inside her. She sits with an arm folded across her middle, struggling to maintain an expression of interested impartiality.

'There may be explanations – diverted by poor winds, or a good wind might perhaps have caused Captain Lamb to decide to press on, and not register at his scheduled ports. These are possibilities, but still, it is unusual. And in any case we should certainly expect the captain to write with updates on progress, which he has not … Ah, I should ask: Captain Lamb has not written to you in the past year, no?' His dark eyes flash shrewdly.

'No. No, I have heard nothing; no more than you have,' Cecilia tells him, glancing out of the window towards the sparkling ocean.

'No. You would tell me, wouldn't you, if … But, no, you say it is not so. Where was I? Ah, yes. You are aware that upon arrival in the West Indies, Captain Lamb's ship was to follow such leads as its captain and master deemed prudent; that is, they could set their own course to pursue whatever profit they saw fit. This makes following a ship's progress more difficult, of course, though by no means impossible. Unless …'

'Unless?'

'Unless the ship perhaps does not want to be found.' He coughs and gives her another curious look. 'Signora Lamb, are you … Do you feel quite well? Perhaps now is not a good time, after all …'

She wipes tears from her eyes. The baby inside is wreaking havoc, like a devil unleashed. It seems to enjoy this man's company as much as Cecilia does. 'No, no. Please go on,' she insists, stifling a wince.

'Just so,' he says with a frown. 'This morning I learned that the company have succeeded in discovering some record of your husband's ship's movements. But what they have found, it is … irregular.'

'What do you mean, irregular?'

'The vessel was sighted where it was not to be expected.'

'I do not understand. If John had leave to decide his own course, then –'

He waves his hand. 'The detail is not so important. What is of substance is that these irregular stops – so far outside the expected route – were some long time ago, now. And since then …' He presses the fingertips of one hand together then explodes them wide: a puff of smoke. 'Nothing. No trace. Therefore, Signora Lamb, ah –' He moves his fingers to his lips, as if silencing himself to consider carefully what he will say next.

'Be assured, signora, that it brings me no pleasure to tell you this. In light of the unwelcome irregularities, and such a long, unexplained delay, the company has this morning taken the final decision to write off Captain Lamb's voyage as lost; and to seek to make reparations accordingly. I am sorry.'

Cecilia remains quite calm, quite still, in spite of the squirming in her belly. 'They believe the voyage to be lost?' she repeats after a pause of several long seconds. Signor Capello, who has stared at the floor through the silence, lifts his eyes to her and inclines his head in affirmation.

'Then you must tell them to be patient, Signor Capello. Surely they can wait a little longer to have their boat back.'

'Indeed I did, Signora Lamb. "Let us not rush to conclusions," said I. A return, and a full explanation, is still possible. But, in point of fact, the company have already shown remarkable forbearance in waiting as long as they have. Now they consider that the evidence speaks too loudly to be ignored. For them the matter is settled, I fear.'

'Evidence? Evidence for what?'

Capello blinks. 'That the ship shall not return, signora.'

'Why should John not return? Does he not have maps, sextants, to find his way home? Has my husband not sailed the globe before?'

'Ah … I think you misunderstand me, perhaps. I have used the wrong words, I fear.'

The Italian holds his hands out helplessly and takes a moment to compose his next sentence. She knows what he really means to say, of course. She is no fool. In truth, she too has been amazed that the company has waited this long.

But she wants to hear him speak the words aloud. For some reason she cannot explain, she wants to hear him say it.

As Capello struggles for words, from the corner of her eye – and only for a second – she sees him. John is there, in the corner of their parlour, seated at the edge of Cecilia's vision and behind his lawyer's back. He lounges in a chair, hands folded in his lap and legs stretched out before him in an attitude of easy relaxation. He catches his wife's eye, and he winks; and then he is gone again. She puts her hand to her mouth and almost laughs.

Capello looks at her, his dark eyes softening with unexpected compassion. Perhaps he has mistaken her gesture for an act of distress. He finds his voice again: clipped and matter-of-fact. 'The company has concluded that Captain Lamb's ship has been sunk, most likely due to misadventure, and all hands aboard lost. The entire crew, dead. There are alternative possibilities, of course: mutiny, or dereliction of duty, some form of abandonment … But none of these are very much preferable prospects, I think, and we need hardly dwell upon them. Signora,' he sighs, 'ships go down all the time. I am sure you are aware. It is … most likely that this is what has happened.'

'Of course I know the risks,' Cecilia breaks in. 'But this is a mistake. John's ship has not been sunk.'

'We may hope and pray that yet proves to be the case.' Another pause, and then Capello's severe brow raises by a fraction. 'But is it possible – are you aware of any facts that I have not yet covered? Have you, perhaps, heard some word of Captain Lamb, after all?'

'No, I have not,' she admits, and folds her arms over the lashing infant.

'No … no, indeed not,' Capello nods. 'But if you did know anything, anything at all – if, say, you *had* heard from Captain Lamb – then I would counsel you to tell me immediately. But, ah, I fear I am only confusing the issue, and clouding your poor mind. There remains a most likely outcome which we should all, now, accept to be the truth. The company has already made up its mind. And now –' He coughs, again, and his eyes skip away, avoiding her steady gaze. 'I fear there is another matter, less comfortable still. The matter of Captain Lamb's debts. There are … not insignificant accounts to be settled, I fear.'

'John has debts? I have never heard of this.'

'Every man has debts, signora. Some more than others. In Captain Lamb's case … Well, he had high hopes for this venture. He borrowed considerable amounts against the anticipated profit of his voyage. As it is, well, alternative funds must be looked for.'

His cold eyes slowly circle the walls of her home – like a prowling shark, she thinks – taking in every furnishing, every detail; cutting and costing every square inch of her and John's property.

Cecilia feels her cheeks grow cold and clammy as the blood drains from her face. She knew nothing about John borrowing money against his expedition; but then, it is true that she had been content not to know much about his business affairs. He had always seemed so sure of himself that she had simply assumed everything was under control. Her gaze flits again to the chair in the far corner of the room, but it sits empty; her husband is nowhere to be seen.

She stands up, suddenly – so suddenly that her eyes swim for a moment as the blood rushes back to her head. 'If John has debts,' she tells Capello, 'then they shall be settled when he returns. This is … Signor Capello, I find this all quite inexplicable. I simply cannot understand why the company should be so hasty to write off its investments. If they would only wait, then my husband shall indeed bring them the profits which they, and you, so crave. Please tell them this … Tell them only to be patient, and John shall return forthwith. You can tell the same to whatever creditors he supposedly has, as well.'

'Signora, you must understand –'

'They must wait, as I have waited. There is no need for this, for any of this … crawling around here, like ghouls.'

Capello is on his feet, too, and he takes a step backward. 'Signora, I have upset you. I apologize.'

'I am not upset. If you had come here today with any real news, a single word of substance regarding my husband's whereabouts – any actual evidence of his supposed fate – then that might, perhaps, have been cause for tragedy. As it is, you have told me only what I already know: that my husband's ship is overdue, off its intended course and detained by as yet unknown forces. Why should I conclude that he is gone forever? Why do you? If I was upset – if anything should upset me – it is only the discovery that my husband's business partners could be so premature and incautious in their practices.'

A long silence weighs heavily upon the room. Cecilia's voice has risen to almost a shout, and in the sudden quiet that follows, she hears the floorboards creak on the other side of the parlour door; Rosalie is waiting outside, listening. Capello stares at her, not shocked precisely, but sort of stunned into inaction. Inside her belly the child floats, suddenly calm and tranquil.

Capello bows. 'As you have it, signora. As you would have it. I will pass on your message, and will do what I can. I do admire your conviction, Mrs Lamb … I pray that it shall help you in the days that are to come. As I shall pray for Captain Lamb's safe return. That is – if you would permit the prayers of a Catholic.' He offers one of his rare, wan smiles, and bows a final time.

With that the lawyer departs, vanishing out the door like a wisp of smoke. Cecilia remains standing motionless for quite some time longer, staring blankly into the shadows and cracks of her empty parlour. Then, at last, she sits back down, and she wipes her eyes.

20.

The doctor calls later that same day – or perhaps he comes the day after Signor Capello's visit. It is difficult for Cecilia to be sure. After Rosalie admits him, Doctor Clement Mayberry stands in the doorway of her parlour, looking about the room with a guileless curiosity.

'Doctor Mayberry, come in. Won't you sit down?' Cecilia says.

'I am glad to see you again, Mrs Lamb. I have been thinking about you … That is, I mean to say, I have been anxious about your health since I saw you last.'

'Indeed, I have been anticipating your visit. But, doctor, you need not worry. I am feeling quite well. A little tired, perhaps.'

They smile at each other pleasantly, but the doctor's eyes betray a suspicious concern. 'By my count that is twice, now, that you have fallen ill while in my company. It would be unforgivable of me not to check on you. May I?' He takes the seat next to her and reaches out. She lets him take her by the hand and place his fingers against her wrist. Her outstretched arm looks almost blue in the afternoon light. The child shivers and kicks inside, making her flinch slightly and jerk her arm. The doctor frowns.

'Have you been feeling dizzy at all? Any headaches?' he asks.

'No, nothing like that. Just tired, as I say.'

She expects the examination to continue, but after a few moments the doctor releases her wrist and settles back into his seat. He stares out of the window, towards the bay. When he speaks again, his voice is low and mild. 'At the castle, Mrs Lamb, you were speaking about the battlements. You seemed to think you had fallen from the wall. Do you remember?'

She nods. 'And before that,' he goes on, 'you asked if there was someone else there with us, inside the ruin. When I first met you, down by the harbour, you spoke of a ship leaving port – you were anxious to catch a glimpse of it. I thought little of it – of any of these points – at the time. You did not strike me as delirious. You seemed certain. Did you see another person at the castle?'

'I … I am not sure. No, I did not. There was no one else there.'

'I do not believe that there was.'

'But, doctor … there might have been, might there not? A local … Some sort of hermit, perhaps. There could have been someone there.'

'So you did see someone.'

She pauses. She cannot meet his gaze. 'I thought I did. But now I think that I didn't. It was a trick of my eyes, I expect.'

'I expect so,' he agrees gently. 'Mrs Lamb, I must make a confession to you. I have spoken with Mrs Delahunty, concerning you. Or perhaps I should say that Mrs Delahunty did most of the speaking … The poor lady is most vexed.'

'I know she is. She told you, then? About my condition?'

The doctor nods.

'I suppose I should be cross with her,' Cecilia muses, 'but perhaps it is best this way. Though I can only imagine in what terms Mabel explained it all to you. She does not believe that there is a child, does she? Or if there is, it cannot be John's … So she says.'

Doctor Mayberry smiles. 'You know, Mrs Lamb, this is actually a stroke of luck.'

'It is?'

'Maternal medicine is a fascinating new field of study. I took a keen interest in it in college. The old days of superstitions and bunk – midwives and wise women – are at long last being swept away by a tide of progress. It is an area of real research and breakthrough now. I had hoped to specialize in it, you see, but I have never … that is … Well, it is not an area in which I have much in the way of first-hand experience.'

'I see. Then I suppose it is lucky, for you.'

He laughs. 'I hope that you might also benefit from my studies. And so, Mrs Lamb, how long have you known of your situation?'

'I … It is difficult to be certain.'

'Then, when did you cease to be unwell?'

'Cease to be …?' She blinks. 'I have not been unwell, I shouldn't say, except for the tiredness I mentioned.'

'Yes, but … Mrs Lamb, as a woman, when were you last unwell?'

She thinks. 'I had a slight head cold about two months ago, I think.'

'No, no.' The doctor frowns and looks away, seeming to search for inspiration in the wallpaper. 'You misunderstand me, Mrs Lamb. I must speak more plainly. I refer to the routine unwellness that is attendant to the female sex … A cycle that is measured in months. Has it been … interrupted?' A deep blush spreads across his face, and again Cecilia is struck by the strange combination of man and boy: a doctor, professional and disciplined, in the body of a naive young man who blushes to ask about the most basic elements of her biology.

'Oh, I see. I cannot be certain, but it has been at least six or seven months, now, I believe.'

Doctor Mayberry looks relieved, at first, to have moved past the misunderstanding – but then he frowns and shakes his head. 'Six months! Yet no obvious swelling, no outward signs to be observed at all. Are you positive?' He hesitates for a moment, and then reaches out again, asks permission to put his fingers against her abdomen. Now it is Cecilia's turn to blush as he carries out a gentle examination of prods and probes.

The life inside her flits and recoils under the doctor's touch, like a tidal pool when a pebble is dropped into it and all of the tiny organisms startle and dart for safety. She studies the doctor's face. With her heart in her mouth she asks, 'Don't you feel it moving, doctor?'

'Feel it?' He looks at her seriously. 'Mrs Lamb, do you feel movement?'

'Can't you?' She grabs his wrist and presses his hand flat against her stomach, swimming with life.

But the doctor's expression does not change. 'I feel nothing,' he says.

Cecilia shrinks back into her seat and crosses her arms over herself, a clammy sense of dread dropping upon her like a shroud. 'There is something inside me, doctor. You must believe it.'

After a long moment Doctor Mayberry says, 'This branch of medicine remains, alas, frustratingly inexact. For the time being I believe that we must rely on the mother's body as the most accurate instrument we have. I believe you, Mrs Lamb. You feel it moving? Tell me how.'

'It … It swims, back and forth. It churns, around and around. Sometimes it feels like one thing, like I imagine a baby must feel; but other times it feels like many things. The more it moves, the more tired I become – like we share a body, and my energies sustain its movements … It likes it when I stare at the ocean. When I watch the ships come and go from port. I think it watches them too, the ships and the waves, through my eyes. That is the only time it is quiet, more or less.'

The doctor says nothing.

'You think I am mad, don't you?' Cecilia says, tears welling in her eyes.

He shakes his head. 'Not mad. But, Mrs Lamb, in my professional opinion I do not believe that you have conceived a child, either.'

'Either way, you believe I am lying.'

'Only in as much as a belief, honestly held but improperly understood, can be called a lie. Tell me, Mrs Lamb – your husband, Captain Lamb, has been absent at sea for some long time now, has he not? And you have been all alone in the meantime, in this unfamiliar place. I myself know first-hand how daunting finding a way through a new and foreign world can be. And – forgive me – but Captain Lamb's fate remains uncertain, still?'

'Are you also going to tell me that my husband is dead, doctor? You may save your breath – I have already heard.'

'No, I am not. I have no better idea whether Captain Lamb is alive or dead than you do. He has gone away to sea, and that is all we know, correct? Let us say, then, that he lives, with certainty, in your heart and in your mind. You hold on to your resolve that he will return to shore, and your mind makes it so; it provides that feeling with substance and causes it to become real. Does it not?'

'I … I suppose.'

'And if that is so, could the same not be true of the child that you believe you are carrying? Could the movements you describe not in fact be imagined, and given substance only by your mind? Made real enough to trick your body, to deceive your senses and even alter the course of your natural physiology? Mrs Lamb, I have treated sailors and soldiers with missing arms and legs who swear blind that they still feel the sensations of the absent limb. They are driven out of their wits by itches that they may never scratch. The mind is a most powerful deceiver.'

She hesitates. 'I do not know … Perhaps it could be as you say. But why? Why would I imagine such a thing?'

The doctor holds out his hands: You tell me.

Cecilia stares bleakly down towards the flat grey waves in the bay, and the ships drifting in and out on a meandering breeze. *Perhaps it is true*, she thinks. *Perhaps all of it – the baby, the glimpses of John, the sound of his voice at my ear – it all exists only in my fevered, isolated imagination. Perhaps I have known it all along.*

But she cannot believe it. 'Could it not be, doctor, that a person might perceive seemingly impossible things to be real precisely because they *are* real and true – even though … even though they make no logical sense? That someone's senses, their intuitions, could permit them to feel things that others cannot … To know things that they have no earthly way of knowing. Have you ever come across such a thing in your casebook?'

He stares at her, curious and perplexed, but not unsympathetic. He shakes his head. 'No, I have not.'

'And so,' she asks flatly, 'if I have taken leave of my senses as you say, what do you prescribe for me, doctor?'

'Do not worry, your case does not have me reaching for the laudanum bottle just yet,' he tells her, smiling. 'You appear to me in every way lucid and in control of yourself. Remarkably in control. My advice is to rest if your body needs it – but do not overindulge. Stay active, keep your mind stimulated. Do you have any hobbies?'

'Perhaps I should take up botany,' she smiles wryly. The doctor frowns, then nods encouragingly.

Cecilia sighs. 'Doctor, is there no drug that you can give me? I am tired … I am tired of feeling this way.'

But he shakes his head. 'I shall return, as soon as I am able,' Doctor Mayberry promises. 'I have other cases to see – a crew of New England whalers washed into port last week, positively brimming with putrid fever after weeks of freezing ice-rain in the Arctic. I think that they shall all recover – and frankly the business is good – but let me assure you that as a patient I much prefer your company. I shall return in a day or two, Mrs Lamb. Be sure to mark any changes in your condition, any symptoms of which you can be certain. And think about what I have said. I shall return.'

21.

As soon as the doctor has departed, Cecilia goes to her desk. The drawer slides open, and with its motion a smallish object rolls lopsidedly among the leaves of scribbled paper and unsent letters that lie piled within. A faint odour like dried flowers reaches her nose. Cecilia reaches into the drawer and lifts out the heart-shaped locket that Mabel gave to her: the container for the mystic Goa stone.

She undoes the fastening, and the locket falls open in her hand. The unappealing stone sits inside the opened heart, positioned slightly off-centre. Cecilia lifts it between her finger and thumb. It is softer and lighter than she had expected, and feels almost malleable under her fingertips, like a shapeless gobbet of wax.

Mabel told her she should drink a part of it. The idea tastes like revolting fuzz in her throat. But then, Doctor Mayberry has nothing to offer her. Why not trust in the wisdom of Mabel's Jesuit monks? Bezoars are well known to protect against poisons and other ailments. It can do no harm to try. Inside her the child lashes, angry and unsettled.

She drops the stone back into its locket and closes it. The cat, grey and murky as a sky full of rain, has been watching her from the corner of the room impassively. It meows once, then steps to the window, hops up to the ledge, and looks out over the twilight ocean view. Cecilia joins it momentarily.

She has not stood there long before the soft, small hairs upon the nape of her neck rise, and a wave of anticipation shivers across her skin; then she feels the sensation that somebody else is in the room. A shadow standing in the far corner, behind her back. *If I were to turn my head very quickly*, she wonders, *would I be able to catch a glimpse of him, a momentary outline upon the blurred edge of my vision?*

But she does not move a muscle; she only stares out over the town below and the rolling sea, coloured a powdery cobalt in the settling evening light. After some time has passed, her lip twitches into a nervous smile.

'Well – aren't you going to say anything?' she asks.

His voice, when it reaches her from across the room, is so soft that she almost struggles to make out his words. 'I was waiting for you to speak first, lass.'

'Waiting, waiting. How tired I am of waiting.'

'Any day now, Cissy.'

'I know.' Cecilia places her hand to the cat's bristling back; it shudders reflexively beneath her touch, but it does not stir from where it sits. 'John, what I saw at the castle … the things you said, the blood on your wrist … That wasn't really you, was it?'

A pause. 'No, Cissy. Don't mind that.'

'But then – this is not really you, either. You are not really here, now.'

'Am I not?'

'No. It is not possible.' She touches her hand to her stomach. 'None of it is possible.'

'You're confusing yourself, lass. Aren't you? Pay no heed to what you think you heard at the castle … Never mind it now.' There is an impatient edge to the voice. He almost sounds irritated with her.

'I wish I could believe you. I wish I knew what to do.'

John pauses for a long time, and then he says sharply, 'Haven't you done enough already?'

'What do you mean?'

'I know what you've been doing. And I know what you're *about* to do.' The voice is accusing and contemptuous – still her husband's, but as she has never heard him before. And then it is gone. The dialogue is over: the presence has departed the room.

There is a guttural mewl and half a hiss at her side, and the big cat twists and hops away from the window ledge. Cecilia looks dumbly down at her hand and is surprised to see a clump of grey fur that remains behind, caught between her fingers where she had gripped suddenly and unwittingly at the poor creature's back. She spins around in time to see the cat slink haughtily through the empty doorway, out of the room.

'I'm sorry,' she calls after it, quietly.

She is alone now – alone save for the restless motion of the baby she carries. A nervous panic is rising within her, a feeling of powerlessness against the terrible solitude of her own home. She returns to her desk. Mabel's golden locket still lies upon its surface, shut tight. She scoops it up quickly and opens its fastening once more. She gasps aloud as the baby thrashes so hard that she thinks it could perhaps break out of her skin.

She calls for Rosalie, but it is late and her maid must have gone home already, so Cecilia goes downstairs to the kitchen and, wincing and gritting her teeth, prepares a pot of tea herself. She searches for a nutmeg grater or something similar, but she does not know where anything is kept so in the end settles for a butter knife. She fills a teacup and, holding the Goa stone in one hand above the steaming drink, uses the edge of the knife to scrape at the stone's hard surface. Its clammy exterior is more resistant than she had expected and requires some force to break – she accidentally cuts away a larger clump than intended, which lands in the cup with a splash. More carefully, she rubs off a few more flakes that sprinkle down to rest upon the copper surface of the tea. She had imagined that the fragments would dissolve away immediately and vanish into the liquid, but they do not; even after she has stirred it they float there unpleasantly, the larger lump turning around and around in a slow circle and looking altogether like a drowned insect.

She gives it another vigorous stir and, while the water is still swirling and the fragments of stone impossible to see, she swallows the entire cupful down in two unrefined gulps that scald her mouth so badly she cannot tell if the medicine has any taste to it at all.

22.

That night Cecilia dreams that she is being dipped slowly into a cauldron of boiling oil. She screams in agony as the bubbling liquid rises like fire over her body, submerging her up to her ribs – she screams but her throat is voiceless; she tries to writhe and struggle but her limbs are paralyzed. She can do nothing but lie in the unbearable heat as her skin and flesh stews and peels from her bones – she can feel it fall away like well-cooked meat. Even when her body is stripped entirely bare and there is nothing left but bones and hard sinew, no nerves to sense anything at all, she can still feel it – she can still feel it burning.

Next she dreams that she is in a house – not her real house, although it is hers in the dream – and it is on fire, and she is trapped inside, locked in a room with no escape. She curls into a ball, helpless, and feels the flames lick over her crackling skin. When it is all burned to ash, she remains in a smouldering landscape, surrounded by nothing but charred and blackened ruins, the skeletal frames of what was once an entire city. She dreams that ants are crawling all over her, tiny and red and hot as coals, swarming up her naked legs – flesh now intact again, though she wishes it were not – and digging, burrowing inside her. They dig through the wall of her belly, dig into her abdomen to make a nest of it, millions of them swarming inside her until she feels her innards collapse, and when she looks down she is staring at nothing but a seething, burning mass of darkness.

The horror jars her awake but, even though her eyes are open, the burning sensation remains. Her first thought is that the bed itself must be on fire, and she with it, but this delusion lasts only seconds, and just as quickly she understands it is her insides that are aflame. Writhing like a caterpillar upon its back, she kicks the sheets away – she sits up in bed, clambers onto all fours in the hope that it will ease the pain.

Beside the bed she sees the empty teacup, and Mabel's amulet lying open, and the Goa stone inside. She hears Mabel as clearly as if she was standing in the room with her: *It draws out the poison*. Cecilia grits her teeth, and she wonders what she has done.

She curls herself into a foetal ball, groaning and murmuring incoherently and drifting into unconsciousness whenever sheer exhaustion overtakes her – only to jolt back to agonizing wakefulness minutes or seconds later.

The pain does not last the full night. She sleeps for only two or three hours at most, but when Cecilia wakes with the dawn she is fully refreshed; rested and at peace in spite of the horrific pain and visions that haunted her through the night. She feels cleansed, like when a dense, creeping fog that has settled over the town is burned away by the first rays of the morning sun.

A happy twittering chorus of birds sounds outside her window; the cat is already watching them through the glass, its tail twitching. Cecilia lies in her bed, still curled into a ball, and stares at the cat. After a few minutes it turns, slowly, to look at her, and it winks with its good eye. She dares to uncurl her body and stretch her limbs out, cautious in case the pain should return – but there is none. Her body feels loose, light, and free.

She rises and joins the cat at the window to stare at the bay, already bustling with activity since the first light of dawn. Her eyes roam over the white crests of the waves in the harbour, and the dark leviathan ships passing in and out with their greedy bellies brimming with cargo, and up towards the hazy pink light of the distant horizon; she draws her gaze over the view as if she were a fisherman casting his net, to see what might be caught. Inside she feels nothing. There is nothing stirring within her at all.

Rosalie is surprised to see her up and active with the dawn and makes no attempt to hide it: 'Is everything all right, senhora?' she asks. Cecilia smiles at her. Yes, yes, all is well this morning. She eats her breakfast with relish, asking for seconds to Rosalie's continued amazement. It feels like an age since her body has felt so completely her own, her thoughts so free and uncluttered.

There is only one thought that nags at the back of her mind: *If the baby is really gone, does that mean it was never truly there? Or if it was, then where has it gone to?* Once a thing is half-formed, surely it cannot simply return to nothing? When she was a little girl, some local boys had raided a bird's nest and peeled open its eggs. They had dared her to look, and she had fled in tears from the pathetic, eyeless blue things twitching and shivering inside, not yet ready to be born. That memory, long suppressed, comes back to haunt her again and again through the morning and into the afternoon.

She leaves the house, to leave behind such unwelcome thoughts. As soon as she sets foot into the hot sea air and hears the tap of hammers and the rasp of saws and the distant tolling of harbour bells, she realizes just how long it has been since she stepped outside. It has been almost a fortnight since the visit to the fortress, and it feels as if weeks, perhaps even months, have passed since she last made her ritualistic walk to the shore, through the sleepy old town with its walnut-skinned, white-haired inhabitants, down the steep cliff to the chaos and tumult of the docks – or farther out past the edge of the town to the black rocks that point out into the bay with the old squat lighthouse and the patient fishermen. The salt water in her blood stirs, and she starts to walk. Not because any life inside her belly is insisting that she must – but for herself, because *she* wants to.

She descends the slippery cliff road with a skip in her step. Passing through the jumble of the old town, she turns down a side alley and follows it, just to see where it leads. She emerges somewhere new, some corner of the winding market streets where she has never been before; stalls are piled high with fish and other wild and curious sea creatures, fringed with spiked frills and dangling tendrils and jaws lined with wicked fangs – creatures that hardly seem native to this world at all. She peers at them, fascinated, until their glazed eyes and puckered mouths make her skin crawl and she looks away. She hurries on until she comes to a wall of cages, a veritable prison filled with exotic birds in every flashing colour of the rainbow. Some are tiny, no larger than a hen's egg, while others are so tall that they stand stooped within their cages, hardly able to turn or move; they watch her as she passes with a sad comprehension in their black eyes.

She follows whichever paths lead downhill, down towards the water, until the streets fill with errant seamen – sailors teeming around the harbour, heathen and barbarous in their tattoos and calico. They turn and eye her hungrily as she breezes past. Every sight and every sound of the town seems vivid and bright after her period of confinement. At last the streets open onto the bay and the harbour itself, and the wide open ocean, shimmering turquoise under a fiery afternoon sky. Her ears fill with the harsh cry of gulls and the deep, eerie creaks and groans of the ships in port. She takes it all in with a new thrill of discovery – as if she, too, is freshly stepped from the boat and brand new in town.

Cecilia walks until there is no more wharf to walk on. It is only then, as the crowds thin and the hubbub recedes, that she notices the grey cat following behind. It must have trailed her all the way from the house, through the winding, busy streets, without her noticing. Each time she looks back, the cat freezes and looks away. She walks on, and when she looks back five minutes later, it is still there, stopped again, staring at anything except her.

Making such stop-start progress, she and the cat eventually arrive at the old lighthouse built upon its snaggle-tooth jut of blackened rock, where the waves are crashing in a glistening foam of diamonds and sapphires. The old fishermen are there, as permanent a fixture as the lighthouse itself, mutely casting their lines and brushing their fingers through their wiry, sandy beards. Gulls wheel and dive overhead or stand sentry atop old wooden posts or mounds of rotted seaweed that lies in heaped piles along the beach; from their proud perches the birds chatter and throw back their heads to offer full-throated screams to the sky. Cecilia inhales deeply, filling her lungs with the ocean's scent, all vitality and decay: life and death mingling in a single breath.

The afternoon has worn on and the sun is dipping low. A brisk breeze whistles across the rocks, bearing its chilling teeth. The ocean seems angrier, somehow. The tide comes in cresting waves and dashes upon the shore like a battering ram against a citadel gate. Cecilia walks all the way to the end of the finger of black rock, until there is no more land to walk on, and another step would place her into the grasping hands of the ocean to be borne away on its speeding currents. She thinks she hears one of the fishermen calling out to her, warning her to be careful, though she cannot be sure. The cat, still following, huddles beside the old lighthouse for whatever meagre shelter it can offer from the specks of white foam that leap and arc with every wave.

The weather is turning. The ocean is changing. As she watches, dark banks of cloud begin to gather above the horizon, while the waves chop and churn with a direction-less energy, like a wild and panicked animal struggling and twisting upon itself. The water is raging, she thinks. She understands: *It is raging at me*.

Standing far out upon the bank of black rock, exposed to the wildness of the elements and the Atlantic Ocean in all its power and fury, she feels the sense of lightness and high spirits that she had enjoyed through the day all blow away in the blustering headwind. The tide sloshes loosely against the rock she stands on, padding and pawing, soaking her shoes as it tries repeatedly in vain to get a grasp around her ankles. *If only it could take a hold, it would suck me out to sea in an instant*, she thinks. *Is that what it wants?*

Cecilia grits her teeth. 'Why should you spit and rage at me?' she asks. 'What cause have you to be angry? It was not your child that is gone. Was it?'

The tide seethes and hisses.

'I carried it – it was inside *me*. If it was ever really there, then it was mine, and mine to lose. And I never wanted it.' Tears fill her eyes and she feels the trace of a sob ache in her throat at the admission of the truth.

But she holds her chin high, her neck strained like a sail-or's rope. 'You – you have lost nothing. You have only taken. You took my husband, and you still have him. But he is mine, mine. What do you want from him? From me?'

The ocean swirls: a pot ready to bubble and boil. A great white wave crashes across the rocks close to where she stands, swallowing them in its hissing foam and then slith-ering back and receding into the depths. She can hear the men calling to her, telling her to return to the shore, but their words are foreign so she doesn't listen. Her heart is whirling in her breast like a pinwheel in a gale, but she feels calm and unafraid.

'I have done nothing wrong. You are the thief, here, and I am the victim. Give him back to me. Let him come home.'

The white ocean spray flecks against her face. The tide like a hundred grasping hands surges around her feet, trying and trying to gain purchase. *Is that what this is all about*, she wonders – *it has John, and it wants me too? The three of us together: husband, wife, and the infinite ocean.* She has heard it is a painless and peaceful way to go. To drown – it is like falling asleep. Or perhaps that is only what sailors tell each other as a comfort. Because who could know for sure?

Barely conscious of what she is doing, Cecilia lifts one foot a few inches from the slippery rock and lets it hang poised in the air for a moment, a footstep ready to land. She stands like that, balanced upon one leg, as another wave closes around her, biting at her ankle and then retreating. She hesitates for one moment longer, and then her body pivots, and her foot goes down – down onto solid rock, and she turns and walks away. Back towards the land, where the ancient lighthouse rises before her with the ragged grey cat still waiting at its base, pressed close against the stonework. The cat appears tiny against the dramatic scene that threatens to engulf it, but its eyes flash large and bright, wide and round beacons of green that watch her with a keen and uncommon interest.

She throws a final glance over her shoulder towards the ocean, and it is nothing but dark water: wild and barren and hostile, and swimming with deceit. There is nothing out there for her, nothing it can offer – nothing except the very thing that it has stolen. With a slight tremble in her legs she walks back to dry land where a line of fishermen are standing, staring at her through startled eyes. She passes them by and makes her way back towards the town, followed all the while by the discreet shadow of a cat.

23.

Even once she has walked back to the harbour from the black rocks, Cecilia still does not turn homeward. She has walked all afternoon without rest or food, but she keeps walking. The port is quieting down now, most of the labour done for the day, and the town is coming to life as the tired seamen turn to drinking and gambling and whoring. She walks the half-deserted wharf, sparing only the briefest of glances for the ships as she passes; she knows that John's is not among them, not yet.

She feels a restless desire to roam, an alley cat's curiosity, which leads her to wander idly down unfamiliar side streets, turning into alleyways and peering onto quaint little market squares hidden in corners of the old town that she has never visited before. On an otherwise deserted street on the outskirts of town she crosses paths with a pair of young women – locals, by their appearance. As they draw closer, the girls take in Cecilia slyly through the corners of their eyes, while continuing to chatter uninterrupted, back and forth in their expressive dialect. Each holds a basket tucked under one bare, sun-browned arm, while their free limb waves and gesticulates in flamboyant enhancement to their words.

Cecilia stops, and turns and watches as the girls continue down the street. They walk like dancers; their movement has a freedom, a carelessness, an uninhibited quality to it that is completely alien to her. She has a sudden, impulsive desire to talk to these girls, to be a part of their world. She wants to know what they are talking about – what it is that is making them throw back their heads and laugh, now, with carefree abandon. She wants to know where they are going with their baskets – where they live, and how – what they do with their days, and their nights? How they came to talk, and walk, and dress the way they do.

On an impulse she finds herself reversing her course and walking back the way she had just come, following some distance behind the local women, down the quiet street through a part of town she does not know, left and right until her sense of direction is entirely confused. A view of the bay glimpsed through a gap between buildings reveals that the girls are leading her inland, following the course of the river upstream and away from the busy harbour. Upriver – farther and farther from her home.

The character of the streets changes. The buildings become more modern, though not like the opulent houses built high on the clifftop. These are simple homes where normal people live. Without much fanfare one of the girls bids the other a goodnight with a kiss and a wave, and vanishes into one of the nondescript dwellings. Cecilia waits in a shadowed corner until the girl is gone; she glances back, but there is no sign of the grey cat now. Probably returned up the cliff to pester Rosalie for some supper, she supposes.

The remaining young woman continues her route upriver, and Cecilia follows unseen. Now that she is alone – or at least thinks she is alone – the girl's posture changes, and her pace quickens so that Cecilia struggles to keep up. The night is drawing in, quick and dark. They turn a corner, and then another; and then, somehow, the girl is gone.

She simply vanishes. When Cecilia rounds the corner, the girl is nowhere to be seen. She must have stepped into one of the darkened doorways that line each side of the street like shadowy tombstones, though there was no sound of a door opening or closing. Cecilia hesitates. Her eyes glide from one side of the street to the other, back and forth. With a chill she realizes that, perhaps, the girl knew she was being followed all along and has slipped out of sight with a deliberate evasiveness. *Perhaps she is watching me, even now.*

She takes a few uncertain steps down the street, for no reason except that it feels wrong to stand motionless as the night gathers around her. It is only then she realizes how dark it has become – and how dark the night can be, when you are alone and don't know where you are. The sensible thing would be to retrace her steps homeward, but she could not hope to remember the route. She wonders if she should call out – perhaps the woman would come to her aid if she saw that she was only a wandering, lost English girl; but Cecilia is afraid of who else might hear her if she were to cry for help.

At the far end of the road on which she now stands Cecilia can make out the river, slithering noiselessly under the moonlight like a glistening eel. Inspiration strikes her: to find her way back to the familiar environs of the harbour, and thence homeward, she needs simply to follow the flow of the water towards the bay. The river must lead back home.

She begins to walk, as quickly as her tired legs can. She has been walking all day, but it is only now that her feet begin to ache and twitch, and her stomach starts to whine with hunger. Hunger – but something else, too. A familiar, stabbing twist of anxiousness that begins to poke in the pit of her stomach: the sixth sense that she recognizes immediately. A cold sweat breaks on her forehead as she realizes that something bad is on its way.

She keeps walking – what else is there to do? The road extends all the way to the riverbank where a small jetty has been constructed. A riverboat with a sail is tied there, bobbing and swaying with the current. She can see figures moving silently in the darkness. They appear to be loading casks onto the boat, working by the light of just two burning torches that illuminate their movements in fleeting, orange glimpses. As she draws closer, she can hear the straining creak of ropes and the heavy thud of the casks as they are dropped onto the boat, and the men speaking in hushed whispers. A gap in the clouds permits the moon to briefly flood the scene with its ghostly, pale glow, and at that moment it dawns on Cecilia that what she is witnessing is almost certainly something illicit. The twisting premonition in her gut tightens, and a voice in her head tells her: *You should have run away when you had the chance.*

As if on cue – and perhaps alerted to her presence by the moon's light, for she has made no effort to conceal her approach – two figures peel away from the scene and walk towards her: shadows in the shapes of men. Cecilia simply stands and waits. There does not seem to be any point in trying to escape now. Even before their features are visible through the gloom, it is plain that the figures are not labourers – their silhouettes give them away, long coats and ruffles tied at their necks. They prowl out of the shadows like wolves draped in embroidered finery. One of them, she sees with a sickening chill, is openly carrying a dagger. Not the narrow, foreign stiletto she might have expected, but something with a wide blade: a Jacobean stage-prop of a weapon that dangles carelessly from his slender fingers as he saunters closer.

It is the unarmed man who speaks first, in smooth but unpolished English. 'Good evening to you, my dear lady. What brings you so far this night?'

'Good evening ... I fear that I have become a little lost.'

'I say it is so. You have come very far, for an English woman.'

She wants to ask him how he knows she is English. She wonders if the girl she had been following is still hiding, still watching. And these other houses – there must be people about. *If I were to scream, would any of them raise a hand to help me?*

'I live above the town,' she tells him, as if that were an explanation. 'At the top of the cliff. My husband is a sea captain for one of the merchant companies. I was walking ... But I must have taken a wrong turn, and now it is dark. Perhaps ... If you could perhaps direct me back towards my home, I am certain I would be most grateful.'

'At the top of the cliff. Yes, I know where you live. The new houses, *sim*? Very fine, for a fine and *bonito* lady like yourself. Your husband is a *capitão*, yes? But I do not see him here. This part of town,' he tuts, 'is not so fine. But do not worry, *bonito senhora*. My friend and I, we shall take care of you.'

Cecilia forces her voice to remain calm. She thanks him: '*Obrigado*. But I need only know the route. I am sure I can make my own way –'

But the man shakes his head. 'It is dark. It is not safe, not clever to be alone. This is not a safe place. Not for you ... Not for an Englishwoman.'

He raises his hand and Cecilia shrinks back reflexively. His hand hangs in the space between them, and through the darkness she sees the thin white line of his teeth as a smile spreads across his face.

'You should come with us now,' he says softly.

His accomplice, who has been picking at his fingernails with his dagger while he waits, now groans loudly and says something in their language. They exchange a brief, bickering back-and-forth of syllables, and then they both glower quickly in her direction. The armed man curls his lip and tilts his head backwards in a sneer, and stalks back towards the river.

'My friend,' the first man says ruefully, 'he is all for business.' He winks. 'Here, there is a way – a faster way, by the river, that will take you to your fine house at the top of the cliff. Home and safe, yes? I can take you.' His hand moves quickly and the soft leather of his glove wraps around her elbow in a gentle but insistent hold.

'No,' she tells him, but the man's grip is tight and he is pulling her – not hard, but still pulling, drawing her towards the river, or the boat tied there – she cannot guess his intention. With a surge of panicked strength she snatches her arm free from his grasp and takes a step backwards, but the young man is far too fast. He lunges forward and snatches both of her wrists, one in each of his gloves, as tight and cold as a pair of manacles.

He hisses like a viper: 'Come with me or you will not be safe.'

At that moment two things happen. First, Cecilia sees something dart across the street, over the man's shoulder. Left to right, shadow to shadow – something small and dark and blurred scurries from one side of the road to the other, passing almost directly beneath the boots of the man with the dagger, who is still sauntering back towards the boat, though he does not appear to notice it at all. Possibly it is because his attention is drawn by a commotion that simultaneously begins to unfold among the men at the dark jetty. A chorus of cries and shouts goes up, enough that the man holding Cecilia frowns and turns to look too.

Before she can even understand what is going on, both men – the dagger-wielder and the English-speaker – are sprinting away from her, towards the riverbank. Cecilia squints into the gloom after them, too bewildered to make good her escape there and then. At last, she sees that the small riverboat loaded with its clandestine cargo is slowly but steadily careening away from its jetty in an uncontrolled spin, being pulled downriver, loose ropes trailing after it across the dark surface of the water like a jellyfish's dangling tendrils. The men on the shore try to grab at the vanishing ropes in vain; a lone man stands on the boat's deck, waving his arms and crying out to his comrades in an unproductive panic as the boat drifts farther and farther away, gathering speed. There is a splash as one of the well-dressed young men wades out into the water, leather boots and silken breeches and all – slogging through the murky slop in a vain attempt to give chase to his vanishing goods as they are swept irresistibly towards the open ocean.

Then there is a voice at her ear – a woman's voice, speaking in English. It hisses urgently, '*Run, lost girl.*' She wheels around and there is a face very close to her own – it might be the face of the girl she had been following, who led her to this bizarre scene, or it might be someone else entirely. Cecilia nods once, and whispers a thank-you, and then she flees from the riverbank as fast as her legs will allow.

How she manages to find her way home that night she will never understand. Like a drunkard guided by nothing but blind faith and dumb instinct, somehow her feet follow their own path homeward, independent of her thrumming and terrified mind. She is pursued the entire way by imaginary, stalking shadows, thin and cruel with smiles and daggers that seem to lurch violently from every obscured doorway. With each step she anticipates a harsh voice at her ear, a breath on her neck, a hand seizing hold of her arm and cold steel sliding under her ribs from behind.

It is not until her trembling legs bring her at last to the top of the cliff, and through the white haze of her vision she can see her own house again, that she is able to relax by a fraction. What manner of fate she has escaped from – what those sleek men might have done with her – she can only guess at, and the guessing is a frightening business.

Beside her front door the bulky grey cat is patiently waiting for her; it looks up at her as she approaches through its one-and-a-half eyes. Cecilia looks down at it, and she thinks of the blurred, furry *something* that she had seen dart across the street. 'Was that you?' she asks.

The cat winks, and then it blinks.

Cecilia shakes her head. The idea is too absurd. But she still whispers, 'Thank you,' as she steps past the cat and enters her house. The cat remains outside, refusing to come in with her.

She has no idea what the hour is, but she had been half-expecting to find Rosalie still waiting, worried as to her mistress's whereabouts; but the maid is nowhere to be found. She crosses the hall, towards the stairs and her bedchamber. But before she can even place her hand to the banister, the hairs upon the back of her neck raise and she can feel her stomach twisting with anxious expectation again; if, indeed, it ever stopped. She hesitates and looks around, but her hallway looks much the same as it always does.

She climbs the stairs slowly, the spiralling anticipation growing with every step. As she touches her bedchamber door, another electric shudder moves through her; her fingers can hardly seem to find a grip upon the handle to turn it.

The door relents to her push, swinging open noiselessly. She steps through. Inside, the room is lit by moonlight that washes in through the open window, painting everything it touches with an ethereal glow; a lone candle rests upon the windowsill, sputtering upwards and adding a flickering yellow tint to the scene. There is a figure standing at the window. A man. She recognizes his height and stature immediately, even if he perhaps stands with more of a hunch than when she saw him last. Long brown hair falls in greasy curls over his collar, almost touching his shoulders.

He stands facing out of the window, towards the sea; but in the reflection of the windowpane she can see his face, illuminated a jaundiced yellow by the candle's meagre flare. The eyes in the reflection meet with hers – they widen, slightly, white and round as the shining moon.

One of Cecilia's hands still rests upon the door handle; now the other moves to join it, and the door creaks and sways under her weight as her legs threaten to give way from beneath her. She moves her hand up the edge of the door, caressing the wood, squeezing its grain beneath her fingertips to make sure that this moment is real and not a dream.

At last her voice escapes as a gasp. 'John!'

Her husband turns from the window to face her – her husband: living, corporeal; more gaunt than she remembers, and his coat is ragged and dirty, and he has fresh oily scoops of darkness beneath both of his eyes. A rusty-red beard hangs scraggly from his chin. But it is her husband all the same.

John stares at her. 'Cecilia,' he says, raspingly. 'I am back. Blood of Christ, woman, where have you been?'

Part Two

24.

The next morning Cecilia lies alone in bed. On waking she had supposed that everything that happened yesterday must have been a dream. All of it: the raging sea upon the black rocks; the two local girls she followed and the sinister young men they unwittingly led her to; the boat being loaded with contraband in the night and then breaking inexplicably free of its moorings. And then John, home again, waiting in their bedchamber looking haggard and haunted. It all seems too unreal to have truly happened. But the details come back to her one by one with a sort of lucid, undeniable coherence, and she knows that it was all real.

She sits up in bed and smooths her hair from her face, blinks, and rubs the sleep out of her eyes. She looks at the empty space beside her – John's vacant half of the bed. Rumpled, displaced sheets mark where another has slept. She reaches out a hand, but the sheets are cool to touch; whoever has lain there rose some time ago. She can still smell him, though – a dank, damp smell, rich and briny, as though tidal waters had flushed through her bed during the night. She wonders if he didn't even bother to wash when he first arrived home.

Arrived home. He is home. John is back. John, her husband, has returned. She can hardly believe it. This is the day that she has wished for, for so long – too long, it seems, for it to have possibly arrived. And yet here it is. Last night, he came home.

Why didn't he wake me, she wonders, and then she worries that perhaps he tried but she was in too deep and insensible a slumber after the long day and night that came before. Even now she is exhausted, her body crimped and pinched with aches and pains all over. She aches from her long walk, but from John, too. He had been insatiable, like a famished animal. Not that she hadn't expected it, but even so … It had not been how she had imagined. She did not expect him to be so insistent when the hour of their reunion was so late, and they both so tired – so tired they had hardly spoken a word, even though there was so much to be said. She realizes with a blush: *I think I fell asleep while he was still at it*.

Her heavy eyelids droop, and she lays her head back down onto the pillow. *Just ten minutes more*, she tells herself. From somewhere downstairs she hears the sound of a man's laughter, echoing through her home.

When next she opens her eyes, the room is filled with light. Not the hazy, lethargic glow of dawn, but the brisk and insistent brightness of a fully risen sun shining upon a new day. She realizes she must have slept for another hour, at least, and drags herself from bed at once, flexing and stretching her tired body like a cat. She rubs her fingers down her arm, where the skin stings just below her elbow: a sting in the shape of a handprint, where grasping fingers had pressed into her flesh. Was that John, or the oily youth who had grabbed at her? She decides in that instant: *I shall never tell my husband about what happened last night*. The frightening memory shall not ruin their happy reunion –

and besides, she does not know how she could begin to explain it all.

In any case, it is over and done and of no matter now, she tells herself as she quickly dresses and hurries downstairs. There are voices in the kitchen. She pauses before rounding the doorway; she hears John's voice, certainly, but she cannot understand a word he is saying. He sounds like he is speaking in tongues – but, no, it has the vowels and consonants of a language, though in a form that is not quite French, nor Spanish, nor even Portuguese. Then she hears a woman reply, in a similarly confusing fashion, and then they both laugh.

She finds John seated at the table eating breakfast, with Rosalie standing beside him, conversing in this strange tongue and laughing. John rises at once. 'Cecilia! You are awake at last. Come in, Mrs Lamb, and let me see you now.'

He is washed and rested and appears less wild than he did last night – a wolf-man loosed inside her home – although he still wears his unkempt beard, and she can see now what a rich shade of copper the sun has burned his skin during the months they have been apart.

She has so many questions, but the one that emerges from her lips in that moment is: 'What language were you speaking just then?'

'Ah – Euskara, the language of the Basques. Did you know that Rosalie here speaks it? From her grandfather.'

Rosalie smiles at her mistress and shrugs modestly.

'I did not know that *you* spoke it, John,' Cecilia says, sitting down. She did not even know there was such a language.

'There was a man on board, our sea-cook. A favourite with the crew, as any good cook must be. He would teach the men the odd phrase here and there. I learned a smattering from him. Rosalie was putting me through my paces.'

Rosalie places some tea and breakfast on the table in front of Cecilia and ducks her head awkwardly. 'I speak only a little,' she says.

'It sounded to me like you were both conversing fluently. I never knew you had such an ear for languages,' Cecilia tells her husband. She takes a bite of pastry and asks: 'So you arrived home last night?' Then she laughs out loud. The question seems so small, so entirely inadequate after such a long-protracted absence.

John does not laugh. 'Aye, in the evening ... at some hour. I don't know. It takes so long, between arriving in port and unloading, and then there are questions, and matters to attend to ... I was stuck at the dock for hours before they would let me away. It was late when I came to the house. I expected to find you at home. Where were you last night?'

Cecilia has anticipated the question. 'I had gone for a walk, that is all. I suppose that I got a little lost, and did not realize the hour ... But it hardly matters now. If I had only known you were here, waiting, I should have ... Oh, John!' she exclaims. 'You have been gone so long – where have you been? What on earth happened to you?'

His upper lip twitches. 'The voyage was waylaid,' he tells her curtly. And then, with a harshness she has never predicted in all of her imagined rehearsals of this reunion, 'Don't look at me like that, Cecilia. You know as well as I that plans laid for the sea are never reliable. You prepare as best you can, and then you make do. We were beset by hardships from the off. It was ... Damn it, I have already recounted this to the company till I was blue in the face, last night. Must I be interrogated in my own home as well?'

'Interrogated!' She laughs, hoping to ease the tension by keeping her own mood light. Rosalie has been moving around the room, placing and clearing dishes, but now the maid discreetly exits and leaves them in peace. 'I should hardly call it an interrogation. Can you blame me for being curious? At least tell me, did you reach the West Indies?'

'Of course I did,' he grunts. Then his tone softens, a little. 'It was a trial from the start, which I have no wish to relive. I have dreamed of nothing but my home, my wife, for so many long nights ... Just spare me the questions for a day or two, won't you?'

'I understand, but ... Were you injured? Your ship and your crew, did they return too?' Her burning curiosity overcomes her instinct for cautiousness or delicacy.

John bites into a hunk of bread and chews. Finally he answers, quietly. 'Aye. I returned every Jack Tar that sailed under me, as intact as the vessel that carried them.'

'Well then, it cannot have been a total disaster. And did your ventures turn a profit?'

His nostrils flare with a sudden, fresh surge of anger. 'Did I not already say that we were beset by trouble? How could any man turn a profit when the odds are stacked against him?' John's eyes rove over the plates of food that Rosalie has left spread across the table, as if he finds their very presence confounding.

There is a pause before Cecilia speaks again. 'To have my husband back safe and unharmed is all the profit I could ask for,' she tells him.

'Would that my employers carried such low expectations.'

The kitchen falls into silence. There is only the sound of John's jaw as it works on his mouthful of bread, and the laboured snort of his breathing. Cecilia's breakfast grows cold before her. She stares at her husband with his scraggly red beard flecked with crumbs and dark hoops below his eyes and thinks, *How many times have I played out this scene in the theatre of my mind? Never once did John look like that. Never once did my fingers tremble so.*

After he has finished eating, John wipes the crumbs from his woolly chin and stands. 'I need to go to the offices,' he declares.

'So soon? But I have only just got you back –'

'Aye. There are matters to attend to. But first …' John's eyes brighten, suddenly, and he turns to his wife with an expression filled with expectation. 'Before that – let me see him. Where is he, Cecilia? Where is the child?'

The blood turns to ice in Cecilia's veins; her vision swims for a moment as she tries to comprehend what she has just heard. With an effort of will she manages to retain her composure, stares at her husband with a frightened smile and asks, 'My darling – what child is that?'

John's enthusiasm remains undimmed. 'Our child, naturally. So where is he?'

She licks her dry, bloodless lips. She cannot think what to say. 'John, we have no child, as well you know … Is this a joke?'

A spectre of confusion flits across John's eyes. His smile remains fixed rigid upon his face, but the joy and enthusiasm has gone out of it, like a snuffed candle. His jaw moves a little. 'Of course,' he says, softly. 'Of course. It was only a joke. Nothing more.'

Her throat is tight, and inside her chest her heart is thumping. In an unconscious movement she touches her hand to her belly. 'Is that what you expected?' she asks. 'Did you think you should return home to find a child?'

John says nothing. He turns away suddenly and moves his hand to his face; she understands that he means to hide his emotion from her, but what emotion he feels, she cannot be sure. 'No. A joke. That is all it is … A sailor's jape, you know. A man goes to sea and returns to find a new mouth to feed. All the sailors tell it. It is just a foolish jape they play. Nothing more.'

'John –' she says – but he has already stood from the table and walked out of the room.

25.

John refuses to shave his beard for the entire first week that he is back on land. Whenever Cecilia mentions it, he frowns and runs his hand through its thick, curly bristles, shades of brown and red like leaves in autumn. It grows in patches and tufts and does not seem to fit his face – as if he is wearing a mask. But he only laughs at her when she tells him this.

Seven days pass and she learns almost nothing about his voyage. The expedition was a failure. The company set them off poorly equipped and the elements were fixed against them; this is all she can glean. How and why the voyage came to be extended to over twice its reckoned duration – how a six-month journey became more than a year's odyssey; and how he came to return empty-handed, with no riches to show for such a long absence – John will explain none of these things. His mood turns so sour the instant she brings up the subject that she finds she hardly cares. *What matters is that he is returned to me now*, she tells herself.

Her curiosity is more consumed by the question he asked that first morning back: *Where is the child?* She tries to downplay the memory, convince herself it was just a joke as he claimed, but it is impossible. The hopeful anticipation, swiftly turned to bitter, pained disappointment had been written across his face all too plainly. No, it was no sailor's joke, she is positive. But John had no reason to suppose she was expecting before he went away. Nor what happened while he was away: the child made of salt and water that writhed and squirmed within her belly … There is no way John could have known about that. And it was never truly there, besides. *It was never truly there, and John cannot have known.*

It is much easier to tease and pester him about his unbecoming facial hair than it is to dwell on either of those subjects. In the end she succeeds in persuading him to at least trim the beard into a form that is halfway presentable.

He inspects the results in the looking glass, turning his reflection this way and that, and scowls. 'I don't look like myself any more,' he says. In the end he relents and shaves the whole thing off. Running his hand over his smooth chin, he laments, 'Now I don't feel like myself.'

She puts her arms around him and says, 'Well, you look more like my husband again.' John pats her arm, then disentangles himself and turns to leave the room – and almost trips over the cat which lies stretched out across the doorway. It dodges his boot with a yowl and skitters downstairs on heavy paws.

'What is that damned cat that's always roaming around?' he demands, flustered and angry.

'It is as you have described: a cat.'

He rolls his eyes and grunts. 'Damn it, must you be so provoking?'

She isn't sure whether he means her or the cat. Through the open door she can see its squashed feline face reappear at the top of the staircase, peering back at them gormlessly.

'It is always glaring at me,' John fumes. 'Look at it. This morning the damned thing flopped beside me as though it wished me to stroke it on its side, and I thought I might do so. But then it seized and bit my hand as soon as I got close.'

She cannot help but laugh. 'It does that to me, too. They are contrary creatures. Didn't you ever have a kitten, growing up?'

'Kitten, indeed. It is an ugly beast.'

'I believe this one was a stray ... I suppose it does not fully trust people yet.'

'If it is a stray, then what is it doing in my house?' John grumbles and stalks from the room, sending the cat scrambling downstairs again in fright from the onward march of his feet.

What John does with his time back on land remains something of a mystery. Every day he returns to the docks, to visit the company offices or to consult with his friend Mr Fitzgibbon, who secured him his captaincy when they first arrived in Portugal. Cecilia presumes that the company must still be questioning him – where he has been, what took him so long, what went wrong, and why their investment has not been returned. She wishes she could be a fly upon the wall and hear his answers. Mr Fitzgibbon must be advising John in some capacity, she assumes.

She wonders how much trouble her husband is in. She remembers what Signor Capello told her: John has debts, supposedly. Every evening he returns bleak and uncommunicative. More than once his eyes are red and his breath stinks of liquor.

Cecilia prefers it when he is out of the house. It is a source of guilt for her, but the fact is that when he is home, she doesn't know what to do with herself. The nothing that she filled her long days with before is no longer acceptable. She cannot stand at the window and stare at the ocean for hours on end, or write letters she will not send, or walk aimlessly down to stand upon the shore and listen to the waves and watch the little black fish. She finds herself missing her solitude, missing the days when her time was hers and hers alone. She has to remind herself that this is what it means to be married.

She tries to busy herself assisting and directing Rosalie about the house, who seems surprised and faintly amused by the sudden attention, though does not complain. Her maid looks at her sideways and says, 'It is a good thing, no, that Senhor Lamb is back.'

Somehow she does not phrase it as a question, but Cecilia answers it as one regardless. 'Of course it is,' she says.

She and Rosalie put the dining room into order, dusting and polishing and rearranging the furniture. The room has seldom been used since they moved in – with John at sea Cecilia did not like to sit at the large table on her own, and so she took to eating most of her meals in the kitchen or parlour or even her bedchamber at times. But those days are behind them now.

'I expect we shall have the Delahuntys over, and the Hardings,' she tells Rosalie. 'The house must be ready. And you should think about whether you will need help with the service. More staff. We have become too accustomed to it being just the two of us around here, Rosalie.'

'Yes, senhora,' Rosalie agrees.

Cecilia hears the front door slam as John returns from his day's business. He thuds through the entry hall, and then another door is slammed open and shut, and then another. Finally he calls to her. 'Cecilia? Where are you, wife?'

'We are in the dining room, my love,' she replies. She hears him grumble something, and then another door knocks open and closed in the distance – then, at last, John locates the correct door.

'What are you doing in here?'

'Rosalie and I were just making preparations. We should begin taking our meals in here again. And we should invite the Delahuntys and the Hardings over sometime, to thank –'

She stops. John stands frozen in the doorway, one foot stepped into the room. His eyes are darting back and forth across the walls with a wild, overawed energy. His sun-blistered face is pale and even more gaunt than usual, and his lips are quivering as if he would speak if he were able, his mouth opening and closing like a fish plucked from the water.

'Darling, what is wrong?'

After several seconds he licks his lips and in a dry voice says, 'What … what is the meaning of this?'

She looks around, following his stupefied gaze. The dining room walls are hung with flock wallpaper in a vivid wine-red pattern, decorated with splashes of blossoming burgundy flowers against an ivory backdrop. It is a design they had picked out together when they first arrived. Cecilia had admired the rich boldness of the pattern and the colour – unconventional for a social room, but certainly a talking point.

'The meaning of … the wallpaper, do you mean? Do you not recall the pattern? We chose it together.'

John raises his hand to his mouth and seems surprised not to find a beard there to rub; he pulls his hand away and stares at his own fingers. He looks around the room once more, then shudders and turns his back.

'I dislike it. I detest it,' he says.

Cecilia hurries through the doorway so she can see his face. 'We chose it together, John. Don't you remember? It was hung before you set sail.'

His complexion is still a ghastly pallor, and a line of sweat has broken all along his upper lip. 'I … I must have forgotten. It has a … a sickly tone. It is morbid – who could want a room to look that way?'

'You liked it at the time. I liked the red flowers in bloom.'

He is already walking away from her. It is how most of their conversations end these days. Over his shoulder he says dismissively, 'Keep it if you must, but I shan't eat in there.'

'I do not understand,' she says, hurrying after him through their house, 'but if you dislike the design now, I will have Rosalie take it down. But it is brand new, near enough, and wallpaper is so expensive –'

'Then keep it, I care not! But I tell you it is an ugly shade, not fit for guests. I shouldn't have to instruct you on such homely matters, Cecilia. Speak to Delahunty's wife – she has an eye for trivial things.'

She bites her tongue and measures her reply carefully. 'As you like, John. I shall have it changed, as you prefer it. I just … I do not understand, that is all.'

Cecilia follows John to his study, where maps and nautical charts lay spread across the desk. He places his knuckles against the desktop and stands bent over them for some time, while Cecilia waits at the door. Finally she asks, 'Did you want something from me, John?'

He turns in surprise, as if he had already forgotten she were there.

'Didn't you call for me?' she reminds him.

'I … I forget what I wanted,' he grunts. 'Leave me to this, Cecilia, won't you? Can I not have some damned peace in my own house?'

'That is another thing, John. You must refrain from all of this swearing,' she scolds. 'You are not at sea amongst your men any longer.'

'Aye, and it's as well for you that we're not.'

'What?'

He stares at her darkly. 'If one of my men talked to me half as saucily as you do, wife, then I'd have him whipped.'

She folds her arms. 'All the more reason for you to remember that we are not aboard your boat, and I am certainly *not* one of your shipmates.' John has never raised a hand against her, not once, and she does not believe that he would. Not even now, with all of this strange, frustrated anger that he seems to have brought with him back to shore.

John seethes but does not offer a reply. He returns his attention to his sea charts. Cecilia continues to linger – she does not want the moment to end on such a note, with them both unhappy and cross at each other.

'What are you looking at?' she asks him, after a minute or two. She sees his shoulder twitch slightly, and she steps closer to stand by his side. On his coat she can still smell the salty traces of his voyage, as well as a fresh scent of gin. Spread across his maps she recognizes the coastline of North America, stretching down to the Caribbean Sea. 'What are you doing?'

'Planning the next route. The next voyage.'

'Already? But you are only just returned to me; I shall not allow it,' she tries to joke, to lighten the atmosphere in the stifling room.

He looks at her. 'You will not? But we do need money, Cecilia. You said it yourself: wallpaper is expensive.' Then he sighs, and rubs at his raw eye sockets. 'But you need not worry. The company are in agreement with you. They will not have me sail again, either.'

'Of course they won't, not yet. You need rest, John. What you have endured … You have been away for so long. You must be allowed to recuperate here, with me.'

'But I have to get back. I must return to sea.'

'You need to? Why, John?'

He shakes his head. 'Forget it. You never could understand.'

Gently – afraid of provoking him again when his mood has been soothed – Cecilia reaches past and pushes the opened map across the desk, away from them. 'The ocean may be singing to you again,' she says, 'but she has had you for long enough. It is my turn to hold on to you.'

He stares at her with dull eyes, unmoved. 'And how are we to eat, Cecilia? Sitting idle on land does not put food upon the table. It does not pay your maid's wages. And besides that, how am I to endure what they say ... I must prove my worth out there, upon the waves.'

'What are they saying, John?'

'They blame *me* for the failure of the voyage. Emmerich blames me.'

'Emmerich?'

'Aye, Mr Emmerich. The ship's master. The company's man on board. He tells everyone that it was my leadership that failed. How can I let that slide? I must go back. I must prove him wrong.'

'But, John –'

'What kind of man am I if I do not defend myself? If I cannot provide for my family ... Hell, if I *have* no family, not even a son and heir to continue my name, damn it.'

She takes a step back and narrows her eyes. 'A son? John – you *did* mean what you said that first morning, didn't you?'

He flinches, and keeps his eyes fixed upon his desktop. It takes him a moment to reply. 'What now?'

'At the breakfast table, when you asked to see our child. You really meant it. You believed that we had a baby, and that it would be waiting for you ashore. Didn't you?'

'Are you still harping upon that? I told you, it was nothing but a sailor's joke.'

'No.' She shakes her head. 'No, John, I do not believe you meant to joke. But I have been going over and over in my memory, trying to understand what could have given you the notion to expect a child. I can find nothing. Why were you so sure? What made you think that we had a baby?'

'It is not so strange, is it, to believe I should have put a child into you?' he asks crudely. 'Aren't we married two years, now?'

'Two years, yes – over half of which have been spent apart.'

He gives a sort of snort, as if that were somehow her fault. 'The men aboard … the men under my command, those of them that were married … each and every one already had a son. Every last one – except me. They laughed about it. They made it a joke.' A crimson blush spreads across his peeling, sunburned cheeks, and his shoulders sag like a sulky child's.

'I still don't understand. The men on your ship made jokes … and that made you suppose that you should have a son, too?'

'Not so simple as you make it sound,' he grumbles. 'You were not there – how could you know what it is like? I was their captain, yet they made out like I was still a boy. I was supposed to be – I *was* in command: they should have had more respect. Besides, I am near enough to thirty, and with no children to my name. It is not right.'

She could almost laugh, he looks so hopeless as he mumbles his dubious explanation like a schoolboy. She wants to believe him. Perhaps his question that morning really was nothing more than a misplaced glimmer of hope, distorted by his many months of absence. 'You are not so near to thirty, not yet,' she tells him. 'There is still time for that, if that is what we wish …'

Perhaps John sees the laughter hidden on his wife's lips, or hears a condescending note in her voice; perhaps he just feels vindictive, having been forced into admitting his own insecurity. A malicious glint flashes in his eye.

'The truth is … I should be thankful that I didn't return to find any wee brats waiting for me, shouldn't I?' he says. 'After all … I never could've known if it was truly mine or not. A child born while the husband's away could be of any man's seed, couldn't it?'

'John! How can you say such a thing?'

'Oh, don't blush. Ha, you think I don't know what you wives do while your men toil before the mast? That's another thing men talk of at sea, you know. Aye, better no child at all than one that's born black-haired and dark-eyed and gabbling in the local lingo. But then I don't suppose you'd ever be so careless as that, would you, Cecilia?'

'I …' She is speechless, doubly filled with shock and anger. 'I hate to even hear you talk like this, John –'.

'But you don't speak a word to deny it, do you? Ah, it's all right. I cannot linger on land – I'll be back to sea before long, just you wait. I'll just have to be certain to put one of mine inside you before I go, that's all. It's the only way I'll be able to be sure, no matter how many other men come after –'

She hears no more. She turns on her heel and storms from the room, tears in her eyes: angry and as confused as ever as to what demons have made a home in her husband's confounded head. Behind her she can hear John's bitter, humourless laugh echoing after her, until the door to his study closes with a slam.

26.

'I cannot imagine what could have possessed him to think such awful things, much less speak them. He must know that I could never be unfaithful to him.'

'I am as horrified as you, truly, my dear,' Mabel agrees. 'I never took Captain Lamb to be of such a jealous disposition. But, dear Mrs Lamb, I am afraid that it is quite ordinary for our men to grow disgustingly coarse while they are at sea. It is the near squalor that they live in, with only the company of other men for months on end. No wonder that they should degenerate like they do.'

Cecilia sits rigid on the Delahunty's chaise longue, an untouched cup of tea balanced upon her knee. A night has passed since John's crude, accusatory words, but she cannot stop reciting them, over and over in her mind. 'He never *was* jealous, before,' she says. 'At least, I don't think that he was. Of course there were times when he lost his temper, but he was never coarse, nor cruel. I never imagined he could be – least of all to me.'

'And he will tell you nothing at all of where his voyage took him? How vexing!'

'No. He seems determined to keep it a secret, although I cannot guess why. Perhaps ... Has Mr Delahunty heard anything about John's expedition?' she asks hopefully.

But Mabel shakes her head. 'He has only told me that it was unsuccessful. To be frank with you, my dear, he used the word *disaster*. But I suppose we knew that already. I shall keep working on him, find out what more he knows.'

Cecilia sighs and stares into her tea as if it might hold answers. The coppery surface ripples slightly with the anxious twitching of her leg. 'John has been drinking more than he ever did as well.'

Mabel nods sympathetically. 'All bad habits picked up on his voyage – and they might soon be corrected.'

'He has been to sea many times before, though, and never returned so … agitated.'

'Indeed, but never so long an expedition, I think?' Mabel lifts her teacup and makes a careful examination of its rim for several seconds, and then she says, 'It *is* curious, though, that Captain Lamb should say such nasty things, when you yourself had a similar confusion … I mean to say, you *did* believe that you were in the family way, didn't you? Does Captain Lamb know of that little matter? I can see how that could cause a misunderstanding.'

'No, no. Goodness, no. I have told him nothing about that. Even if he was more himself, I should not tell him; besides, all that is over and done. Only yourself and Doctor Mayberry knew, and I trust neither of you have breathed a word.'

Mabel touches a hand to her chest as if to say: I should sooner swallow poison.

Cecilia had handed the Goa stone back to Mabel when she first arrived that afternoon, telling her that she no longer had need of its remedial powers. 'My mind is much clearer now; I feel much more myself,' she had said, and then she had leaned closer and whispered, even though they were alone: 'Besides, my courses have started again –

which is not so welcome, although at least it is a sort of answer.' Mabel had smiled and nodded, and taken the golden amulet back with no further enquiry.

Now Cecilia says firmly, 'John was on his boat, who-even-knows-where; there is no way he could have known about all of that.' She shakes her head and changes the subject: 'When Mr Delahunty used to sail, did he ever return from sea similarly changed?'

'Oh, my word, yes. His language – well, I shan't repeat any of it. And the drinking! It took a great many weeks to wean him off that, when finally he could sail no longer. He hates to hear me say it, but I do believe his leg injury was the best thing that could have happened to him, the poor dear. They get used to being in command, you know – to having a troupe of sailors ready to hop to and go about at their every word. They come to expect the same when they are back ashore, in their homes. Does Captain Lamb hit you?'

'No, never.'

'Oh, you are lucky,' Mabel replies blandly. She flips open her fan and begins aggressively wafting. 'Open the windows a little wider, will you, please?' she instructs a passing maid. 'Mrs Lamb is entirely uncomfortable in this heat.'

'Now John is already planning his next voyage, as if he cannot wait to be away from land again. Away from me. I never thought … I knew when I married a sailor that I must always compete with the ocean for his attentions and affection; John never made any illusion of his adventurous spirit. But I thought that whenever he did come home, to me, it would be an occasion filled with joy. I should … I should be the light that guides him back, the anchor that fastens him to the shore, not just another frustration to turn his back on.'

She rubs her eyes. Mabel is right; the heat is bothering her, and the sun, so relentlessly bright. She has had little sleep since John returned, between his lascivious, animal attentions deep into the night and the hot summer mornings that arrive far too early.

'I cannot believe my own feelings,' she confesses. 'For a year and more I have pined and mooned around, longing for my husband's return, and now here he is – delivered by little less than a miracle, against all the odds, I know … And yet I feel hollowed-out. Like a wooden doll. I feel nothing, as if he had not returned at all.'

'But he *has* returned, my dear,' Mabel tells her soothingly.

'I know. But I am afraid.'

'Afraid?'

'Yes. I am afraid that the ocean took something from me, and it has not yet given all of it back.'

Mabel stares at her for some time. When she speaks, it is in the same light, reassuring tone. 'Captain Lamb's difficulties shall soon be remedied. If he has forgotten why he has returned to land, then you must remind him. Months of roughness and hardship have worked to make him rough and hard – but he can be softened, believe me.'

Her expression brightens suddenly. 'We must have you over for a meal, soon. The Hardings, too. Yes, yes, all six of us again. My, I can't imagine why we haven't already done so. Some decent company and polite conversation shall soon remind Captain Lamb of the civilized way to behave. My dear, you may mark my words on it.'

Cecilia cannot help but smile at Mrs Delahunty's determined faith in the power of a polite dinner with friends to solve all of life's problems – but she consents to the idea readily enough. A dinner with all the families together again could be enjoyable, and it may well do John the good that Mabel predicts. Surely, she supposes, it can do him no harm.

* * *

The next day Cecilia stands in her dining room, watching as the old man who sometimes helps Rosalie around the house takes down the striking crimson wallpaper from its hangings. He arrived prepared not only for the job but armed with a brand-new wallpaper to be hung in its place: a bland white backdrop with golden vertical stripes, decorated with small sprigs of pale green ferns. 'It is better, yes?' Rosalie had asked, and Cecilia had nodded mutely. It is a design that her Aunt Lara might have picked.

As the man takes down the old sheets, he drops them carefully into a growing heap beside the door; folds of rich red and ivory piled one atop the other. Cecilia stares down at it. It looks almost like a mound of flayed skin. *Perhaps John was right*, she thinks. *Perhaps the colour was morbid.*

The new paper goes up, and the room grows dull and unremarkable around her. She wanders away, leaving the old man and Rosalie to it. She calls for John, for no particular reason except to see if he is in the house or not – he comes and goes so irregularly that it is difficult to be sure, and she dislikes being surprised by him. There is no reply. He must be down at the harbour offices, or else the taverns.

In the parlour she finds the cat sprawled across the settee in a blissful slumber, taking up almost the entire length with its considerable bulk. John has taken to chasing it out of any room he finds it in, but for now it may sleep in comfort. Cecilia cannot resist tickling the cat's ears as she passes, and it stretches and half-lifts its head to squint at her with a contented purr. She walks to the window and stands by it for a time, staring across the bay, happy to just do nothing. It will likely be hours before John returns – she has the afternoon to herself.

Several long minutes pass by. She gazes towards the water and listens to the cat that continues to purr behind her, a sonorous hum that gradually fades away to nothing. Then, from nowhere, she feels an agitation begin to grow in the pit of her stomach. Her pulse quickens in her veins and her heart begins to race. The air in the room changes; the walls seem to close in, and the floor shifts and sways like the planks of a ship.

She squints her eyes and focuses on the view, thinking – or hoping – that perhaps what she feels is a danger outside her house: a sinking ship or a fire in the town, for instance. But the scene outside remains as static as a painting. No … A cold perspiration collects around her neck as she realizes that whatever she can sense is somewhere inside her home.

Next comes the prickling knowledge that she is not alone. A sensation she has felt before, many times. She spins away from the window, expecting to see someone or something behind her, but the room is empty. The cat sits upright, poised and interested but staring at nothing in particular. Somewhere in the distance she can hear men laughing, and the knock of hammers on nails.

'Rosalie?' she calls, but there is no answer. Everything looks washed-out and grey in the waning afternoon light. The cat watches her curiously as she crosses the room and opens the door to call for Rosalie again; but as the door swings open, a shiver runs down the length of her spine, making her gasp – as if a skeletal finger had reached out and traced a line down her back.

She wheels around and, directly behind her, where less than a second ago there had been no one, is John. He is standing before the cold ashes in the fireplace. Or his likeness is; this is not John, she understands, but a vision of him only. He appears dishevelled and unkempt, his clothes creased and stained down the front like some gin-soaked caricature. His face is contorted with spite, sallow and marred by a rusty-coloured, week-old stubble. He is not facing her – he stands side-on, feet spread apart, one arm hanging by his side while the other is raised towards the room, and at the end of his outstretched arm he clutches a pistol. Its barrel is aimed roughly towards where the grey cat is sitting, oblivious. In his bleary, drunken eyes she can see nothing but cruelty and rage.

Her eyes scarcely have time to register this scene before it is gone again. The vision is over; the room is empty once more. She staggers to the settee and drops beside the cat, which stands up immediately and steps towards her, as if to offer comfort. She runs a trembling hand through the soft, dense fur of its back and looks into its one-and-a-half ocean-coloured eyes.

'Why should I see such a thing?' she asks. 'Why would I imagine it?'

But the cat will not say, and Cecilia can only sit and wonder. Sometimes, she knows, she sees things that might be, and sometimes she sees things that will be. Sometimes what she sees can be changed, avoided, prevented. Sometimes it cannot.

Though the vision passed almost as quickly as it came, she is haunted by its memory all through the afternoon and into the night. Except, in her memory, the image grows and becomes more terrible still. She sees John standing there in all his squalor, pistol trained upon someone or something unseen with what she cannot doubt is murderous intent; but his eyes are turned deep and black as coal pits, like abscessed wounds that have sucked two holes into his face. Though she is sure they were not there at the time, in her memory two horns sprout from beneath the long hair matted across his head, and from his back dark tendrils spread and float like awful, nightmarish wings. She sees the walls of the room shaking and pulsating, ready to cave in from the pressure of the briny water that is streaming down from the floor above, pouring down the walls of her home like a dam about to burst – as the entire house threatens to collapse beneath the weight of an ocean of bitterness and hatred which has long since submerged it.

27.

A card soon arrives from the Hardings inviting Cecilia and John to dinner – evidently it is Frances's turn to host. John stands in their hallway and holds the invitation at arm's length, as if it might be contagious. Once he would have been the one enthused by any such social invitation, and she the reticent party. Now their roles are reversed.

'They're *your* friends. But I suppose I am obligated to put in an appearance,' John complains.

'They are our friends – it was you who first introduced me to them, remember? In any case, I am glad of it,' Cecilia tells him. 'We have hardly been seen together since you returned. It shall do us good to dine with other couples.'

John mutters something unflattering about Frances Harding. 'Well, you like Captain Harding, don't you?' she points out. 'And the Delahuntys will be there, too.'

Privately she wonders if Doctor Mayberry has been invited as well. At first she hopes that he has – but then she realizes this would bring John and he together, and she decides it would be better if he were not there after all. It is only at that moment that she realizes she has not seen the doctor since they discussed the child that never was, even though he had promised to call on her again. She supposes he must have heard that her husband has returned and opted to discreetly stay away.

'It would be better if Fitzgibbon were there – but I don't suppose the Hardings would have a scoundrel like him. Nor any of the fine fellows at the club,' John says, and he chuckles at some private joke.

'What club?' she asks.

'Oh, just some fellows I meet with. Sailing men, men who know what's what.'

'Is that where you spend your days – carousing with these men?'

John rolls his eyes and does not reply. Cecilia steps closer to take the invitation from him; she sniffs and wrinkles her nose. 'I don't know how many times I can have Rosalie scrub your clothes, yet they still stink of the ocean,' she says. She plucks at the linen of his shirt; it is soft and clean, and yet the overpowering scent of brine and rot still lingers.

John isn't listening. 'Captain Harding shall provide some conversation, at least,' he grumbles. 'And thank the devil it's not the Delahuntys to host, or we should have to sit through a display of their tiresome offspring. Who wants to watch a bairn play with a hoop?'

'I thought you were all in favour of families and children now?'

'Hardly. A married man should have a family; it's only right. But keep them away from me till they're of an age to sail or drink, I say. Before that they're women's work – reeking, noisy brats that are hardly fit for civilized company.'

'That being so, John, I am surprised you do not feel more at home with them.'

He scowls and rubs his chin. Then his face breaks into a smile, and he lets out a cackling laugh and turns and walks away.

* * *

The Delahuntys have already arrived by the time Cecilia and John reach the Hardings' house, but there is no sign of Doctor Mayberry. The husbands stand by the window engaged in some deep and sober discussion; John immediately breaks from his wife's side to join them. Cecilia watches him go. She has no idea whether Mr Delahunty or Captain Harding have even laid eyes on her husband since his return to port, in defiance of all their expectations; but if this is their first reunion, then there is nothing in their muted, impersonal greetings to betray that fact.

She joins Frances and Mabel where they are seated on the far side of the room. In Frances's lap sits a small brown monkey with bright orange, almost golden fur on its hands and feet. It grimaces at Cecilia with long, needle-like teeth as she sits down. Around its neck is a dainty red collar attached to a thin chain, the other end of which is clasped firmly in Frances's clenched fist. Frances is handing the monkey purple grapes, which it snatches with its tiny fingers and devours in one, two, three quick bites, without ever taking its terrified eyes off the unfamiliar faces that are now dotted around the room.

'Isn't it a *delight*?' Mabel enthuses, and squeezes her hands together with pleasure. The monkey flinches at the sound of her voice and lets out a tiny shriek.

Cecilia is not sure what to say. 'Does it have a name?' she asks.

'Certainly not. It is a tamarin, from the Spanish Americas,' Frances Harding explains, as if that were sufficient designation for the animal. Frances is watching it carefully while it eats, like a governess monitoring a small child.

'I call it darling,' says Mabel, and reaches out to stroke the silky, mottled brown-red fur of the primate's back; it ducks from her hand at first, but then accepts the caress with apparent indifference. Frances thrusts another grape in front of its nose, which it only sniffs at and then turns its head away. Frances shrugs and drops the fruit back into the bowl.

'Where did it come from?' Cecilia asks.

'I purchased it from a French commander in port,' James Harding answers from across the room. The men approach, as one. 'He had bought it as a sort of pet, but I suppose the novelty wore off quickly on a long voyage. I suspect he would've drowned the poor chap if I hadn't stepped in – he practically paid me to take it.'

'It is quite the specimen,' Frances says proudly.

'Don't bring it to the table, though, dear,' says James. 'It still has a sailor's habits and hasn't been domesticated yet.' He laughs at his own joke, and all three men make their way towards the dining room where a bell has just been rung. The monkey, apparently with a mind to follow, drops to the floor and begins to totter after them on two legs until its chain grows taut and almost pulls it over backwards. It stops, stranded in the middle of the parlour floor, and stares about in confusion.

Frances hands the chain to her maid. 'You had best take it away, Charlotte,' she says. 'It has eaten too many grapes; I expect it shall have the runs very soon.'

As the women follow the men towards the dining room, Cecilia asks quietly, 'Will Doctor Mayberry not be joining us? I had supposed that I might see him again.'

'The young African doctor?' Frances replies, surprised. 'No, I did not think to invite him.'

Throughout dinner John appears bored and makes little effort to hide it. Cecilia watches him reach for his wine glass again and again, motioning for it to be refreshed whenever it is in danger of growing dry. Cecilia had expected the group to show an interest in John's voyage – in fact, she had been hoping that some social pressure, along with the interest of fellow sailing men, might coax her husband to divulge more concerning his travels than he has so far been willing to share with her. But through the first three courses no one references his absence at all, except to raise a toast to his return. John responds with a tight-lipped nod.

It is only at the end of the meal, after their plates have been cleared but before the women have withdrawn, that Captain Harding finally introduces the topic, albeit indirectly. He turns to Cecilia, seated to his right. 'Mrs Lamb, I daresay you must be well pleased to see your husband safely home again? The last few months have weighed on you heavily, I am sure'. He speaks quietly, his question intended for her alone to hear, but owing to a natural lull in conversation everybody hears him. Now they all turn to look and await her reply. Everybody except John, who stares into the pool of his half-emptied wine glass.

'Of course,' Cecilia says. 'It was a great relief when he returned at last. It had been so long … It was difficult not to worry.'

'Poor Mrs Lamb; but you bore it with great dignity, dear,' declares Mabel, a little tipsy. She turns to John. 'You men have no idea how we wives must suffer while you gallivant across the oceans. No idea! But, you know, now that I think of it, I realize that I have not yet heard the story of your reunion, when Captain Lamb first arrived home. It must have been very romantic?'

Cecilia laughs. 'In truth, Mrs Delahunty, it was probably not as you imagine. It was already late in the night. I had gone out for a walk that evening and had become slightly lost. By the time I arrived home, I could conceive of no thought but to go to my bed – and then there was John, entirely unexpected. It was so late, and we both so tired, that I am afraid that is really all there is to it.'

'How romantic!' Mabel declares anyway.

'Late at night?' Samuel Delahunty murmurs thoughtfully. He looks at John. 'But did not your ship come in close to midday? I can hardly forget my surprise – and, er, relief, at the moment of hearing the news.'

John takes a drink. 'That is right. But I was much waylaid at the docks. You know how it is,' he says, turning to Captain Harding as if he were the only one present who could possibly comprehend. 'The bureaucracy and the questions after a long voyage are very nearly endless.'

Cecilia keeps her gaze upon Samuel Delahunty. He looks as if he is about to speak, but then his cheeks puff out and he exhales, slowly and uncomfortably. He refills his brandy glass and takes a long drink.

'Of course, even after many hours being cross-examined by my paymasters, when I could finally return home that evening, I discovered my house cold and empty – my good wife nowhere to be found. You never did tell me where you were that night, Cecilia,' says John, smiling slickly at her across the table.

'Indeed, and you have never told me what it was that your employers had so many questions about,' she replies, emboldened by the company of others as well as the wine inside her – they are all several glasses in by this time.

Frances breaks the chilly silence. 'I am positive that I speak for all of us when I say that it is a great relief to have you delivered safely back to us, Captain Lamb.' All four toast to that.

Mabel glances at Cecilia somewhat anxiously, and then at John, and she asks, 'Captain Lamb, will you tell us, was your voyage very arduous? When Mr Delahunty used to go to sea, I simply hated to hear of all the hardships he experienced. And you were away for so very long, one could not help but think –'

'Mabel,' Samuel warns, refilling his brandy, 'I am certain that Captain Lamb has no wish to dwell on matters past.'

John continues to stare bleakly into his glass, a thin, somewhat ironic smile on his lips. Cecilia stirs restlessly and pipes up again: 'Indeed, I believe my husband is determined to pretend that his voyage never happened at all. He has told me nothing whatsoever about it since he came home, though I am dying to find out. It all remains quite a mystery –'

John's voice cuts across her in a low, drunken drawl. 'There is no great mystery,' he says coldly.

There is a pause – a hush brimming with anticipation. All eyes turn to John's end of the table. 'It is a common enough tale. Not pleasant talk for the dining table, perhaps … But you ladies are all sailors' wives and wise to the world, are you not? And – ha, look at your eyes, all so desperate to hear what I have to tell. So be it.'

He drains his glass. 'None of it was my fault. Of that I am positive – no captain could have done different than I. The voyage was poorly outfitted from the start. It was a farce; a ship requiring two dozen hands was provided with twenty, and rations enough for sixteen. Still, I brought her across the Atlantic as charged. Even the wind was against us from that first crossing, and we were taken considerably off course. But such is commonplace.

'It was when we arrived in the West Indies that the troubles truly began. The fine wines we had carried over were not fit to be sold, they told us – some issue with the proper stamps or the like … I don't know. That was Emmerich, he was supposed to fix that.' John's face folds into a deep frown.

Samuel Delahunty says quietly, 'Mr Emmerich is a capable and honest man in such affairs,' and John shoots him a glare filled with venom.

'We had to sail to a different port, a different island – and then another, just to offload our initial cargo,' John goes on. 'We finally traded it for many crates filled with birds – some kind of savage chicken, I don't know – an unwelcome cargo, and half the birds had perished from disease before we were even a day out of port. I should've turned around and wrung that swindling trader's neck for him, but Mr Emmerich said they could still be sold for the meat if we did not delay ... Anyway, on and on we went, up and down the Americas following leads, trading this for that and just trying to turn a profit. I thought, if only I kept sailing, my luck *had* to change.'

He lifts his eyes from his glass and to Cecilia, as if his next words are addressed to her alone. 'But you're still thinking a fool's errand up and down the American coastline can hardly be the whole story, can it? No, dear wife, you're right. The devil still had his ace in the pack to deal me.' He chuckles mirthlessly. 'We did have a turn of good luck, in the end ... And with the hold at last filled with a profitable load, we turned for home with a great sigh of relief.'

He falls silent for a moment, and they watch spellbound as he shakes his head with a sudden, impulsive jerk, and then swipes up his glass to raise it to his lips, only to seem bewildered to find it empty. Captain Harding makes a motion and a servant steps forward quickly with a decanter.

After his lips have been wet, John continues with a renewed and fiery energy. 'It was somewhere in the mid-Atlantic that the wind turned against us once more. It blew with a bitterness I had never known, shunting us this way and that, helpless for hours on end. Keeping a hold of the wheel was impossible, as was any attempt to maintain our bearings. For fourteen days we were caught up in that continual gale – blown off course and deeper and deeper into the wild ocean, turning in helpless circles in a place where the sight of land was just a memory.

'All you could hear was the wind screaming across the waves and howling like a banshee between the masts. It tore the words from our lips; we had to shout until our throats were raw, just to be heard. That sound ... It gives me shudders to remember it now, to call to mind its terrible wail. Like the long, strangled notes of the dying church organ in my home town, filling our ears all night and all day. Some of the men said it was the devil himself, piping a tune that would blow us all the way down to hell. I kept what order I could. But in those hellish nights I confess that I wondered to myself if it could be true.'

John goes on, his voice growing more cracked and distorted with every word. 'Perhaps worse than that, though, was the silence that came after. The winds finally fell and the waters were still – deathly still – and we could reckon our bearings again by the stars. We positioned ourselves a good way south of the dreaded doldrums, yet all the same there was no breeze at all. Not a trace of a current to stir us from where we floated. From the frying pan to the fire ... We were nought but a ghost ship, a useless hulk cast adrift. We set every scrap of canvas; we whistled for a wind till our lips were cracked and bloody. For eighteen weeks I did nothing but score out the date in my captain's journal – days that passed without news or hope. Eighteen weeks floating in that empty, watery purgatory, with nothing to be seen but water, salt, and sky.'

'Good heavens,' Mabel murmurs, and glances at Cecilia.

'You never told me this,' she says, too quietly for anyone to hear her.

'The provisions ran out swiftly, of course. There was no space ... The hold was filled, and I had intended a swift crossing on light rations. The rats made away with as much as the men ate. We were soon down to biscuits and grog, and then nothing but crumbs. The ship's cat was bit to death by the rats; and the men, they caught and ate the rats in turn. I know they did, though no one would admit to me that it was so. It was so silent upon those waters I could hear the rumble of every empty belly, every groan of discontent ... And every mutinous murmur, too. There was scant work to put the men to, stranded as we were ...

Nothing to keep their idle hands and minds occupied. Nought to do but lie in the sun and burn. Below decks it was even worse, the stink of death and disease, down where the sun's light could not reach. In the deepest darkness … In the dark …' He stops, and passes his hand over his eyes momentarily.

'It was all I could do to keep discipline. To maintain order. I knew … I knew that without it we were lost. Every day for those cursed months I dished out some new punishment upon the crew. There wasn't a one of them that didn't feel my lash. They didn't deserve it; they were not bad lads, not when we set sail – but they would have gutted each other like fishes had I not come down on them so strong. Of that I have no doubt.'

He rubs at his shoulder, then drains the final dregs of his glass, scratches his eyes, and concludes with a comment seemingly addressed to no one and to everyone all at once: 'Damn it all to hell.'

Cecilia stares at her husband across the table. She does not doubt that the tale he has told is the truth – or at least part of the truth. His haunted and harrowed visage seems impossible to doubt. She might have felt pity for him in that moment, for the wretched fate that he has described – had he appeared in any way pitiable. But all through his story his countenance has been twisted and twitching with a barely suppressed rage, his eyes wet and red with fury, his lips stained crimson from the wine. All the while that he spoke, his trembling hands lay upon the tabletop, opening and closing into fists.

As she listened, within her own heart she could feel an angry indignation rising. If the story was the truth; if that was really all there was to it – poor trading and unfortunate winds – *Why then, John, did you clutch your secret so close for so long?* She stares at her husband and wonders, *Why share this now, surrounded by acquaintances for whom you claim little affection, when you could not tell it to your own wife?*

There must be more to the tale, she is sure. She glances again at Samuel Delahunty, who is staring at the tablecloth thoughtfully.

It is Captain Harding who breaks the long silence. 'A fearful tale,' he says. 'I have heard much of the horrors of a still ocean, though never experienced it myself. But it is as you say: without discipline, all is lost. And in spite of all hardships faced you brought her home, with all hands accounted for. It speaks highly of your leadership, sir.' He raps his hand upon the tabletop, like a patter of applause.

John flinches, and stares at the captain with something like disgust. 'Not a soul,' he repeats. 'Aye, every head accounted for. And look how they thank me. I bring back my crew and the company asks me, "But where is the profit?"'

Cecilia clears her throat. Every face turns to her. 'I have a question, John,' she says. 'You said that when you turned for home, your hold was filled. Why, then, was your venture unsuccessful? What happened to your cargo?'

Samuel nods. 'It's true, the ship arrived without goods to register.'

'The ocean took it,' John growls, without looking at them. 'We dropped our cargo into the sea. We had to, to … to lighten the load and speed our final return. Emmerich disagreed. He said it was a waste. But the goods were spoiled … worthless.'

'Let the clerks worry about such things,' says Captain Harding, with a slightly forced brightness. 'You did right by your men, that is what matters most.'

'I did,' John mutters. He drains his drink. 'Every man among them was saved. I brought them all back.'

28.

Not long after John has finished recounting the tale of his year-long absence, Mrs Harding makes a signal that it is time for the ladies to retire. They leave the men to console their returned companion and share tales of hardships on the waves, and whatever else it is that men say in such circumstances.

'Where is my tamarin?' Frances asks a maid in the parlour, who explains that the monkey has become poorly and ill-tempered. 'Oh, well keep it away, then,' she says.

'Captain Lamb has endured such a terrible ordeal,' cries Mabel. 'It breaks my heart just to think of it. Had he truly told you nothing about it? Did you really have no idea?'

'Truly, I knew nothing until now,' Cecilia replies. 'He revealed that the voyage had been financially unsuccessful. I knew that they had struggled to turn a profit. But of being caught up in such a storm and becoming stranded for so many weeks … of that he told me nothing. Nothing whatsoever. I cannot understand it.'

'My poor dear, it must have been simply terrible for you to hear.'

'I hated to see his face as he spoke,' she replies. She glances at Mabel and sees that she is close to tears almost.

Even Frances appears pale and withdrawn, and remains unusually silent. Cecilia wonders if she, too, should feel more moved, having heard of her own husband's suffering. *I would be*, she tells herself, *if only I did not have so many questions that remain unanswered*.

'It is no wonder Captain Lamb's disposition has turned sour, after all that he has suffered,' observes Mabel.

'It might certainly explain why he has not been himself since his return,' Cecilia agrees. 'I did not like to hear,' she says, thinking aloud, 'of how he treated his own crew so harshly. I have never heard John speak like that. He did not believe in it … He told me that when he was a young sailor, not long in the Navy, his first captain was a cruel and vicious man. He was cut from old cloth and would dish out punishment for the smallest error. John was his mate, and the old captain even punished him for not being harsh enough with the men. John said … He told me that all the crew hated that captain, himself included, and that he would never be the same way. He would lead by example, not fear – he believed in that so strongly.'

'A fine sentiment,' says Frances. 'But surely, Mrs Lamb, you must agree that in such a dire situation a firmer hand was necessary? Why, Captain Lamb's harshness undoubtedly saved lives. You should be proud that he proved to be the man the occasion demanded.'

'Perhaps. All the same, I did not like to hear it.'

There are raised voices from the other room. The men are shouting; it is John's voice that rants and raves the loudest, drunk and hostile. Cecilia puts her hands over her eyes. She cannot make out much of what is said through two closed doors, but she hears John cry more than once, 'You were not there!' And a foreign word – no, a name, repeated by both John and Samuel Delahunty: *Mr Emmerich*.

Speaking loudly and somewhat shrilly in an attempt to drown out the male voices, Mabel begins to say, 'I read in the newspapers that there will very soon be war with the French over our territory in Virginia. What on earth they think they are doing, I cannot imagine –'

The parlour door bangs open, interrupting her. John steps through and then pauses, swaying unsteadily on his feet in the doorway and staring at the three women like a man bewitched.

He licks his lips, and his swaying gaze roves from Cecilia, to Frances, to Mabel. Words fall from his mouth, loose and slurred. 'It is time to leave. They do not care for my company any longer – nor I theirs. And so … which one of you fine ladies shall accompany me home?'

'I believe that I should,' Cecilia says quickly, rising to her feet. Mrs Harding and Mrs Delahunty look away quickly, embarrassed, and murmur some polite farewells.

Frances insists that they borrow her carriage for the short homeward journey. Cecilia and John are alone in the small compartment, and still only halfway home, when he begins trying to undress her. She pushes his hands away easily. 'John, you are drunk.'

'Aye, and so? Come on, don't keep me waiting.'

She gives him a firm shove back to his side of the carriage; he does not resist, slumping back into his seat where he continues to stare at her hungrily, like a wolf. 'Damn it all – a year away and look how she treats me,' he mutters to no one. 'What are you for, wife, if not a little pleasure? Aren't I due it? No doubt *you've* been well satisfied while I was away.'

'John! I shall not hear this nonsense again.'

'Well,' he shrugs. 'I know how it is. It's plain as … as the moon in the sky, out there. What did those two say to you – Delahunty and Harding's wives, eh? They've been speaking about me, no doubt. Damn their eyes.'

'They had only words of sympathy for the troubles you faced at sea. They showed nothing but kindness, and you embarrassed me with your behaviour. I am glad that they cannot see you as you are now.'

He stares out from the carriage window, pretending not to hear. 'I suppose they know how to keep their husbands satisfied ... What do I need you for, wife, if you give me no pleasure and produce me no offspring?'

She folds her arms. 'Perhaps you shall need me to save you from destroying yourself, John, the way you are going. I don't want to hear any of your disgusting ideas any more. Tell me, why were you arguing with Captain Harding and Mr Delahunty?'

'It was just a disagreement. They have no stomach for harsh truths, it seems.'

'Your disagreement was so loud that we could hear you in the parlour. I am ashamed of the way you behaved tonight, John.'

They ride on in silence for a short while. The distance between the Hardings' house and their own is not far, but the journey seems to stretch on interminably. John mumbles and shifts agitatedly on his side of the carriage. Once or twice his hands flex and shift in his lap, and she thinks he will start trying to grope at her again, but he does not.

Still burning with a shameful anger at her husband, and giddy with the wine she has drunk, she asks, 'What you told everyone, of becoming lost and stranded on the calm ocean – was it true?'

'Damn it, of course it was.'

'If that was what became of you ... If that was the only reason ... Why, then, couldn't you tell me? Why did I have to hear of it for the first time tonight, in front of everyone?'

'Why should I have told you?' he asks, genuinely puzzled. 'To what end? It is not something you could understand.'

'And why not? You seem to think me some silly child,

but I have known sailors all of my life. I know how weather can ruin a voyage, how merciless the sea can be.'

He laughs cruelly. 'Aye, is that so? You know how it feels, do you, to sizzle and roast beneath the sun on deck, like meat on a gridiron? You know what it's like to stare over a thousand leagues of calm water, helpless to stir yourself even an inch towards salvation?'

She thinks of her own long year, alone and adrift in this strange, foreign town, with almost no one to talk to and only her own increasingly untethered thoughts for company. 'Perhaps our experiences in the last year have had more in common than you think, John. Perhaps you would know that if you had cared to ask.'

He leers at her. 'Your experiences? What are you wittering about, woman? I don't want to know what you've been up to. How could it compare? How could … Hell's teeth, I don't want to know what you've been doing, or who you've been doing it with.'

She rolls her eyes. 'You are impossible. You are drunk.'

'Aye. Tell me one more time, damn it, and see if it makes me sober.'

In the rich stillness of the night, she wakes. She sits up in bed and looks to where John lies restlessly asleep beside her. She still finds herself mildly surprised to find him there, even many days after his return. He lies with his face turned away, so she can only see one half of his expression, which is tightened into a serious frown, like a small boy presented with a difficult problem. He looks almost innocent in his sleep.

She watches him for a while, studying the familiar lines of his nose, and cheeks, and mouth, watching the veins and muscles twitch beneath the thinness of his skin, listening to the soft hum of his breath that comes in wordless murmurs through twitching, cracked lips. For some reason she has a devilish impulse to try to wake him: to whisper his name and see whether he responds.

She silently swings her legs out from beneath the covers and drops her bare feet to the cool floor. Their bedchamber is hot and stifling, the air fragranced with stale wine and John's briny scent.

She walks around the room aimlessly, looking at her possessions in the dark. Everything looks different and somehow unfamiliar in the pale shadows. She had been in a deep sleep only minutes earlier, dreaming about something fantastic, which she has already forgotten. Now she feels wide awake, ready to start the day and greet a dawn that will not break for many hours. Even the drowsiness of last night's alcohol has already left her system. She tries to remember if there was something in her dreams that summoned her to wakefulness, but if there was, it is gone and forgotten now.

The window pulls her closer. She lifts the thin curtain and looks out into the night. Below her the town is a jumble of shadows, at the base of which sinks a deep well of blackness that is the sea. There are no stars and no moon in the sky. The horizon flickers and flashes as a storm rages over the ocean many miles away; thin spider-webs of lightning which hang there – jagged gossamer strands of neon blue and aquamarine that chase each other through the darkened sky – they flash bright and then fade forever, far out over the edge of the world. She wonders if any other soul in the town is awake at this moment and watching this same scene. Or perhaps its splendour is meant for her and her alone.

Behind her John jerks and calls out some meaningless phrase in his sleep. She lets the curtain fall and turns back to the bed. As she turns, a feather-light sensation tingles through her insides in a fluttering spiral, then softly up her back, past her shoulder, and gently brushes her hair back so that it might speak into her ear.

'Aren't you glad to have me back, lass?'

In front of her John lies in a deep sleep, his eyes squeezed shut, his mouth a worried line. Cecilia stands frozen to the spot.

'Who are you?' she asks.

'Don't you know me, Cissy?' says the voice behind her, teasing.

'I do not. You are not John. He is home again. I don't need to hear or see you any more. Why do you continue to come to me?' She speaks in a whisper because she does not want to wake John, and she cannot be certain whether she is really speaking out loud or not.

'You think so? Well, I'll be going soon enough, don't worry. Not much longer now.'

'Wait,' she says. 'Wait. Don't go yet. If I hear you ... and John is there, then either you are not John ... or –'

'Or who is that lying in your bed, eh, Cissy?' the voice chuckles.

'But ...'

'But – you don't really believe that, do you?'

She peers through the darkness at her husband's face, thin and haggard, sunburned and blotched where skin has peeled and mended, and blood vessels have ruptured purple and red beneath its surface. But it is her husband's face, all the same.

'No,' she says, without certainty. 'I don't think that I do. And I also think ... You don't mean me any harm, do you? Whoever you are. Whatever. So what is it that you want? Why do you keep coming to me?'

'Perhaps you are the only one who can answer that, lass. Perhaps you are only hearing me because you want to. You called me here.'

'Why?'

'Perhaps because of something you've missed. Questions that remain unanswered.'

'The child,' she says, with a lump in her throat. 'What it was that I felt moving inside me. I know I didn't imagine it. And how did John know to expect a baby? Where has he been, and what did he do, overseas?'

'So many questions,' he chuckles.

'Can you help me?'

The voice answers with some regret. 'No. I can only tell you what you already know. Sometimes things that you've forgotten. Loose threads in the tapestry. Threads ... or a stray hair, perhaps.'

'A hair? You mean John's ring.'

'I cannot linger, Cecilia.'

'Wait,' she says – but she can tell that the presence is already departing. 'You are leaving me – for good?'

'Perhaps.' There is a smile in the voice, she thinks. 'Perhaps I will still be around, should you need to find a lost glove or the like. But not unless you need it. I hope that you do not.'

'Wait –' Cecilia gasps again. But the presence is already gone. She feels it withdraw, like a shadow subsumed into the night. She stands alone in her bedroom in the darkness, while outside the storm continues to flicker and flare, and before her, her husband lies in their bed, snoring and murmuring, and beside him an empty space just waiting for her to crawl back in.

29.

Cecilia says to Rosalie, 'What do you suppose could happen to a man, far out at sea, that might change his nature entirely?'

'Senhora?' Rosalie replies, and at first Cecilia supposes that she has not understood the question. But when she looks into Rosalie's dark brown eyes, wide with curiosity and surprise, and – she thinks – something like relief, she can see that her maid has understood her completely.

'You think of Captain Lamb?' Rosalie asks. They speak gently; John is somewhere in the house, moving around downstairs.

'Yes. I don't suppose you knew him very well, did you, before he went away on his voyage? I wish that you had, Rosalie. He was … a different man then, I think. Kinder. Patient, and good-humoured. What do you suppose could change that?'

Rosalie smiles sadly, and shrugs: the question is too huge for an answer.

'I believe that some event must have occurred on his voyage,' Cecilia goes on. 'Something terrible – even worse than what he has already spoken of. Something crueller than the run of bad luck that he confesses to. And yet, he is desperate to go back to sea. It is all he speaks of, almost. As if his mind can know no peace until he is back upon the waves, despite how he has already suffered. I cannot understand it.'

Rosalie nods. 'That happens. Men, they go to sea, and when they come back they are different. I have seen this, many times. My brothers, they went to sea, also. Like Captain Lamb. Again and again … Until, at last, they do not come back any more.'

'I did not know that you had brothers,' says Cecilia. She tells herself, *Of course I didn't; I never even thought to ask*. 'I am sorry for your loss.'

'They are not dead, senhora. At least, I think not. But the sea took them away. They are still out there, still looking. Looking for the thing that men look for.'

'What is that? Rosalie, what did your brothers go looking for?'

'I do not know. I do not believe that they know, either. I think they would not even recognize it if they found it. But … the world is a difficult and dangerous place, they say. Everywhere it is the same. They say that over the seas, to the west and to the east, there is very much beauty: in the land, and the weather, the plants and the animals; it seems very strange and magical. But even in these different and magical places, the people are the same. Perhaps the truth is that these sailors find nothing. Only different lands with the same people, where life is still hard and to survive you can only do what you must.'

There is a crash downstairs – John slamming a door or throwing something, and then cursing loudly. Both women turn their heads towards the sound, and then look at one another again. Rosalie closes her eyes. 'I think,' she says, 'that I would not like to travel so far, to discover only that.'

* * *

John stops visiting the shipping company offices, or the dockside taverns, with as much regularity as he once did. In fact, following their unfortunate dinner with the Hardings and Delahuntys, John ceases to go anywhere much at all. The business which had demanded his attention day after day seems to halt abruptly and with no resolution, at least as far as Cecilia can tell. John's mood becomes withdrawn and sullen – even more so than before. He hangs about the house all day and all night, doing nothing, haunting the place like a ghost or an unhappy memory.

Her husband's thoughts seem to run in only three directions. He commiserates with himself at his own wretched fortune, stranded on land with no readily available boat to sail away on. He rants and blames others for what has happened to him – Mr Emmerich most of all. Cecilia hears the name almost daily, spoken like a curse. Third among his obsessions, he casts slights and aspersions on Cecilia herself for not furnishing him with a family.

'It is not natural,' he says. 'What sort of wife provides no children? What age are you at now? I should send for a doctor to look at you.'

'I don't know what you expect *me* to do about it,' she tells him defiantly. For all that he complains, John does little to make his declared desires come true. He does not come to their bed often at all any more; he falls asleep downstairs, propped up with a bottle at his desk strewn with sea charts, or else sunk into an armchair, deep in his melancholy dreams. When he does deign to visit their marital bed, he is inevitably too drunk to complete his part, or even to get started. Once he simply rutted uselessly against the bedsheets until he was finished, apparently oblivious to what he was doing.

Whenever she talks back or ignores his demands, he swears at her and calls her saucy and insolent, but Cecilia finds that she is not afraid of her husband – not at all. As much as he resembles the passionate, sometimes imposing man whom she married, he seems a diminished version: shrunken, cowed, and furtive, capable only of bullying and boasting with no force to back up his threats. Sometimes when she moves close to him, he actually shrinks away from her, as if he fears her touch.

Cecilia tries to keep busy around the house. She and Rosalie have settled into a sort of complementary routine, and there is always something to do now that John is back. She sorts through his clothes and his personal things – most have either been spoiled by his long voyage and not yet thrown away, or are being ruined by his current slovenly habits. John stands in the doorway and watches her. He does this sometimes, in the afternoon hours: he stands on the edges of rooms, observing her blankly while she busies herself with tedious household tasks. It is irritating, but at least he is quiet.

'Where are all of your things, John?' she asks, staring into his cabinet. 'There were good clothes in here that were still usable. You had a winter cloak and knit gloves that would do when the evenings grow cold, as they will soon. That silk waistcoat that your aunt gave you. And where are your good knee buckles we bought from Brighton?'

He stares at her as if she were a stranger accosting him. 'I don't know.'

'They were in here, I know it. Why would you have moved them? You need decent clothes, John, if you are ever to recover your standing.'

His eyes slope sideways. 'Perhaps that maid stole them,' he mumbles.

She understands immediately. 'You sold them, didn't you? Sold what fine clothes you had left – why, to pay off your debts?'

'Not sold,' he says. 'They were only lost at cards. I'll get them back.'

She shakes her head. 'Lost to gambling. Down at your club, I suppose?' She closes the door and moves to his dresser; his crushed tricorn hat rests on its top, along with a scant few dress buckles and buttons, a pair of gloves with a lengthways hole in one side, which she thinks looks more like a slash than a tear. 'Where is the pocket watch that my father gave you as a wedding gift?'

'Damn your eyes,' John grumbles without passion, 'What does it matter? Why are you searching through my things anyway? What are you looking for?'

'A ring,' she tells him. Then she says slowly, as if she were talking to a child, 'Do you recall the ring that you took with you upon your voyage? A ring … with a lock of my hair shut inside. You bought it as a keepsake, and you cut a curl from my head to take with you all around the world. Do you remember that, John? What became of it? I have not seen it since you returned.'

John had been rubbing his stubbly chin; now his hand falls to his side and he looks at her warily. 'What now? A ring?'

'Yes. You remember.'

'I don't recall it.'

'You do. The ring which you took with you, and my hair inside it. A memento.'

He blinks, and his jaw shifts slightly. 'Oh, yes … I suppose that I do know it. That was lost, I believe, on the voyage.'

'You lost it? How? It slipped from your finger? Or you took it off and misplaced it?'

'No, neither … How should I know? I did not keep track of such a trinket.'

'Then how do you know it was lost?'

'I …' His eyes flash with frustration, and with a defiant shrug he says, 'It was not lost. I gave it away.'

'You gave it away?' The soft hairs upon the nape of her neck are all standing on end. In her stomach she feels a tightening knot, a cold lump of anticipation that she can almost taste at the back of her throat, dry and metallic.

'Yes, I gave it … You see … It was a sort of payment.'

She frowns. 'You gave away our ring as payment? Whatever for?'

John sighs and his shoulders sag. The stubbornness seems to go out of him, and when he speaks his voice is reluctant but resigned – as if he does not wish to tell her what comes next, but for some reason he is powerless to resist.

'There was a woman … an old woman. A sort of fortune-teller, or a wisewoman, I suppose.'

'Where was this?'

'Abroad,' he says tetchily. 'A port in the Americas. Some of the men went to see her. They said she was the real article. So I went also. At first I was only curious …'

'What did you ask her?'

'I asked … I asked whether I would have a son. I … It was all I could think of at the time. The whole voyage over, it niggled at my consciousness. All the crew had sons, so why not I?'

The coppery nervousness that Cecilia had tasted now fills her mouth; it numbs her tastebuds as she feels a dizzying rush of blood flow to her head. 'And what did she tell you?' she asks, feeling as if she were in a dream.

'She told me it would happen,' he says simply. 'She told me that my son would be waiting for me when I returned home.'

'And you gave her that ring, with a lock of my hair, as a payment?'

He nods. 'It was the only payment she would accept.'

'You traded it away for the sake of her promise? Why would you do such a thing?'

'It did not seem right,' he mumbles, 'that every man should have it but me.'

She stares at him coldly. 'Was it only her words that you

paid for, John, or … did this woman say she could *make* it happen? That she could conjure a child for you across the ocean … inside me?'

'She promised me that it would be real. If the price was right.'

'And the price was the ring – my hair – my body?'

'It was only a trinket.'

'How could you make such a deal, John? That first morning back … you truly believed you had bought a baby, didn't you? Bought it with this fortune-teller's magic … But what did you think that would do to *me*? What sort of child did you think such a bargain could create? Did it even occur to you to ask?'

She realizes that her hands are clutched to her belly, and for a moment she can feel it again: churning, twisting, a frothing swell of life bursting forth from deep within. But it is only a frightful memory. She snatches her hands away and squeezes them into angry fists. John is staring at her, a dark furrow of confusion between his eyebrows. Her anger and her despair are things he cannot understand.

Cecilia wheels around, turning her back on him. In her heart she feels a coldness she never could have imagined. 'You sold a piece of me for an illusion, John. Traded part of me away, and you didn't even think twice, did you? Ask yourself: what did this fortune-teller really get for her part of the bargain, besides a cheap ring?' She remembers the long days of sapping fatigue, too exhausted to do anything but stare at the ocean for hours on end. Feeling her true self slipping farther and farther away, like the cresting waves carried far out to sea.

'I thought I understood you, but this I cannot … How could you do it? I can never forgive you. And … it was all for nothing. There was no child. Your deal was as worthless as the rest of your voyage. There never was a son for you, John. There never was.'

His rage bubbles up again then, all his contrite self-pity vanished in an instant. An angry hand slams down upon the dresser. 'I know it! For God's sake, don't you think I know it? What more would you have me say?'

Still with her back turned, she listens to his heavy tread as he lurches to leave the room. But he pauses. After a moment he says in a faint voice, 'When we were stranded upon the still waters … lost, out of hope and … abandoned by God … there were days then, Cissy, when there was nothing that kept me alive but the promise of one day meeting my son. I swear it.'

30.

For a week husband and wife do not say a word to each other. They hardly lay eyes on each other, even. They orchestrate their movements around their home like dancers in an elaborate court ballet, listening and watching for the stirrings of the other and moving from room to room, exchanging places while avoiding crossing paths. Whenever Cecilia does glimpse her husband, it comes as an unpleasant shock – a stranger in her home, wearing a familiar face.

John barely leaves the house for all this time, but Cecilia does – just like she used to. She resumes her walking, down to the shore and around the town. She is pleased to discover she can still find a quiet pleasure in reading the names of the ships in the harbour and admiring their liveries and figureheads; even now there is no hope that one of the great ships will be the one that returns the man she loved to her. She walks around the harbour and the wharfs, not caring if anybody were to see and recognize her and wonder what her business is.

The first thing John says to her, after their confrontation about the ring, is to tell her he has invited some men to the house to play cards. She shrugs her shoulders and tells him he may do as he wishes; but privately she thinks that it is perhaps a good sign that he wishes for some male company again. It has to be better than him sulking around the house every hour of the day.

Mr Fitzgibbon comes, as does Signor Capello, and two other men whom she does not know – men who look like bankers or civil servants, with accents she cannot place and faces she forgets almost as soon as she sees them. Capello gives a weak smile and nod to Cecilia as he arrives.

Mr Fitzgibbon greets her enthusiastically. He is an old friend of John's, a fellow Scotsman and seafarer; although how precisely the two met she has never quite been sure. Mr Fitzgibbon has lived overseas for some time – John used to like to tell her that he was some sort of secret Jacobite general living in exile, though she is almost certain he was only teasing.

'Mrs Lamb, it is good to see you,' Mr Fitzgibbon says, taking her hand in both of his own. 'You are as fair as ever, my dear.'

'I am glad to see you too, Mr Fitzgibbon. It has been a long time.'

She intends nothing by the polite phrase, but he cringes slightly in response. 'It has been too long,' he admits guiltily. 'I should have visited you, while your man there was away,' he nods towards John who is standing impatiently shuffling cards. The other players are already seated around the dining table, the only suitable space they have in the house. Mr Fitzgibbon leans closer so as to not be overheard. 'I was overseas myself, for some of the time that John was. But I should have called when I returned, to see how you fared. I cannot even think, now, why I did not.'

'You are kind to think of me,' she tells him. 'But it is my husband who is in need of your friendship. He is not himself, Mr Fitzgibbon. I am sure you must have noticed?'

A shadow passes over his broad, friendly face, and he is about to say something when John calls impatiently for

Fitzgibbon to join them at the table. He squeezes Cecilia's hand, nods once, then turns and joins the other men. She watches him enter her dining room – now decorated in its bland, insipid wallpaper – and a vague sensation washes over her that it is not her room at all any more. As if her home has become a battleground, and that territory must be counted as lost. John's eyes meet with hers momentarily as he swings the double doors closed.

Cecilia retreats upstairs to her drawing room, relieved to have an afternoon left to her own devices without John's haunting and unpredictable presence. The weather outside is too insufferably hot to walk in, so she remains in her room, reading and drawing little line sketches of the view of the bay for her own amusement. Voices and laughter, the clink of glasses, and the pungent scent of foreign cigarettes comes rising through the floorboards. It is strange to hear such activity within the walls of her home.

The cat seems not to enjoy it. It sits at the corner of the window surveying the bay, its entire body perfectly still save the tip of its tale that flicks and twitches with irritation every time a raised voice or a peal of ribald laughter bubbles up from downstairs. Cecilia has been in her room for some time before she even realizes that the cat is with her. 'Where have you been?' she asks, scratching the back of its head with her fingertips and eliciting a minuscule flicker of its left ear in response. 'I do not seem to see you about so often as I did. I suppose that you have been avoiding John as well? I wonder if you have other homes that you go to?'

A chorus of celebration or excitement, or anger or confrontation – it is impossible to tell which – comes from the men, and the cat flinches away from her hand.

'Well,' she sighs, 'I am glad to have the company at this moment.'

Afternoon grows to evening and evening to night, and the gamblers get louder and rowdier. Somehow she had not expected that their games would continue so late, though it comes as no surprise when they do. By now the muggy air inside her home, downstairs and up, is thick with the smell of smoke and alcoholic vapours. Outside the sky grows dark, lit only by the thinnest sliver of a crescent moon, and across the bay hundreds of lamps and lanterns light up and glimmer like a sky of stars. There is one voice which she hears cutting above the hubbub downstairs with more grating regularity than the others: the loudest voice, the coarsest, and the most abrasive to her ear. At first she does not even recognize it as her husband's.

Rosalie enters with her evening meal. She is flushed and angry, and wastes no time in declaring to Cecilia that she shall wait upon the men no longer.

'They are all drunk. They behave like *cacharros*. Like dogs. This is not why I am paid,' Rosalie tells her, indignant. Cecilia has never seen her maid so put out – Rosalie even exchanges a glance with the cat, which still sits upon the window ledge despite the darkness outside, without narrowing her eyes in loathing at the creature.

'It's all right, Rosalie,' Cecilia says. 'You don't have to look after them, tonight or any other. I am quite positive that they can pour their own drinks. If you are finished, you can go home now, thank you.'

Rosalie nods. 'Thank you, senhora.' Another peal of discordant laughter rings up the stairs, and she rolls her eyes exaggeratedly and shakes her head, before taking her leave.

Perhaps an hour later there is another knock upon her drawing room door. Cecilia is surprised, thinking that Rosalie must still be working – but when the door opens, it is Signor Capello who enters.

'Signora Lamb.' The small lawyer bows to her. He is dressed to depart, and in his long black coat appears as some sort of revenant, fresh from the funeral and now standing inside the threshold of her bedchamber in the half-light. 'I apologize for disturbing you. I came only to say farewell. I think that you shall not see me here again, after tonight.' His expression seems even more drawn and serious than usual. Downstairs she can hear that play is continuing; Capello seems to shrink from the noise.

'You are leaving? Goodnight, Signor Capello,' she says, a little confused that he should trouble himself to offer her a formal farewell.

'Just so. I wanted to wish you well for the future, signora. I do not suppose that we shall have cause to meet again.'

'No? You will not be working with John any longer?'

He shakes his head solemnly. 'Our business interests do not now converge. Captain –' he clicks his tongue and corrects himself, '*Signor* Lamb is no longer employed by the company – as I am sure you know. I came tonight because I wanted to show my support as a friend. However … it is clear to me now that it is not my sort of friendship that he seeks, at this time.'

Cecilia had been sitting at her writing desk – she stands, now, and takes a step towards him. For all the disgust she feels in her heart towards John, she still finds herself speaking words to defend him – to defend their marriage, and their status and prospects in this foreign port. 'I cannot claim to understand what is happening in my husband's mind any more than you do,' she says. 'Though I live in hope that his current mood is a lowness that will pass. His ambition remains to return to the sea. Perhaps, when he is employed to sail again, he shall have need of your services once more. I hope that you will not think unkindly of him in the future because of the bad habits he has fallen into in the present –'

But Capello shakes his head. 'It is not his current hardships that come between us. Drinking, gambling, it is not uncommon. Not to my tastes, but I do not presume to judge. But there are some deeds which I cannot look past. I … It is not for me to say, but perhaps you have heard some rumour? What John did, I –' He stops himself, and his dark eyes flash like obsidian as he shoots an inquiring glance at her. *Do you know?* His eyes question her: *Do you know what your husband did while he was at sea?*

It is upon her tongue to ask. Right at that very moment, she could ask Capello what happened on John's voyage, and he would tell her all he knows. It seems that he *wants* her to ask, to unburden himself of the secret. But she does not. She presses her lips together and shuts the burning question inside.

The fact is that she does not want to hear it from Capello – nor Mr Delahunty, nor Mr Fitzgibbon, nor even from Mr Emmerich if she were able to track his whereabouts down. She does not want to hear from any of the men who could no doubt tell her whatever hearsay and half-truths float around the docks. No. If John has a secret – a confession – then she would hear it from him, and him alone. Face to face, husband to wife.

Capello speaks again, to fill the silence. 'I hope … I do hope that Signor Lamb is able to sail again someday. He was a fine young captain. Very promising. Ambitious. He had placed such high hopes in this venture –'

'Goodnight, Signor Capello,' says Cecilia. 'Have a safe journey home.'

He bows. 'And to you, Mrs Lamb. And to you also.'

31.

Cecilia falls asleep that night to the sound of laughter and cursing still ringing downstairs as John and his associates continue to play cards, long past the midnight hour.

She is woken while it is still dark by the bedroom door creaking open. It is John; she can tell from his smell: the distant trace of the sea, clothes and skin bathed in salt and baked beneath the sun – a scent that she can still pick out over the fug of liquor and tobacco smoke that drifts through her house and scratches at her nose and throat. The house is quiet now; his visitors must have all finally gone home.

Cecilia pretends she is still asleep. She listens to him walk over to the bed. She can feel him standing over her, hear his hoarse and boozy breathing above where she lies. He tries to rouse her: 'Cecilia … Wake up, wife …' – and then, with a drunken curse, he undresses and falls into bed by her side, and is asleep almost instantly.

When she is certain that John's eyes are firmly closed, she opens her own. She lies there for some time, unable to sleep, listening to her husband's laboured and uneven breathing. His snores become words, muttered snatches of phrases that make no sense. He has spoken in his sleep like this almost every night since he returned to shore. Tonight, though, there is a word that he forms distinctly and unmistakeably over and over again: 'Emmerich. Emmerich.'

She rolls over, lifts herself onto one elbow and watches him sleep. Doubts and worries chase each other over his features as fractured dreams run through his unconsciousness. As quietly as she can Cecilia whispers to him, 'What do you wish of Mr Emmerich?'

'Hang him,' John replies immediately, still asleep. He moans. 'Hang him for what he made us do.'

'What did Mr Emmerich make you do?'

He stirs slightly then rolls away with a discontented grumble. A moment later he speaks again, clear words with form and purpose. At first she thinks he has woken up, but what he says makes no sense except within his dreams.

'It cannot last forever, lads,' he murmurs. 'It cannot … Whistle us something cheerful, now.'

He rolls onto his back so she can see his face by the moonlight. 'Won't … won't any man among you whistle a tune? Mister Jones? Sing us a song from home. To lift our spirits – let us hear it.'

He falls silent. Perhaps it is the strained, desperate expression that remains on his face; perhaps it is only morbid curiosity – whatever the reason Cecilia begins to hum a tune. Some old sailors' song that John used to sing from time to time. She cannot remember the words, exactly, so she half-hums, half-sings the melody, very softly into his ear.

John sighs blissfully. 'Aye, aye. Very nice, lads.' He rolls away again and falls silent, and she thinks that his dream is done. She lays her head back to the pillow and her own thoughts begin to drift off as they will. She is almost asleep herself, when, with an abrupt spasm, John's body shakes from head to toe and he speaks again.

'The hold … the hold, Mister Castellano.' His voice comes out as though there were an invisible hand pressed down upon his throat, strangling him. Cecilia sits upright in their bed and stares at her husband in alarm. His eyes are still screwed shut.

'The hold,' he gasps, 'is it locked, Mister Castellano? Be sure to lock it tight. Is it locked, now?'

For a moment the room is silent. Then, hesitantly, Cecilia whispers a reply. 'Yes, it is locked,' she says.

'Good,' John answers immediately. His throat clenches as he swallows. 'But – check again, won't you, Mister Castellano? See that it is locked tight, now.'

She leans closer. 'What is in the hold?' she asks. There is a pause, a silence that drifts through the gloom like a static charge. John's shoulder jerks slightly, but he does not reply.

She asks again, louder: 'What is locked in the hold?'

John sits bolt upright in bed, hauled to attention as if snagged and reeled on the end of a fishing line. He sits up, his face a bloodless death-mask in the pale light, and his head swivels crookedly upon his shoulders until he is staring directly at her. His eyes are wide open now, but glassy and unseeing: still locked inside his dreams. In the deep circles of his eyes she sees nothing but absolute terror. A voice which she can scarcely recognize emerges from somewhere deep at the back of his throat, a ghastly, tortured croak.

'Keep it locked,' he groans. 'Keep it locked up tight. Do not go in there.' His blank eyes stare lifelessly into her own, and then he simply drops backwards, back onto the bed, where he lands with such a heavy thud she is sure that the shock must jar him awake. But a moment later his snoring resumes, and he is deep asleep again, and he does not breathe another word all through what remains of the night.

* * *

John's acquaintances return over and over again to gamble over increasingly rowdy games of cards. At first it is every few days, then it is every day. They arrive late in the afternoon and play on until the small hours of night. Rosalie refuses to even attempt to keep the remnants of the dining room clean or in any sort of order. 'There is no point, senhora,' she complains. 'Tomorrow the pigs come again, and it is filthy again.' It is difficult to disagree.

The men that come to gamble change day by day, though somehow their faces remain the same. Different men with the same manners. There are only two types: some are like the dull, unmemorable bureaucrats who played with Fitzgibbon and Capello that first night. Men who, Cecilia suspects, sneak away from their wives and families to indulge in a little vice from time to time. The other type is much less benign. Men who make a habit of vice, with ravaged, dangerous faces. None of the players ever seem to say very much; they only come to life when the doors have closed and the gaming has started, and then it is all shouts and jeers and challenges and laughter, until they leave by starlight, jangling coins in their pockets.

When she asks John how he knows them, he shrugs and shirks the question. 'They're men who aren't afraid to play a little cards, that's all.' Sometimes Mr Fitzgibbon comes too, and sometimes he doesn't. Captain Harding joins once, but like Signor Capello he does not return for a second round. It makes Cecilia burn with embarrassment to imagine what he might report to his wife, Frances, about the state of her home and her husband. She has not heard from Frances or Mabel since the evening of Frances's dinner – she can only assume they were scandalized by John's drunken behaviour that night, as well as his doubtless growing and laughable reputation around the port. Sometimes she wants to talk to Mabel, and seek her advice on what she should do, but Cecilia feels too ashamed herself to reach out to her friend.

She imagines writing home, finally, to explain all that has happened – or almost all of it – and beg for help from her father or her sister's husband. She composes a letter in her head but does not write a word of it down on paper. She would not wish to be a burden on Louisa's young family. But surely her father would bring her home if he knew that her husband was a drunkard, a gambler and – no doubt worst of all to her father's mind – close to penniless. Better to hide a disgraced daughter at home than let her become a laughingstock abroad.

She tries to imagine a life back in England. She is twenty years old now. That is still young, and surely her tale is deserving of pity, not scorn. But of what use can she be to anyone? She cannot marry again while John still lives. She does not know how to cook or sew particularly well, and she has no patience or aptitude to be a governess. And what if John were to track her down, come and fetch her? The possibility could never be discounted. The law would be on his side, of course, and she believes that she would have no choice but to go with him.

But what if, she thinks, *I were to go somewhere that he would never find me?* The ocean leads to more places than just England. The ocean can take you anywhere. And when you arrive, you might be someone else completely.

It is a tempting notion. But for the time being she is shackled to John, like an anchor looped around her ankle. She cannot imagine loving him ever again, but that does not necessarily mean that their marriage must be a failure.

When John is sober Cecilia tries to persuade him that he needs to look for work – that he cannot continue to live like this, neither of them can. 'There are other companies, surely, that you can sail with? They cannot all have closed their doors to you?'

'What do you know of it?' he grunts dismissively.

'Didn't you tell me yourself that you longed to return to sea? But what are you doing about it, John? No one will give you a ship to sail when you are locked in there playing cards all night, and drunk.'

'You don't understand what you're talking about. It is not just as easy as you make it sound. Go and find a commission, ha! And how am I to do that, pray tell, when that bastard Emmerich speaks against me to anyone who will listen?'

'And no wonder, when you call him every blue name under the sun. Hardly a day passes that I do not hear you curse Mr Emmerich.'

'It is not only that,' John says bleakly. 'He calls me a poor captain. He says I am not a fit sailor. He blames *me*, if you can credit it. At least he says he does, to save his own skin. Blames me for what happened, when wasn't it all his idea in the first place? How could I ... I could not have known what it would come to. What else could I have done?'

'Blames you for what? What really happened on your voyage, John?'

'No ... No.'

'Perhaps I should speak to Mr Emmerich myself, then. Perhaps he shall explain it to me.'

'No!' he cries. For a moment his eyes flare with rage and she sees before her the ruined, murderous image of her husband that she has glimpsed in fleeting visions, now made flesh. For all his drunken ranting she seldom feels afraid of John, but in that moment she takes a step back, overawed.

'No ... Keep away from him. I'd see all three of us dead before I let you hear a word of his lies,' he tells her, curling his hand into a fist.

Cecilia swallows, and waits a moment to regain her composure. 'Then I shall hold on until I have heard the truth from my husband. I can wait. I have much experience of waiting,' she tells him coldly.

He lurches away, and a few moments later she hears the pop of a bottle in another room, and the glug of its content as it pours. *Yes – I can wait*, she tells herself. In the meantime, though, her imagination does a good job of providing a terrifying array of possible explanations – of what it is that Mr Emmerich blames John for, and what sin has made Signor Capello turn away. Of what it was that was locked inside the ship's hold. Some of the possibilities she can conceive are fantastical and far-fetched, some are horrifyingly banal. She dreads that the actual tale is worse than any of them. Some truths are better left unheard, she fears. *Do not go in there.*

32.

One evening as the latest roster of gamblers arrives, Cecilia hears a voice among them that she recognizes. She rushes to the top of the stairs to steal a glance down, and standing in her hallway she spies a friendly face, looking lost and innocent among the menacing scowls of John's associates.

'Doctor Mayberry!' she calls from the top of the stairs, and his face turns wonderingly towards the sound. He breaks into a warm, surprised smile upon seeing her.

John is already ushering the men towards the table and Cecilia can see him eyeing the doctor and herself sharply, but she pays him no mind as she walks halfway down the stairs. The doctor breaks away from the other men and stands by the bottom step.

'Why, Mrs Lamb,' he says, 'it is a pleasure to meet you again. I knew this house had a familiar air to it, though I could not bring to mind why I might recognize it. I feel foolish; it had somehow not even crossed my mind that the Mr Lamb I was invited to play with should be your husband. I trust that you are well?' His cheerful bedside smile is impeccable, but he cannot have failed to notice how foul the air of her home has turned since he first visited her some months previously. His confusion and alarm is visible in his slightly forced smile and wincing eyes.

'Doctor Mayberry,' she asks, 'what are you doing here?'

'Why, I was invited to play cards. I am not much of a gambler, truth be told. But for the sake of a little companionship I can muddle through.'

'You know my husband?' she asks anxiously, placing her fingertips to her throat.

'Only by reputation – ah, that is to say … some colleagues of mine have played here from time to time, and they invited me. As I say, I am not much of a player, but it might make a change for an evening.'

John had wandered into the dining room, and now his voice comes rumbling out through the opened doors: 'Are you here to play, doctor, or only to sweet talk my wife?' The doctor's rigid smile twitches with confusion, unsure whether it is a joke or not.

Cecilia quickly runs to the bottom of the stairs so she may speak without being overheard. 'Doctor,' she says urgently, 'be careful in there. It is not a friendly game that my husband plays. Those men … They play to win, and not for the pleasure of each other's company. I urge you to watch your wallet … and yourself. Please.'

The doctor's expression turns serious, and he nods. 'Thank you. Consider me warned; I shall be careful. Although,' he flashes her another grin, 'if they hope to take me for every penny I'm worth, they might be disappointed when they count their winnings. I am glad to have had this chance to see you again, Mrs Lamb, unexpected though it is. Even if the cards do not favour me tonight, I shall count this a profitable visit.'

She watches him move into the dining room and hears John's harsh voice from within: 'Shut that door, will you?' Even after the doors are closed, she waits outside a while longer, listening to the muted sounds of the games beginning within – like standing outside the lion's den and listening to their stomachs rumble.

Normally after John's friends arrive, she will go for an evening walk through the hazy remnants of the afternoon's searing heat. But tonight, knowing that the young doctor is among their number, she stays at home and listens intently to the sounds of her house, alert and anxious for any disagreement or confrontation.

After two hours or so, when the moon is not yet in the sky, she hears the double doors to the gaming room open and close, and then the tread of footsteps climbing the stairs. She listens for the telltale creak of the step third from the top, which has come to serve as her alarm on the nights that John makes his way towards their marital bed. But on this night the step creaks and then all falls silent, as whoever has climbed the stairs goes no farther.

After a moment she opens her bedroom door. Doctor Mayberry is standing at the top of her staircase looking somewhat lost.

'Mrs Lamb,' he says, squinting at her through the half-light, 'I am sorry if I intruded. I wished to say goodnight and tell you that I am leaving. I did not know if it was proper, to come to you … But I mentioned it to your husband and he did not seem to mind.'

'I don't expect that it distracted him from his game, no.'

'Well,' he hesitates. 'Goodnight, Mrs Lamb. I do not believe I shall return to your husband's table, in truth. You were right to warn me – the way those gentlemen play is not for me.'

'That you call them gentlemen only proves that fact,' she tells him. 'You are leaving now?'

'This moment.'

'Then I shall take a walk with you, if you do not object. It is not yet very dark, and the fresh night air will do me good.'

She insists on accompanying him out of the house, despite the doctor's polite but not entirely convincing attempts to object. A few minutes later they are walking side by side along a street overlooking the bay, where the final sliver of sun is melting into the sea like a burning fire of scarlet and indigo.

'Has my husband lost very much money tonight?' Cecilia asks.

'Some. What luck he started with seemed to run out quickly. Every fourth or fifth hand he wins a little back; the pattern is quite remarkably consistent.' The doctor keeps his eyes upon the bay, embarrassed to look at her. 'He is losing in the long run, there can be no doubt. I had thought there was an element of chance in playing cards, but with those men I see that I was mistaken.'

'I actually believe John knows they are cheating him, and yet he still invites them back, night after night. I am ashamed that you have met my husband as he is now, doctor. He was not always this way. I hope that you do not think too unkindly of me, to see what sort of home I keep –'

'No,' he says quickly. 'No, I can think no such thing. It is plain that the household is not of your making. Are you hurt, Mrs Lamb?'

The abruptness of the question surprises her. 'No, he does not lay a finger on me. I feel like he is afraid to, somehow.'

'That is good. But there are other types of hurt, beyond physical misuse,' he tells her gently.

'You must hear things, doctor – what do they say about John, around the harbour?'

'It is known that he runs a liberal card game … I have heard his name more than once, among my patients with poor habits,' Doctor Mayberry admits. 'More than that … Well, it is not all bad, or else I should not have come tonight.'

She smiles. 'You did not call on me again, doctor, after the last time we spoke. I wondered what had become of you.'

He laughs sheepishly and adjusts his collar. 'Yes, I am sorry. I heard from Mrs Delahunty that your husband had returned, and that ... the matter which we discussed on that previous occasion had resolved itself, so to speak. So I thought it should perhaps be prudent to stay away. She told me all about her bezoar and its magical properties, and how it had eased your mind. I cannot condone the superstitious method, but I am pleased with the outcome nonetheless.'

'You have spoken to Mrs Delahunty? How is she?'

'Well enough. She speaks of you a great deal. She would have called herself, except she is chained to the bedside of a poorly son. The boy will recover though, have no fear.'

'Poor Mrs Delahunty; I should have been the one to visit her, except I feel so ashamed. The things she must have heard about John and I ...' She glances around to check that they are alone. 'Doctor Mayberry, I confess that I did not wish to walk with you tonight only for the pleasure of your company. The matter which we discussed when last we spoke ... my condition ... I have been wondering ...'

She sees his head turn sharply in the corner of her eye, and she adds quickly, 'Mabel is correct: I do not believe myself in the family way any longer. But ... You may think me foolish to ask, but: for a woman to be made with child ... there is only one way, isn't there?'

'There is certainly only one method that I am aware of,' he says, and clears his throat awkwardly.

'But other ways could be possible, couldn't they? I have heard of standing stones in Penzance that will put a woman in the family way just by walking between them ... Or like the medicine in Mrs Delahunty's Goa stone. Perhaps there are old ways, ways we might not fully understand, by which it might be done?'

'These are myths and legends, Mrs Lamb. They have no substance. They go against all principles of modern natural philosophy.'

'I suppose. You are much more learned than I am, of course, doctor. But still it seems to me that there are a great many more strange things in this world that cannot yet be explained, than there are that can. I wonder how much damage science could wreak with a single lock of hair?'

'I do not think that I follow.'

'John told me that on his travels he gave away a cut of my hair, and a ring which he had purchased for both of us. He traded them for a service –' She shies away from mentioning the slithering child again, or detailing her most outlandish fears – although, by the thoughtful look on his face the doctor perhaps guesses the direction that her thoughts run in. 'Perhaps it sounds like no great matter when I say it aloud, now. Perhaps I am being foolish. But when he admitted what he had done, I felt it grievously. Like a great part of myself was being torn away. Doctor Mayberry, what sort of service do you suppose could be bought for such a price?'

He considers the question. 'Truthfully? Nothing but hocus-pocus, Mrs Lamb. Certainly nothing that could do harm to you.'

'Yes, doctor.'

'Or perhaps I should say, nothing that could harm you physically. I can tell what a breach of trust this was between you and your husband. Not all harm leaves a mark that we can see with the naked eye.'

'Indeed. Look,' Cecilia says, 'we are near the edge of the old town. I suppose we must say goodnight, doctor; though I am sorry to see you go so soon.'

'You know, Mrs Lamb,' Doctor Mayberry says, 'it is such a fine evening. I think that I shall walk you back to your home – providing that you permit me.' She smiles and nods, and they both turn around and begin to walk back the way that they have just come.

As they walk back along the edge of the cliffside, the doctor says, 'I do believe there is a cat following us.'

'Yes: my good luck charm,' Cecilia laughs. She looks back to where the grey cat is plodding behind them, trailing some dozen feet distant, paws treading silently across the paving stones. She was aware of the cat following them all the way from the house; now, it follows them on the way back, although after they turned around they somehow did not ever cross paths with it.

'He follows me almost everywhere I go. I always feel that he is protecting me somehow, keeping an eye on me.'

'You should feel honoured – the poor wretch only has the one eye to spare,' the doctor observes.

They walk most of the way in comfortable silence, but as soon as they draw within sight of Cecilia's home once more, she senses Doctor Mayberry's manner become stiff and serious. He says: 'Mrs Lamb, I hesitate to even say this, but … the truth is that I have heard more rumours of Captain Lamb's philandering and mounting debts than I wanted to let on. I tried not to listen, but having seen for myself tonight … Well, with the captain as he is, bound on a path for bodily and financial destruction with seemingly little prospect of change – could you not simply leave? You have family back in England, don't you? Would they be willing to help, to intercede, somehow? If my own financial position were only more tenable, then believe me that I would do what I could –'

But she holds up a hand to stop him and shakes her head. 'I have considered it. But even if I were to write home – even if my father, or my sister's husband, were willing to fetch me from this place, which they might be – I would return to England used goods, with no remaining value. Fit only to help my aunt around the house, or be a companion to some other old madam … What sort of a life is that?'

She sighs. 'For now I am still John's wife, in sickness and in health. I belong here with him. That was true when he was lost and believed dead at sea – it is still true now, as he seeks his ruin in empty bottles and card games. I cannot go. I must see this out.'

The doctor frowns, but he nods in mute acceptance, and they say their goodbyes and he at last departs, walking back into the night alone. Cecilia stares out into the bay for a long time before going indoors. Night has truly fallen now, and all is bathed in darkness. The cat creeps closer and curls itself around her legs as she stands. *It is true*, she thinks. *I cannot leave this place behind. I cannot leave John – not yet. Not until this act has played out to its final scene. Not until I have seen something break.*

33.

One evening as Rosalie is clearing away the used dishes from where Cecilia has eaten, alone, in her drawing room, she catches a glimpse of her maid studying her through the tail of her eye: looking her up and down with a solemn, worried expression upon her face. When Rosalie realizes that she has been noticed, she casts her gaze downward and stops what she is doing.

'What is it?' Cecilia asks.

'*Nada*, senhora. It is nothing.'

'What? Tell me,' Cecilia insists – not angry, but intrigued.

'Senhor Lamb,' says Rosalie. 'He asks me – again and again he asks – whether you are getting bigger.' She holds up her finger and thumb and gradually widens the gap between them, to illustrate her meaning. 'He wants to know if your clothes become too small, around your stomach, your hips – you understand, yes?'

Cecilia nods. 'He hopes I am with child.'

'A baby, yes. He hopes. But I think …' Rosalie hesitates a moment longer, her eyes floating away in thought. 'You know, senhora, there are things you can do, so that it will not happen. Forgive me, but I think it would be better if it did not happen. The senhor wants a child, but' – she frowns and shakes her head – 'if … if you do not wish it … I know women that can help.'

Cecilia smiles sadly. 'Thank you, Rosalie. But the truth is, if John expects a child from me, then he forgets what he must do to make it happen.' She thinks: *Your fortune-teller lies many leagues across the terrible ocean, John.* The only way now is Doctor Mayberry's way; and that will not happen if she has any say in the matter.

'It is the rum. The drinking,' Rosalie says. She looks relieved. 'It ruins everything.'

'Yes. Well, not all of its effects are to be lamented, I suppose. Rosalie … I am sorry that I have not yet been able to pay you this week. When I can, I shall –'

Her dark hair shakes back and forth. 'Not important, senhora. Only when you can.'

Cecilia nods. Downstairs she can hear men arriving for the night's games. 'I will go outside for a walk now, Rosalie. I shan't be too long, I expect. The nights are getting shorter and shorter these days. If you have finished your work, then you may leave – there is no need for you to wait around for those men.'

Rosalie bobs a curtsey. 'Very good, senhora.'

Cecilia walks aimlessly across the black rocks near the old lighthouse, watching the fishermen and the seagulls and listening to the tide break, until there is almost no more light to walk by. She makes her way homeward feeling strangely cool and empty inside. She feels distracted, as if there were something at the back of her mind that she has forgotten to do. It is not until she is nearly at the top of the cliff and home again that she recognizes the cause of her distraction: deep inside her gut, almost too faint to feel, there is a slowly turning helix of foreboding. A sensation she has not felt for some time, now. *Something is about to happen*, she thinks. And then she thinks: *Could this be it, at last?*

As soon as she enters her house, she notices that the double doors to John's gambling room have, unusually, been left wide open. The men inside are deep into their games and also their cups, their coarse voices echoing loudly into her hallway – the same as any other night, except that John is normally insistent on hiding his vice behind a closed door.

Rosalie is waiting in the hall, standing by the parlour door and staring towards the dining room. When she hears Cecilia enter, she turns; Cecilia can immediately see the nervous concern written in her maid's eyes.

'What is going on?' Cecilia asks.

'Senhor Emmerich,' Rosalie replies, simply. 'Tonight, Senhor Emmerich is at the table.'

Both women look towards the open doorway, again, and then Cecilia says, 'I see. Thank you, Rosalie … You should go home; it is late already.'

'You are certain?' Rosalie looks afraid.

'Yes. Thank you. I am sure.'

Rosalie withdraws to the kitchen, and Cecilia moves to go upstairs, but she cannot resist glancing sidelong into the dining room as she passes. The men within are laughing. It is a low, dry laughter without any trace of humour or pleasure to it – but all the same it is not the violent threats nor hissed confrontation which she might have expected, given who now sits at her husband's table.

Mr Emmerich – that name which she has heard cursed and decried almost constantly these past weeks by John. Mr Emmerich, the ship's master on his voyage, both men now blaming the other for all that went so badly wrong – whatever, exactly, that was. Can the pair really now be playing calmly at cards together under her roof?

Cecilia sees little from her passing glimpse into the smoke-shrouded room: just shabby figures of men hunched over a table. So she waits out of view beside the door, listening to the voices, baffled and fascinated. After a few minutes she cannot hold back from taking another peek.

Inside the room is a murk of tobacco smoke, drifting in the dim light thrown by three or four candles that drip gouts of hot wax directly onto the tabletop. The reek of liquor and cigarettes and ripe, unhealthy sweat affronts her nostrils, as if the room stank of sulphur and brimstone. She stares at the unfamiliar faces around the table one by one until she comes to John, when, with a start, she sees that he is looking directly at her. As if he had been watching the door the entire time, just waiting for her face to appear.

His voice rings out, loud and full of bravado – but it is of the forced and false kind: the desperate boasting of a frightened man. 'Who is that now, lurking at the door?' John calls. 'The maid? Show yourself! But look, gentlemen – it is my wife, in the flesh. Come inside, Cecilia, don't be shy. Gentlemen: I introduce to you the good Mrs Lamb. Tsk, well now, don't get up all at once, you worthless curs.'

Reluctant but intrigued, she allows herself to be drawn in by her husband's words and gesturing arm. She skirts around the edge of the room, keeping as far as she can from the men at the table so that the sleeve of her dress brushes against the yellowing wallpaper, until she comes to stand beside John's chair. As soon as she is near enough, he seizes her roughly around her hips and pulls her closer. She feels his fingers press clumsily, lasciviously into her side, flaunting her to the room like a trophy. All of the men at the table are now staring at her. She forces herself to hold her chin high as she stares back. She wants to demand, *Which one of these half-men crumpled around my dining table is Mr Emmerich – whose blood my husband lusts for day and night?*

'See these lousy wasters I am forced to play with, love?' John says. ''Tis a shameful sight for a bonnie lady like yourself. But what brings you creeping to the door of such a den of iniquity? I've never known you to show an interest in our little games before. Do we play too loud for you, is that it?'

'Why don't you introduce me to your friends, my love?' she asks, placing her hand lightly upon his shoulder, which, she notices with a creeping revulsion, is oddly damp. She can endure his pawing hands and his crowing words, if only he would slake her curiosity and point his finger at the mysterious Mr Emmerich for her.

But John is not listening. He is continuing to boast about her supposed charms with a triumph that is quickly becoming aggressive: 'Aye, she's a fair treasure, is my Cecilia. She's too fair a lass for any of you lechers, that's for certain. Keep your eyes off her, now, or I'll put them out, damn you. You'll see if I don't.'

But his guests are rapidly losing interest in her. They turn their heads back to their cards and reach for their glasses. One of them, she doesn't see who, grumbles that they should get back to the game, and John angrily slaps his free hand down upon the table.

The atmosphere in the room is too much. It was a mistake to be drawn in; no good can come from her being here, she quickly realizes. She snakes her way out of John's clumsy embrace and exits the room at a half-run. As she pulls the doors closed behind her, she hears a softly spoken voice say, 'A lovely creature, indeed. Too bad she should be squandered on the likes of you,' and then the table laughs cruelly.

'Say that again, Emmerich. Damn your eyes. Only say it again and I'll knock you about, see if I don't,' John seethes. Cecilia closes the doors with a click, and she does not hear whatever is said next.

Cecilia listens all evening and late into the night to the men playing downstairs – John and Mr Emmerich, dealing hands of cards and getting drunker and drunker on cheap spirits.

Eventually her eyes sag and close and she drifts into sleep, and dreams of placid green waters, cold and endless. When she is wrenched suddenly from her deep slumber, she thinks she feels a movement inside her, a life coiling wetly around her womb, and her skin turns cool with panicked sweat as she half-dreams that the infant has returned. But it is only an illusion. A noise coming from downstairs jolts her fully awake and her insides are empty again.

There is a violent commotion of curses and oaths unfolding downstairs. She sits up in bed and strains to hear what is being said. The men are shouting – John is shouting, cursing at them all and chasing them from the house. He calls them cheats and swine and other words, and they jeer in protest, call him a drunk and a fool. There are tramping footsteps, doors slamming – and then the house falls deathly silent.

Cecilia slips out from the bedsheets and hurries downstairs, still wearing only her shift. Her heart is pounding too heavily, and her imagination is running too loose and wild for her to possibly return to sleep, or to resist investigating. As she descends the staircase the house is so quiet that she wonders if John has disappeared out into the night as well. But she finds him in the parlour, sprawled in a chair before the empty fireplace.

He does not stir when she enters the room. She moves to stand in front of him so that she can see his face, thinking he might already be asleep – but his eyes are open wide as saucers and he is staring like a madman into the cold, clean iron of the hearth. He clutches his arms around himself as if he were freezing, though the night air is as warm and sticky as ever.

'I heard your friends leave,' Cecilia says. 'Did you have a disagreement?'

John's eyelid twitches and he looks at her. If he is surprised to see her at so late an hour – if he even realizes what the time is – then he gives no indication.

'Did we wake you?' he asks, almost kindly, but then he sneers, 'Friends, ha – they're no friends of mine.'

'Yet you invite them back, night after night. And tonight Mr Emmerich played with you, didn't he?'

The effect of his name is instantaneous. John winces, then grinds his teeth. 'Emmerich, that bilge rat. I never thought he'd have the gall to show his face.'

'Didn't you invite him?'

'Aye, but I didn't expect he'd come. I only hoped … I hoped that he would.'

He sits forward with a sudden agitation and looks her up and down. 'Cecilia. Do you know what else I hoped?'

'No … Tell me, John.'

He shifts his arm from where he has been holding it pressed against his ribs, curled around his body like a bat's wing; his hand slips from inside his jacket, drawing with it a small silver pistol. It is a compact, neat thing, so small in his hand it almost looks like a toy. A weapon designed to be concealed: an assassin's tool. He holds it out to her balanced on his palm, as if he were presenting a gift.

'How d'you like this?' John cackles mirthlessly. 'It's been here all along, hidden upon my person all night. Right where I can reach it. All the while as we played cards, I could not help but press my hand against it time and again – just to feel its weight against my heart.'

He looks away suddenly, startled by some imagined noise. His voice becomes flat and emotionless. 'I invited Emmerich tonight for just one purpose. I hoped to catch him cheating, or even just to have the chance to accuse him … or for any other reason, to be able to confront him. I wished to shoot him dead, right there at the table.' He nods and stares ahead blankly, as if he can see the murderous deed being performed right before his eyes. 'I wanted to kill him here tonight, under my own roof, in front of all those men. Tell me, wife, how do you like that?'

For a moment she cannot speak. When she does, she is surprised at how clear and firm her voice is. 'I do not like it at all,' she says. 'What has possessed you, John, to think such evil thoughts?'

'She likes it not at all,' he mimics. 'As well you shouldn't. Neither do I. And yet it is all I can think of, day and night. I think only of Emmerich, and how I might end him for what he has done to me. I pray for the opportunity to take his life.'

'What possible good could come from his death? You would be hanged and I would be made a widow. And for what?'

'I might know peace. I might be allowed back to sea.'

'It is not Mr Emmerich's words that keep you from sailing,' she tells him. 'It is your own disgraceful habits. You still have friends who respected you, who would speak for you, if only you were ever sober and willing to receive their aid. I do not see Mr Emmerich's hand pouring that liquor down your throat night after night, nor propping the cards in your trembling fingers for you to deepen your debts. You tell anyone who listens that he slanders your name, but Mr Emmerich has no *need* to ruin you – not when you are doing such a fine job by yourself.'

'You do not understand,' he moans pitifully. 'How could you? It is not only what he says now. It is the whole damned thing … All that happened began with him. It was his idea; he set the course, he swayed the crew. It was his fault, yet I must carry the blame. He wore me down to this. He made me what you see. With every word that you disparage me, Cecilia, you are cursing his foul name, too.'

'How so, John? How? What is it that happened on your long voyage?'

He stares away, mumbling – that it was Emmerich's idea. Emmerich's word. Emmerich's promises.

'John, you must tell me – what was locked inside the ship's hold?'

The question makes him start. Then he laughs. It is a thin, papery sound, like a dusty echo from a tomb. Like a murderer's final wheeze as the noose is tightened around his neck.

'I suppose … Why not?' he says, resigned. 'So be it. If you must know the awful truth, Cecilia … you shall have it.'

34.

'I had promised myself you must never find out,' John says. 'I swore an oath that it must be kept from you, Cissy. Although … for the life of me I cannot remember why. I suppose that I worried what you would think … that it would lower your opinion of me – but I don't suppose that's even possible now, is it?' He sighs. 'I hardly know where to begin.'

'Why don't you begin by telling me what Mr Emmerich's idea was?' Cecilia prompts him, as calmly as she is able. She has sat upon the settee before the fireplace, and watches him side-on as he begins to talk, still staring blankly into the empty hearth.

'You already know the start of our troubles. We were sailing aimlessly from port to port in search of any opportunity to turn a profit. All along the American coastline, from Brazil up to the King's colonies and to every wretched island of the Caribbean, all with no success. Every deal failed, every lead a loose end. But we could not come back empty-handed – I would not allow it. My first expedition as a captain could not return in failure. I was thinking of you, Cecilia.' He glances at her, pained. 'I was thinking of my family … I would not have you know me as a failure.

'Somewhere off the coast of Hispaniola we crossed ways with another ship. A Barbary trading vessel, Moroccans – and Spaniards and Dutch too – who had ventured far from home. But, hell, who hasn't in those tropical waters? They had carried skins and hides all the way from Africa: lions, zebras, and giraffes, fanciful beasts ... The luckless devils had run afoul of pirates, and when we found them they were in a poor state. They had fought off the invaders and kept hold of the valuable cargo, but most of the crew were grievously wounded and the vessel had taken significant damage in the fighting. They were barely keeping afloat and had lost their bearings ... They were in dire need of aid.'

John rasps his yellowed tongue across his lips. 'The expectation was clear. They were a vessel in distress, and we were in a position to help them, even with all of our own misfortune. And yet ... What do rules and traditions really count for out on the open ocean? It was a boon for us, it seemed. The stroke of luck we had been praying for. All of that cargo, just waiting to be claimed. The Moroccans were half-dead in the water, already ... Hell, those heathens had probably sailed across the ocean to play corsair themselves. Why not take their goods? Who would know?'

'So it was you who became a pirate? You robbed the men who needed your aid?' Cecilia asks coldly. 'And this was Mr Emmerich's fault, I suppose?'

He nods. 'Emmerich, aye. This was the start of it. But ... I was for it too, we all were. Take the skins and strike for home, and have done with the entire cursed affair. But what of the witnesses? What to do with the Berber crew ... That was Mr Emmerich's plan. He knew a port, he said. A port not much frequented, on the western coast of Africa; one that is not marked on many maps, you see? A place where anything can be traded, and everything carries a price. Even bodies: good muscle and sinew. Even souls.

Whatever the colour, whatever the creed. A place where men might vanish and never be heard from again.'

'You mean slaves,' Cecilia says. The word rolls like lead on her tongue – like a poisoned bullet. 'Don't you? You are talking about selling those men as slaves. And you went along with it?'

'To save our voyage … The sailors keep their lives, and we turn a profit to boot … Return in glory. It was the best way. There was no need to shed blood. It was to save us.'

'But, John –' she cries, appalled.

He has been quite calm, but now his temper flares. 'Spare me! It was a transaction, Cecilia, nothing more. The crew were for it by a majority, they were so desperate to get home. What choice did I have?'

'But you were the captain, weren't you? You abhor such wickedness. Or you did, once. Remember we put our names to that Quaker petition, together? Our married names …' She looks away, her eyes misting with tears. 'I remember. It was one of the first occasions I had cause to write my new name in ink. And now … You sold your principles so easily, just to save face on one expedition?'

'You little fool, you don't understand what it's like on a ship at all,' John seethes. 'A captain acts for the good of the voyage, and for the sake of his men. The crew must be with you at every step. There is no other way. Emmerich convinced them. He said it would be easy, no one would know. What else could I do? Better than be murderers.'

'No. It may as well be the same thing.'

'Anyway,' he throws up his hand, 'you can save your high and mighty preaching, wife. As you well know, I did not profit a penny for my evil deeds.'

'Yes – your ship returned empty. So what happened next?'

'My God … Can't you guess?' he growls, and he scratches at the rough stubble across his chin like a dog with fleas, and then he falls silent for a very long time.

'You know that we were becalmed. It should have been our final crossing – to Emmerich's port in Africa, and thence homeward. We had taken the hides and locked them and the Berbers below deck, then set their vessel ablaze, left it behind to burn and sink. No trace. But everything carries a price. We were thrown off course by a gale and left stranded, bobbing like flotsam, burning under the sun and … starving. Starving to death. So many weeks we were out there. The stores that we had should have been just enough for the crew to make the crossing, and … and the cargo, too. When we were first stranded, I cut the men to three-quarter rations. Then half, two-fifths, one-fifth … But it wasn't enough. Within weeks we were reduced to crumbs and a sip of fresh water each day. From time to time a raincloud would drift overhead and we would chafe our lips bloody, sucking the moisture straight off the canvas sails.

'I couldn't feed my men, my own crew … Those wretches … those pitiful wretches in the hold, packed into the darkness … There was nothing to share. I had no choice but to keep them locked away while I tried to maintain what order I could above deck. Locked away with nothing at all, in the heat and in the darkness.'

Outside the moon drifts from behind a cloud and the room lights with an eerie, yellowish glow. Cecilia feels as though she is within a dream – *Please, let this be a dream*. 'John, stop – I would hear no more,' she manages to say.

He ignores her. 'We were starving,' he says again. 'And they were starving. Christians and Muslims, and all of us equally damned on that ship. I held the key to the hold, and the one copy was entrusted to my mate. At first I heard whispers. There was food on board, for any bold enough to take it. I turned a deaf ear. I ignored what I heard –' He raises his knuckle to his lips and falls silent for a moment.

'There was an altercation. I was called to the hold. Jesus, the smell … One of the Berbers had seized a man's cutlass

– he looked like a child holding it in his thin and quivering arms. They were at a stand-off. I asked what my men were doing in there; they said they were removing the bodies. The … remains of our captives who had fallen to starvation already. The Berbers, they said they would not allow their fellows to be eaten. They said it had already happened – bodies had been taken away … I don't know, I don't speak French and could only listen to my man translate while all the others were shouting … And the heat, the noise, the stench, I couldn't think … I heard the crew saying, why not? They are already dead, why must we starve too? Or … I think I did. My men, those good lads I had led from their homes, led them to this … I had to do something. I was their captain. I had to decide.'

Cecilia holds her fingertips to her temples. 'What did you do, John?'

'I made the decision for them. I drew my pistol and shot down the man with the cutlass. And then I gave the command. I ordered my men to draw their steel and execute them all. We cut them all down right there in the hold, amongst shrieks and the ring of metal and the chop of flesh, and … blood, blood everywhere, covering the walls, soaking into the cracks and the grain of the wood … When they were all dead, God, what a mess it was.'

John sucks in a quavering breath through tightly pursed lips. 'We dropped the bodies into the sea. Gone. I knew … I only knew that I had to get the meat off the ship, as quickly as possible. The hides, too. Those wonderful hides the Berbers had brought with them – they were ruined. Chewed through by the rats and I suppose by our captives too, for whatever small sustenance they were worth … Whatever hadn't been gnawed at was ruined by some manner of orange rot. I suppose … I suppose that we hadn't stored them with proper care. We cast it all into the cold Atlantic. What a strange and sorry resting place.

Within the week a wind had lifted, and we set a course for home.'

There is a thud as the small silver pistol falls from John's limp fingers onto the floor. He raises his shaking fingers to his face and buries his head in his hands. Outside the birds have begun to chirp and warble with the first rays of the rising dawn.

He turns his head and stares at his wife, wild eyes peering through his dirty fingers. 'Didn't I make the right decision, Cecilia?' he asks. 'Didn't I save my men, save their souls?'

35.

Cecilia is brought to her senses by the pallid glow of morning beginning to wash across her parlour. Dawn is breaking; she has sat through the night listening to John's wretched tale. He sits opposite her, his face still in his hands. She has no idea how long it has been since either of them spoke.

The only sound is the merry chirping of birdsong. At last she breaks their solemn silence. 'You murdered them all, John. How could you … How could you have done any of it?'

He lets his hands drop and stares at her for a moment, and then picks up his story as if he had never left off. 'Yes, we turned for home. Set a course back to Portugal. There were a scant few strips of the animal skins remaining, and … other things, belts and boots and sundries that were left behind. We traded them for food and water at the Canary Islands, enough to see us home at last. Returned with nothing. I had the men scrub the hold clean, again and again. It seemed to me that the blood remained plain to see, no matter how many times they washed it, but … the innards of a ship are dark, and cargo men have seen worse. All the crew agreed never to speak the truth of it – never to confess to what had taken place. I suppose that their captain has broken his vow now. Although,' he smiles morbidly, 'from the black looks they throw me around the harbourside, I am surely not the first.'

'You are a coward, John, to hide from your crimes.'

'Maybe I am at that. But it seemed the only course at the time. And look how I pay for it now.'

His expression has been drawn and miserable all through his tale but now twists back into his more familiar mask of spiteful self-pity. 'Before we had even made it back to land, Master Emmerich had started to blame me. I believe he wanted to turn the men against me while the horror was still fresh. He said that there was no call for them all to die – that we could still have delivered the goods, turned a profit. He said I couldn't hold my nerve. As if … As if he could not see as plainly as I how the crew were crying out for their own taste of meat. As if he could not hear their empty stomachs rumbling, just as I could. I did what I had to do. Had I not stamped the thought from their minds that instant …'

He turns his eyes to her imploringly. 'You tell me, Cecilia. I know that I must answer for my sins in the next life. I dread what surely awaits me. But how am I to be blamed for what happened? I cannot prevent a calm ocean – I cannot fill the sails with wind. How can I be blamed for directing us to a port that only Master Emmerich knew about? I did the only thing I could do. And … and didn't I bring my crew back, all of them, back from the mouth of hell itself? Didn't I make the right decision? Well?'

'I do not know,' she replies. 'What do you want to hear from me, John? Do you want me to forgive you? To absolve you of all of your crimes? You need a priest for that, not a wife. Perhaps you are right, and I simply cannot comprehend what it is like to be a man sailing with other men, far from home. But I can never imagine making the same decisions that you made. Do not claim that Mr Emmerich forced your hand when you alone were captain of the voyage. I cannot forgive you. I will not.'

John's raw eyes blink once, and he nods. He stands from the armchair on unsteady legs and begins to pace around the room. 'Aye. Aye, you've the right of it. Yes, you say it fair, wife. I've no right to ask for forgiveness. There's none who can give it to me. I'm too far gone for that.'

'I did not say that. I said that *I* cannot forgive you. But no one is beyond forgiveness. A life can always be turned around, made worthwhile again. Perhaps if you –'

'No,' John snaps. 'It's just like you say, Cissy. A man cannot undo the things that he has done. These things do not rub off. I am stained on the inside now, just like the ship. Just like the ship.' He paces this way and that, his voice dropping to a low and inaudible mutter – words that do not make sense, giving voice to thoughts that are lost beyond reason.

Though it is morning outside, Cecilia is dog-tired. Her sleepless night is coming back to make its demands of her now, and her forehead is beginning to ache. She would retreat to her bed to sleep and leave John to his frantic pacing, if only she were not afraid of the dreams that must surely come after all she has heard.

Before she can stir, a noise from the corner of the room makes them both jump. 'How now!' John cries. He had paused beside the fireplace, and he bends and snatches the pistol from where it had fallen. 'Who goes there? Show yourself, damn it!' he commands, his voice quivering like a leaf.

A small form emerges from the shadows at the far end of the room – it is only the grey cat, appearing from wherever it has been hiding. It takes a few steps across the floor, oblivious to the pistol that John now holds trained upon it.

'Hell's teeth,' John says. 'That skulking beast again. Everywhere I go, it's watching me.'

'It is only a cat,' Cecilia replies flatly. 'It does no harm.'

'No harm, indeed. See how it glowers at me now.'

She rubs her tired eyes. That her husband's outrage and fury can flit so capriciously from the appalling story he has just told to the innocent attentions of a cat seems entirely absurd. She could laugh if she weren't so exhausted. 'Listen to yourself, John,' she sighs.

But John's pain and rage are crystallizing inside him. His wrath is hardening into something sharp and cruel and dangerous. He extends his arm, taking aim at the creature with his small pocket-pistol. The cat stands where it is, uncaring.

He only means to scare me; he is posturing, nothing more, Cecilia thinks. But she says nervously, 'Please, John, it is only a little cat – what can it do to you?'

The cat takes a step forward. A pink tongue flicks out and tastes the sour air. John maintains his aim as it takes a few more steps across the room. Then, at last, he curses and lowers his weapon.

'Christ, you look like a scared bairn,' he says, glancing at Cecilia with disdain. 'Calm down, woman. I wouldn't waste the bullet on the thing.'

The cat brushes close to where she sits, curling its tail up around her calves with an affectionate, lingering swish. She bends to stroke its head, and it pauses a moment to accept the affection then moves on, past the settee and John's armchair and to the window. With a neat hop it alights upon the windowsill and looks out to where the birds are singing tunelessly in the trees.

After a moment John says, 'Look, it wants to go outside.'

He takes a step towards the window, and then another. His gait is slow and unsteady. The cat does not stir, just continues to gaze out the window, even when John is right behind it. With both hands he grips the sash window's hooks and lifts it open with a creak.

A skewer of foreboding stabs through Cecilia's body. 'What are you doing?' she asks, her nerves jangling.

'Just letting the cat outside,' John replies. 'Tsk, get on. Go out, you cur. Go and chase those chattering birds.' He removes one hand from the window's base and tries to shoo the cat outside without touching it.

The cat turns its head languidly and looks at John, and then at Cecilia. Its ear flicks slightly, and then it stands and places one paw onto the dewy ledge outside the window.

'That's right – be off with you,' John says gently.

Cecilia raises her hand. 'John, please –'

The cat puts its other paw forward, so that it is standing half-in and half-out of the opened window. With a scrape the sash comes down, slamming onto its back with a sickening crunch; its back snaps in an instant, before it can even make a sound. She can feel it – its life being cut in two, its death instantaneous. Cecilia screams and looks away, covering her eyes. But an instant later she is on her feet, standing before her husband, battering at his chest with her clenched fists, pounding as hard as she can against the rattling hollow of his ribcage.

'*What did you do? What did you do?*' she gasps through her tears. John catches her wrists easily in his hands and holds her arms, not hurting her but preventing her assault from continuing. He stares down at her without emotion.

'Why would you do it? You killed it – it was only an innocent cat!' she sobs.

His gaze is empty, his eyes devoid of compassion or mercy. 'I did not like how it looked at me,' he tells her, then pushes her away, letting go of her wrists. He shrugs and says, 'It dropped outside,' then he stamps heavily from the room.

Quivering, she turns to face the window, somehow expecting to see it pasted with ruby blood and matted grey fur – but there is nothing there, only a closed window, now with a splintered crack running down the centre of the glass like a forked bolt of lightning. A fracture to mark the lethal force with which John had slammed it down.

With her vision swimming with tears, Cecilia steps closer and peers through the glass. For a moment she dares to hope that she might see a sea-green eye staring back at her, the cat still alive, somehow unharmed at the cost of one of its nine lives. But she can make out nothing at all.

Still dressed in only her night shift, she leaves the house by the front door, stepping outside into the rising dawn, the warm air buzzing with the low thrum of insects and the twittering of birds and the rustle of leaves as tiny creatures wake and stir all around. She rounds the house at a run until she stands below the parlour window, where she tramples through the flowerbeds, pushing aside their leaves and snagging her skin on their thorns until she finds it. It looks as if it were only sleeping in the half-light, nestled among the bushes. Sleek fur as grey as a storm cloud, both eyes now fully closed, and a look of peaceful serenity on its face as it lies beneath the window, quite, quite still.

36.

Cecilia watches the old man as he slowly bends, drives his spade into the ground with a dry rasp and lifts out a chunk of soil, then turns and drops it into a pile to one side. He repeats the process methodically, over and over, until there is a hole deep enough. The old man's movements are painfully slow and stiff, and she tries not to grow impatient as she watches. The sun is burning upon her back; she can see the sweat glisten and trickle down the man's neck. His knees click mechanically each time he straightens his posture to empty out another spadeful of soil. The pile of dirt grows higher and higher. In just a few minutes' time it shall go back into the ground, and the hole will become a grave.

A cooling wind wraps itself around her. The sky remains as startlingly blue and bright as it ever does – incongruous weather for a funeral. There is no one present aside from herself and the old man. Cecilia knows it is faintly ridiculous that she has come out to the garden to watch, herself. At least Rosalie's elderly relative was willing to dig a hole for the poor creature. A stray cat should be grateful for even this modicum of dignity.

When the hole is sufficiently deep, the old man uses the tip of his shovel to unceremoniously tip the bundle of remains, wrapped in one of Cecilia's old shawls, into its final resting place. Then he stoops and begins the process again in reverse. Each spadeful lands with a soft thud. A click from his knees and then a thud; a click, then a thud.

Cecilia sighs and wipes the tears from her eyes. She turns away, not bothering to watch the grave be filled. They are stupid tears, she knows. It is stupid to cry for a dead cat with no name. Through her wet eyes she looks at the ocean, visible from her garden above the rooftops of the town. *How is it that you can shed tears for a cat*, she asks herself, *when you have not cried at all for those that died by your husband's hand?* Those nameless souls are not even afforded the dubious honour of a hole in the dry soil of a garden to serve as their memorial – just the unfathomable icy depths of the Atlantic Ocean. When she thinks of them – what John did to them – her heart aches and her mind reels. Yet she cannot summon a single tear.

Then she thinks, *It is foolish to even compare the two. Even an ugly, half-feral cat deserves a few tears, doesn't it?*

The old man shuffles back into the house without a word, but Cecilia lingers outside for a while longer. Too late, a bank of cloud hides the sun and a light rain begins to patter upon the grass. The scene at last becomes as sombre as she feels. She does not want to go back indoors. John might be in there, and she does not think she can look at him. She stares at the ocean and thinks, *It would have been better if he had drowned, after all.*

Cecilia takes a seat at her desk to write a letter home. The time has come, she knows. She must get away now, before things become any worse. She will ask Rosalie or Doctor Mayberry to arrange for the letter to be shipped to England. She wonders how long that will take – double it, at least, before the reply arrives. She tries to imagine what her father might do once he has read it – send men, perhaps, to bring her home? Would he sail here himself? It is difficult to imagine him stepping off a boat into her world. She wonders if John would put up a fight and try to keep her.

Even now she struggles to know what to say. *John gave away a piece of my hair to conjure a water child within me, but then it burned away to nothing. John intended to sell men as slaves, but he did not succeed. He pirated and murdered at sea, but there is no proof of it except his word. He killed a cat that had become a part of my home, here in this foreign place* … The last eighteen months have been too strange to explain.

She writes that her husband is a drunkard and an inveterate gambler, that he has lost his captaincy, and rumours abound that on his last voyage he turned to piracy and slaving. She states that he has set his course firmly towards self-destruction, and that she fears for her safety. She leaves out all of the worst details. What she can bear to write down in ink should be enough to move her father's heart, she thinks.

When she has filled a page, she sets her pen down and goes to the window. The blue tide rolls away endlessly. She watches a ship as it sails out of the bay, its masthead aiming squarely in the direction of the sun. *How much to book passage?* She still has some things she could sell: things that she doesn't need any more. She has never had much in the way of finery or jewels, but what she does own she hid away when the extent of John's vice became clear. *How much will it cost for just one passenger – and where exactly would we be heading?*

Her thoughts are suddenly and violently interrupted by a sharp crack like a circus master's whip which explodes through the house. Cecilia stands up automatically, her hands gripping the edges of the desk; she cocks her head to listen, her every nerve on edge, but the house remains silent save for the lingering reverberations that tremble through the walls and through the floor. Rosalie must be out, for she does not hear her running to investigate. Rosalie is often absent, these days, and Cecilia suspects that she has found a second job somewhere else – one that pays her on time, no doubt. There is no cat to run skittering across the floor in fright. There is only herself.

She ventures downstairs. No sooner has she placed her foot to the ground floor than a second report blasts out, loud and clear, coming from the parlour, accompanied by a shattering explosion. She opens the door. John is inside with a pistol in his hand – not the palm-sized instrument he had concealed murderously in his jacket previously, but a true soldier's sidearm. A plume of smoke rises curling from its barrel. John stands side-on with his arm aimed towards the mantelpiece, where a row of china plates have been balanced standing upright; three remain intact and two are now nothing but a shower of white fragments and dust, blown to pieces by a force that has also left a pair of blackened dents smeared across the wall of their home.

'What – in *heaven's name* – are you doing?' Cecilia manages to exclaim.

John cocks his eyebrow and throws her a haughty glance. 'Practising my aim,' he says.

She grips her head in her hands. 'Why on earth – here, in our own home … Look at the wall! What are you *thinking*?'

'They would not let me shoot at bottles in the tavern,' John tells her, and laughs. His manner is swaggering and infuriating, shed of any trace of the mournful self-pity he had been wallowing in. She assumes that he is drunk.

'Our neighbours – everyone will hear.'

'Hang the neighbours. Hang them all.'

In a daze of confusion Cecilia walks directly into his line of fire. She lifts a fragment of a shattered china plate from where it lies on the mantel. The acrid scent of gun smoke chokes in her nose and throat, and all around her feet the floor is peppered with white specks of exploded crockery.

'I am sorry about your plates, dear wife. But they were a cheap imitation and had no value. I should know – I tried to sell 'em.'

'I don't understand,' Cecilia says helplessly, despairing. 'Where did you get that pistol?'

'A rare weapon, is it not? I purchased a brace of them, look –' He points with the gun barrel towards an opened case lying in an armchair, with a second pistol inside – a deadly twin to the one in his hand. 'Don't screw your face up at me, Cecilia. It is true I spent the last of our cash on them. But it does not matter, not any more.'

She feels a sickly lump rise to her throat. 'What do you mean? What does not matter? Why did you buy those pistols?'

He is trying his best to cover his emotion with a show of bravado and suave confidence, but his face convulses for a moment with pure wrath. 'Emmerich,' he says. 'I am ending it. All that has plagued me. I shall put a stop to it. To him. One way or the other it shall end.'

'You still plot to murder him … No.' She frowns, trying to read his thoughts through his ugly expression. 'You will confront him. A duel? John, you cannot be serious.'

'As serious as I ever was, Cecilia. I must have a resolution. He must answer for all he has done. I heard … Can you believe that he is to take sail again, while I am still stuck here, helpless and stranded in port? I cannot permit him to leave. His ship cannot sail before I have defended myself.'

'Defended yourself!' she exclaims. 'This is absurd. You are absurd. Has he even accepted?'

John nods smartly. 'Of course. He could hardly refuse. Mr Fitzgibbon will be my second. He alone stands by me.'

'And what will you do if you succeed in killing him, John? Will another death ease your conscience by even one inch? Just listen to yourself!' she cries out in despair and frustration. 'Murdering Mr Emmerich will not restore your reputation. It will not make you a better man. And if you lose –'

She pauses for a moment, and John's face colours, deep red like a demon's. 'Ha! Look how your mind works!' he jeers. 'Look at that flash of enthusiasm in your eyes! My sweet and good wife. That's right; should I lose – should I be the one shot dead – then you will be freed, won't you? Free to take up with whomever you please. I'll be cold in the ground, and you'll be hot in the bed of some new fool. So, do you still mean to talk me out of it, Cecilia, or are you reconsidering?'

She hugs her arms around herself and walks to the window. 'You don't know a thing of what I think,' she says. 'I never meant to talk you out of it. You and Mr Emmerich deserve each other – each as foul-hearted as the other.'

John grunts and points his pistol towards the plates. He has been stuffing it with powder and shot while he speaks, and now Cecilia watches as he squints and takes aim. She braces herself for the deafening report, but it does not come. He does not pull the trigger. She sees the oily beads of sweat forming on his forehead, how he bites down on his quivering lip, and how his eyes waver and struggle to focus while the pistol's barrel trembles in his unsteady grip.

'John – do you even wish me to talk you out of it?' she asks. 'Do you … do you even believe that you *can* defeat Mr Emmerich? Or, is that not your intention …'

'What sort of damn fool question is that?' he snarls. 'Of course I shall prevail.'

'Well … And then what?'

'Then I will be back at sea, where I should be.'

'And reconciled with all that you have done? Will you be able to respect yourself, care for yourself, after Mr

Emmerich's blood has been shed, too? What of your real victims – where is their justice, their resolution?'

He stares at her blankly. 'They are at peace now,' he says, grimly. 'How can I help or hurt them any more than I have? But I … I still have work to do. The sea is still calling to me. It gives me no rest.'

'So you will just sail forever, trying to outrun your misdeeds? You will sail until you reach the edge of the map, and then right off it? The world is round, now, John. If you keep sailing, keep running for long enough, then you shall only end up back where you started.'

'Would that I could,' he mutters. He lowers his pistol and stares at it thoughtfully. 'Maybe I *shall* sail off the edge of the map,' he says. 'I'll go until I find the very edge of the world. And then I'll drop right over it. Into the abyss, where I surely belong. Down and down until I hit the bottom of everything, where they'll all be waiting for me.'

37.

Cecilia returns to the waterfront. It is early in the evening and the streets are already crowded and rowdy with labourers at the end of their working day. Men lie sprawled out in the street, drunk or well upon their way, throwing dice and laying bets. Unscrupulous barkers and prostitutes walk among them trying to flog their wares to anyone who will lend an ear. A perfumed lady dressed in red winks at Cecilia and says something she suspects she should be grateful she cannot translate.

Cecilia hurries past, attempting to keep her head down while simultaneously maintaining a watchful eye on her surroundings. This is a part of town she does not know. She slips a card from her sleeve and consults what is written there, then tries to make sense of the street names and numbers on the buildings around her to find her way.

'In need of directions, lovely?' a woman asks. 'Meeting a gentleman? Perhaps you want some company?'

At last she locates the street and then the address that she is looking for. An elderly woman with crinkled skin like leather answers, and Cecilia asks for the English doctor. Doctor Mayberry appears before her an instant later, wearing his sombre black coat and an equally serious expression.

'Thank you for helping me, doctor,' she says.

'I am only glad that I could. Come, we are already running late.'

'Was he very difficult to locate?'

'Not particularly.' He leads them through the busy, narrow lanes. 'Watch your step around here,' the doctor warns. The air reeks of spilled beer and human waste.

'Is this where you live, doctor, or work?'

'Both, I am afraid. I might have chosen a fairer location for my practice had I visited the port in advance – although, it is here that I can do the most good. And in truth I doubt I could afford rooms anywhere grander.'

They twist and turn through the streets until their environment changes. The buildings become grand and ostentatious – this is where the money flows when it washes in with the tide. Doctor Mayberry directs them to a door and knocks. A well-dressed, well-mannered young man answers, confers with the doctor for a moment, takes his card and then permits them inside. There is a small reception area where Cecilia and the doctor wait while the doorman makes his way upstairs.

Twenty minutes go by. The doctor hums and taps his foot. 'I expect that he is a busy man,' he says.

At last the young doorman returns and indicates that they should follow him upstairs, but the doctor hangs back. 'My small part is done, I believe,' he says. 'I shall be waiting here; call if you need me.'

Cecilia follows the young man upstairs and through a fashionable suite of rooms. In the final room, seated behind a prestigious and ornate oak desk, she is met by a solidly built, if slightly portly, middle-aged man with wispy blonde hair who seems to sit swathed in an atmosphere of importance. He is older than she had expected, almost fatherly. Cecilia had anticipated that she might recognize him from her husband's card table, even though she did not get a good look at that time – but the man's face is unfamiliar to her. He looks up at her from his work and frowns.

'Mr Emmerich,' she says, extending her hand. When he reaches out to take it, his hold is surprisingly gentle.

'What is this? I thought I was to meet some doctor?' Mr Emmerich says, guardedly.

'I am sorry for the subterfuge. I did not know if you would agree to see me, and I feared word getting back to my husband. He does not know I have come. This seemed the best way. Mr Emmerich, I am Mrs Cecilia Lamb.'

His eyes widen but his expression remains inscrutable as he processes this information. It does not take him long; a moment later he nods and indicates for her to sit down.

'Very irregular,' he says. 'I imagine that you are correct: I should not have agreed to meet with you had I known. But you are here now.'

She takes a seat on the edge of a comfortable leather chair. It must be strange for him, she supposes, to converse with the woman whom he would make a widow. Mr Emmerich raises his eyebrow expectantly, waiting for her to speak her purpose.

She had not known, until this moment, what she was going to say first – but something in the man's brusque, efficient demeanour seems to cut through any need for sensitivity or caution.

'John told me what happened on your voyage,' she begins bluntly. 'Is it true?'

He stares at her, unmoved. 'Dear lady, how am I to answer that without knowing what your husband has said?' His accent sounds English, even if his name and clothes and mannerisms all suggest otherwise.

Cecilia glances at the young servant, who is now handing Mr Emmerich a slice of cake on a plate. His dark eyes meet with hers. 'Then perhaps,' she says softly, 'I should repeat for you everything that my husband has told me, here and now?'

Emmerich's eyes close. 'No, that won't be necessary,' he says. 'Though the point remains, whatever slander you might have heard, you can hardly expect me to confess to it now, can you?'

She shrugs. 'I shall take that as your answer, then, and conclude that everything my husband said was true. Every detail.'

He looks at her coldly, unmoved.

Cecilia says, 'John says you unjustly blame him for all that went wrong. That you have ruined the good reputation he has spent the last decade, at least, working earnestly and tirelessly to construct. Why?'

'Everything I told our shared masters was the truth,' replies Mr Emmerich. 'It cannot be helped if they choose not to work with Mr Lamb again. And Mrs Lamb, recall that I could level the same accusations against your husband. He has spread the foulest lies about me in every disreputable tavern along the waterfront, to any sot who will listen.'

She cannot doubt that this is true. 'I am not here to make excuses for my husband. He has brought about his own ruin, I know this. My question to you is, why add to it? Why blame him in your reports? Surely your voyage … Even with everything that happened, I can see no need to identify a scapegoat. You all shared in the crime. Every man on board is to blame for what was done.'

Now he does react, slightly; he shifts in his chair and cocks an eyebrow at her, though if he is uncomfortable or ashamed, it is not apparent. 'Mrs Lamb, you are young, and I hope you take this advice to heart: there is *always* a need for a scapegoat. And if you don't know who it is, then you may rest assured that others are pointing the finger at you. The fact is that Mr Lamb was the captain. His rash action squandered valuable cargo, and the expedition turned a loss as a result. Of course he must be the one to blame.'

Cecilia can feel her temper rising, her impatience and ire gathering around her like an electrical charge at this man's careful, arrogant logic. But she forces herself to remain calm. 'You know that my husband is unwell. He is not himself. Do not accept this duel, Mr Emmerich.'

'I have already accepted his challenge. I cannot back out now.'

'Why not? Call him mad; call him ill. Call him a drunkard who has fallen too low for you to fight. No one would judge you harshly for showing pity to a lunatic.'

He sighs and rubs his eyes. This is what he expects her to say, she knows. He expects her to sob and drop to her knees, shaking and begging for her husband's life. *He cannot understand that there is nobody now who despises John more than I.* And yet still she tries to save him.

'Mr Lamb may be intemperate. He may be ill, even. But I do not believe him an imbecile,' Emmerich tells her gravely. 'His campaign of vitriol against me has been anything but lunatic. It has been single-minded and ruthless to the point of obsession. Try to see it from my perspective, Mrs Lamb. Your husband has ensured that every man in this port knows of our quarrel – how can I refuse his challenge or back down now? How would that make me look?'

'So you would shoot down a miserable drunkard just to prove that you are no coward? Would it not be braver still to rise above his jeers, to turn the other cheek?'

Mr Emmerich looks away. It appears that he does not think so.

'John may be wretched beyond hope of redemption. God knows that I, his own wife, have no love for him any more. But he does not deserve to die by your hand, Mr Emmerich. Murdered by his own tormentor. For whatever memory of affection remains within me, I would not see him come to that. Call it off.'

She stares at him fiercely – he continues to look away, apparently unconcerned, but she can see the pinkish blush spread across his cheeks. A minute goes by and neither says a word. Finally Emmerich coughs and looks her in the eye again.

'I will aim to miss if he does first. That is the best I can offer. Mr Lamb must shoot first, and he must fire into the ground. I shall do the same. If you can convince him to do this, then we might have our satisfaction and both walk away with our lives. It is a recognized compromise. It is up to you to convince him, Mrs Lamb. And I warn you … If I think that he is aiming for me – if I think for a moment that he means to kill me – then I shall defend myself.'

'Thank you, Mr Emmerich. I suppose that is all I could expect. Perhaps I can persuade him … somehow.' Cecilia rises from her chair and goes to leave, but she turns back with a final question.

'Mr Emmerich,' she asks, 'have you ever fought in a duel before?'

He lifts his chin to look her steadily in the eye. 'Twice,' he says.

And here you are, she thinks, *still alive to tell the tale*.

38.

John is in no mood to hear Mr Emmerich's offer of a compromise. In the days and hours before his duel he moves restlessly about the house, muttering, staring about madly, sometimes halting his nervous pacing to peer at some corner of the room or through an open doorway as if he has spotted something there, something which only he can see. He does not resume his target practice against their remaining tableware, thank goodness, but he does take his pistols out of their case to examine them reverentially, over and over again.

Of course, Cecilia cannot tell him it is Mr Emmerich himself who has proposed that they both fire into the ground. She dare not admit that she has met with his rival at all – that would undoubtedly only enrage and provoke the most perverse of his present demons. She tries instead to suggest the idea in a way that he might think it was his own. 'I have heard of duels,' she mentions, 'where both men can be satisfied without violence. That if both shoot deliberately to miss – into the ground by their feet – then their honour remains intact and the terms of the duel are met, and everyone walks away with their lives.'

It does no good. 'Trying to get me killed, love?' he jeers. 'Loose my shot into the ground, indeed! You would have him shoot me down like a dog.'

It makes her wonder why she even wishes to preserve his life. After all that he has done, is there anything left worth saving? And – what is more – John was right when he said that if he dies, she will be free. It is difficult even for herself to understand the reason, but she does not want him to die. Not in this way.

But every door, it seems, is closed before her. She tries to appeal to John's sole remaining friend, Mr Fitzgibbon. She dares not tell him of her meeting with Mr Emmerich, either, but she implores him to talk reason into her husband – to convince him to abandon his challenge, or to resolve the dispute bloodlessly.

'If you cannot convince him, then how can I?' he asks her helplessly. 'John knows I am against it. I have said what I will. All a man can do now is stand by his side as a loyal friend.'

'He can hardly focus on what is in front of his face – and that is when he isn't flinching at shadows,' Cecilia pleads. 'He has appointed a time and a date for his own execution, and you well know it. A true friend would stop him.'

Mr Fitzgibbon tries to smile and reassure her. 'John always was an excellent shot. Even with a drink or two in him I never saw his aim falter. And he could hold his nerve under pressure like no other.'

'Be that as it may,' she tells him, 'but, Mr Fitzgibbon, you are speaking about my husband as if he were already dead.'

'You know, there is a good chance that neither man will perish at all. In my experience most such affairs end with no more than a wounding. I believe the outcome might not be as dire as you fear, Mrs Lamb.'

She throws her hands up. 'So I should shut my mouth and pray to God that my husband is merely maimed? And that by some miracle he is content, then, to call a halt to the entire affair; that he will finally know peace with Mr Emmerich's bullet lodged inside him? Truly, my mind reels.'

Cecilia paces around the room angrily. Her gaze falls upon a globe that stands in the corner. She places her fingertips upon its smooth, blue surface and makes the world turn with a gentle push. Landmasses spin beneath her eyes, divided and sectioned by colours and lines, and marked with invented names. The globe slows its spin and stops with Europe staring up at her: a small, knotted growth hanging on to the edge of the world.

'It is a miracle,' she says, 'that men ever managed to take sail in the first place, let alone conquer the globe, when you seem to believe that shooting at each other is the only way to settle a quarrel.'

Mr Fitzgibbon shoves his hands into his pockets. 'You should see how they get on in other parts,' he grumbles.

When Cecilia returns home from visiting Mr Fitzgibbon, Rosalie is waiting to speak with her. Her maid explains that she cannot work for her any more. She hardly has to give her reasons. There is no need to point to the shameful squalor that she has been working in – the den of vice that the household has become. No need to mention the harassment by John and his erstwhile gambling companions, nor the many missing weeks of wages which she is owed. And yet in spite of these many and legitimate grievances which Rosalie could list, she appears genuinely pained to tell her mistress that she must leave.

'Where will you go to?' Cecilia asks her.

'There is always work. For me it shall be easy,' Rosalie says. Then she looks Cecilia directly in the eye and says, 'Senhora Lamb, I do not want to go and leave you here – but I cannot stay. I wish that you would go away, also. You understand? You do not need to stay, either. But' – she sighs and looks away – 'if you think that you must, then please, be careful. The *capitão* … Senhor Lamb, he is not well. His mind is not healthy.'

Cecilia nods. What is there to say? 'I shall be careful. Thank you, Rosalie.'

'I will work until the end of the week. Then I must go.'

Cecilia blushes and says, 'I shall find what money I can, but … I cannot pay you all that is owed. You should know that. If you need to leave at this moment, then I would not blame you at all.'

But Rosalie shakes her head. 'To the end of the week,' she tells her, then she walks to the door and touches the handle. But she stops, and stands for a moment, then turns back to Cecilia with a strange expression.

'Perhaps one more week is all that will be necessary, no?' she says.

Cecilia nods. 'Perhaps. Yes, I think you may be right. Thank you, Rosalie.'

39.

The day of the duel arrives. There are days when the weather seems to understand what is required of it – when the sun and sky seem to recognize the ambience that is called for. So it is today. The sky is a sheer canopy of steel-grey cloud, and everything beneath it appears dull and subdued. The sun is up there shining somewhere, but it dares not show its face. Even the ocean in the bay is calm and level, untroubled by the lifeless breeze that stirs through the air.

Cecilia finds John asleep in his armchair, dishevelled and stinking like vinegar. When she wakes him, his eyes jolt open immediately. 'It is time?' he asks.

She crouches down at his elbow and places her finger-tips upon his forearm. 'John, listen to me,' she implores. She has tossed and turned all night, thinking of what she can say in a last-ditch attempt to turn things around. To prevent what she knows must happen from happening. 'If you have ever listened to your wife, it must be now. You know that the odds are stacked against you in this duel. The alcohol has ruined you. You know it is true. But I have heard … I have heard that Mr Emmerich will not shoot you if you do not shoot at him. If you miss your first shot

– fire it into the ground, by your feet – then he will do the same. It is his wish that the matter could be settled peaceably. Please, you must try. It is your best hope. Please, John.'

But his eyes widen and he shakes his head. 'No, no. Tell Emmerich that if he is to aim anywhere, he must aim here –' He leans forward and raps a long yellow fingernail twice against his forehead, directly between his red-rimmed eyes. 'Tell him to put his bullet right there. That way when I awake in the next life, wherever that may be … perhaps I shall not remember.'

She closes her eyes and prays that her words might yet penetrate his closed mind. 'Shoot into the ground, John. For my sake, shoot into the ground.'

John seems surprised when she tells him she will accompany him to the site of his confrontation. He tries half-heartedly to forbid her but acquiesces almost immediately. She has to be there. Whatever is to happen she must see it with her own eyes. In the days leading up to this moment she has tried to call upon any foresight that she can in order to envision what the future holds. She has strained her ears listening for voices from the shadowy corners of her house, focused her mind and tried to will the spiralling sensation of premonition into the deepest core of her insides. But that is not how these things work. Not for her, anyway. She has no idea what will happen next.

They set off walking together, husband and wife, side by side, following a road along the cliff edge with the gloomy bay spread out below them. Neither one of them glances even once at the ships that float slowly in and out of port, their sails hanging limp with only the faintest flutter of wind.

They walk in silence until their destination appears before them – a dusty copse of thin trees situated somewhere on the outskirts of the town. For some reason Cecilia had imagined that John's confrontation with Mr Emmerich must unfold somewhere along the waterfront – a space cleared on the busy wharf for just this purpose, or perhaps out upon the prehistoric black rocks on the edge of the bay with the waves crashing dramatically in the background. But of course their chosen site is nowhere so public.

It is then that Cecilia hears herself say, 'You know, John, there *was* a child.'

She does not know why she tells him. This might well be her last chance, and perhaps she simply needs him to know the damage and hurt his actions have caused. The long, lonesome, and frightening weeks and months she spent not knowing, not understanding what was happening to her own body. She must share the secret while she can – to make herself feel better, or to make him feel worse. Perhaps both.

'The child you wished for. It was real; I carried it for many weeks. Everyone told me it was impossible, that it could not be, with you so far away and for so long. But I know what I felt. I did not imagine it. I know that it was your child, no one else's. It can only have been yours.

'But … it was no natural child, John. It was nothing good that I carried inside me. It was a wicked thing, foul and corrupt – corrupting me from the inside. Corrupt, just like the bargain you struck to put it there. I was glad when it went away. I was so relieved, I did not mourn it for one second. I never wanted it; it was *your* wish, not mine. But you never even asked me. That child … that wicked child. You might have been its father, John. But I was never its mother.'

He listens silently. She does not know how she expects him to react. After she has finished, he says nothing, and they continue towards the trees in silence for some time more. When they are almost beneath the branches, he says faintly, 'It went away ... I can't even remember why I wanted it now. I'm sorry, Cissy. Just another rotten deal to mark against my name.'

They enter the quaint grove of trees and in the centre come to a small clearing with a ruined stone fountain, overgrown with creeping moss – they must be in some sort of long-abandoned garden or public park, Cecilia supposes. There are no waves, no calling seabirds to hear – just the faint whispering rustle of the leaves above their heads as they stir and shake in the breeze.

There are three men and three horses already waiting in the clearing. As soon as John and Cecilia arrive, Mr Fitzgibbon approaches them. He scarcely nods to John before turning to her, alarmed. 'Mrs Lamb, you have come too? This is hardly the time nor place –'

John cuts in. 'Don't bother – she may watch if she likes.'

The words have barely left his lips before another cry of objection rings from the far side of the grove. Mr Emmerich stands there with a man who must be his second. Both are staring at Cecilia with hostile incredulity.

John and Fitzgibbon walk slowly across the clearing to join their opponents. Cecilia remains where she is, her gloved hands folded in front of her, listening to the crunch of dry, dead leaves beneath the men's boots as they walk and the shy whinnies of the horses that stand nearby. The morning is so overcast and grim they could almost be back in England.

The four men form a square and begin to talk, their voices low, quick, and urgent. She cannot make out what they are saying but sees them looking and pointing towards her; evidently Emmerich objects to her presence. The older man lifts his head and stares directly at her, his distant eyes shining like keen white pinpoints. She meets his gaze steadily. She hears John shout, angry and impatient: 'She is my wife and will do as she pleases. What damned difference does it make?'

Finally Emmerich holds his hands out and appears to relent. But their conference is not over. The men point and indicate distances and spots around the clearing; they pace around testing the light and examining eyelines from different angles and perspectives – scoping out any possible unfair advantages and reaching a consensus on the most even ground over which they might shoot, she supposes.

Finally Mr Fitzgibbon and Emmerich's second stand back to back and measure out a distance of paces, then lay their handkerchiefs upon the ground where they each stand. The four men gather for one final discussion, and then John and Fitzgibbon make their way back towards her.

'You both remain determined to go through with this foolishness?' Cecilia asks as they draw close. She wants to laugh in their serious faces. The entire situation seems so absurd: the ridiculous ritual the men have just performed, their sombre drawing up and agreement of the terms and conditions for attempted murder.

'It shall soon be over and done,' Mr Fitzgibbon tells her. John is tight-lipped, his face as pale as a ghost's.

She watches across the clearing as Mr Emmerich's second opens a case and produces a pair of pistols. He breeches and loads one, and then the other. Mr Fitzgibbon does the same for John. As he does he recites the rules of the duel in a solemn monotone: the two men will face each other at their appointed marks, a pistol in each hand; at the signal they will advance and fire as they see fit; whoever fires first must wait for their opponent's return before using their second shot; victory shall be declared upon the instant of the first successful hit.

Mr Fitzgibbon hands the loaded pistols to John. 'You must check them,' he reminds him gently. John nods and obediently turns the guns around in his hands, staring at them without recognition or understanding, as if they were artefacts which had just fallen down from the moon. He keeps glancing over at the small figure of Emmerich, who is checking his own weapons. John looks at him again and again, as if he is afraid that the other man might vanish altogether if he takes his eyes off him for too long, like a mirage. In the pale daylight her husband looks sober and afraid.

'John,' Cecilia says, but no one seems to hear her. The time has come.

As if summoned by a signal only they can hear, all four men turn and march mechanically towards the centre of the clearing, their backs straight and rigid like tin soldiers. John and Emmerich take their marks on the handkerchiefs, while their seconds stand to the sides, well clear. Emmerich's man holds his arm high, gripping in his fingertips a third, crimson handkerchief, which stands out boldly against the colourless surroundings.

For a few long seconds nothing moves. The world is frozen. Emmerich stands side-on, one pistol dangling by his hip, his other arm folded behind himself. John faces his opponent squarely, shoulders hunched like a tavern brawler. A bird warbles in the trees; another takes flight on fluttering wings. In the quilt of cloud high above their heads a split forms, tearing open gradually until a window of bright blue sky can be seen. Through the gap a sparkling shaft of sunlight sweeps over the treetops like a blade of divine judgement; it swings above their heads once, and then it is gone. Across the clearing from where she stands, huddled among the roots of the trees, Cecilia spies a cat. Its green eyes meet with hers, and then it looks up, and she does too. She sees that all around where the cat is sitting there are people standing among the trees. Dozens of them, the slender shapes of men, pale and indistinct like shadows. They do not move – their feet remain planted in the dry ground, as if they were trees themselves – but they resolve into view slowly, their arms dangling lifelessly by their sides, their sorrowful eyes fixed upon the scene that is about to play out in front of them.

A pistol shot rings out, seizing her back to her senses. The cat is gone and so are the people. They were never really there. The crimson handkerchief lies upon the ground. John and Emmerich are moving towards one another; she did not see who fired first, but John's arm is extended towards his opponent and smoke is pouring from the barrel of his gun. His bloodshot eyes are wide and wild and staring at his empty pistol in disbelief. All other eyes turn to Emmerich, who is still advancing in cautious sidesteps. He is unharmed: John's shot did not connect. An uncertain voice declares, 'A misfire!'

Mr Emmerich raises his arm slowly, pauses for a moment, and fires. The second sound makes her jump even more than the first. For a moment she thinks that he has missed too – that he has fired wide, as he said he might. But then John cries out, a strangled groan of animal rage, and there is a clunk as his spent pistol falls to the dirt and his now empty hand clutches at his arm, just above the elbow.

Emmerich's second shouts, 'A hit! It is done!' and all three men advance at once upon John, holding their hands out towards him – hands of commiseration and concern, as if they were only children playing a game that has got out of hand.

'It's a fair hit and a clean wound,' she hears Mr Fitzgibbon say. John is still on his feet. He removes his fingers from his arm and holds them before his eyes, staring confusedly at his own sticky red blood.

'It is done, John,' Fitzgibbon says. The men have almost reached him now. Cecilia remains rooted where she is, a detached and impassive observer – she is not a part of their play.

A guttural roar burbles up from John's throat. 'Back!' he cries. 'It is not over. We have our second shots.'

'The terms were clear; Mr Emmerich has first blood,' the others protest.

'I can still stand – I would fight on. Or are you afraid to?' John jeers.

'For Christ's sake, Lamb,' says Mr Emmerich. 'It is over. I have no desire to kill you.'

'I have not had my satisfaction.'

'John, resign with dignity,' Fitzgibbon urges.

'I have no dignity left. He has taken it.'

Emmerich arches his shoulders and turns away. 'Gentlemen, we are finished here –'

John cries out again, a howl of rage from the very pit of his being, more wolf than man. He lifts his arm – his injured arm – and aims his remaining pistol almost point-blank at Mr Emmerich, and he fires. Another report roars out, another cloud of smoke splutters, but there is no impact. Another misfire.

The men all recoil in horror. 'You see this man?' Mr Emmerich shouts, 'You all see what he is capable of? He would shoot me down in cold blood!'

John's second pistol clatters to the ground by his feet. He drops into a crouch and then straightens, drawing something concealed from his boot, something long and sharp and shining; he throws himself at his foe, swinging a dagger down in a murderous arc. Emmerich cries and raises his arms to protect himself, and the others rush to his aid, but too late. When John pulls back, both men's shirts are covered in blood. Fitzgibbon and the other man try to restrain him, but John hisses and flails, writhes and lashes until he is free of their grasp. Emmerich collapses to his knees and the men turn to his aid instead. Only Cecilia continues to watch as her husband turns and runs fleeing into the trees, bounding through the branches and the falling leaves, bent and cavorting like a maddened thing, and never once looking back.

40.

Dear Mrs Lamb

I hope that my letter finds you well in body and in mind. I can only imagine how the events of the weeks past must weigh upon you. Though, if I may be permitted to say, when I spoke to you last, you appeared in remarkably healthy spirits all things considered.

I have looked into the matters which you asked of me, to the best of my somewhat limited capabilities. There is no sign of your husband. I have asked around among what contacts I have in this place. Everyone, I fear to say, appears to have heard of what unfolded between Mr Lamb and Mr Emmerich, and yet no one has seen nor heard a word of Mr Lamb since. The popular belief appears to be that he has gone to sea again, under the guise of another name and employed as a common sailor. I am reliably assured that such deception is not difficult to achieve. 'The gallows and the ocean turn away no man', as they say. A glancing arm wound would not attract much attention. If this is true, then I suppose that he could be almost anywhere in the Atlantic by now.

I should add that my attempted enquiries brought me to the desk of Mr Samuel Delahunty, who passes on his kindest regards and begs that you must contact him if he can render any assistance whatsoever. I am told that his good wife asks after you most anxiously.

As to the other party concerned, Mr Emmerich is not dead. I conferred with his physician, doctor to doctor, and I understand that his wounds were neither deep nor serious, and failed to penetrate any vital organs. However, the knife used has poisoned his blood, and he remains confined to his bed in a fever. The physician does not believe that Mr Lamb's weapon was envenomed for this purpose – rather, it was merely dirty. Mr Emmerich is expected to recover, though he shall be lucky if he ever walks again, let alone takes sail.

Concerning the other matters which you explained to me, I hardly know where to begin. I have had several days to think over the crimes you described, committed by Mr Lamb and his crew on their long voyage. Crimes piled atop crimes, conflated by circumstance. And yet I still do not know if I have reached any sort of perspective. I suppose that there is a kind of justice to the mutual fates of Mr Lamb and Mr Emmerich. If one had been shot down and the other walked away from their duel, free and absolved in society's eyes ... Well, I do not like to imagine such an outcome.

But at the same time I cannot shake off the feeling that two more ruined lives does nothing to rebalance the scales of justice. It cannot provide any measure of comfort, or ease the onward path of those who died so unjustly upon the waves. Theirs is the real tragedy here, that much seems clear. And yet we do not even know their names, their stories, where they came from, or who they were. Perhaps they have loved ones who still await their return from sea, ignorant of their miserable fates. We cannot know, and we cannot help them.

It is sometimes difficult to see the hand of God in the events that unfold upon his earth. But then I suppose that it is vanity to even look, is it not? I must imagine that in the span of human history your husband's tale is nothing very unusual. Terrible things have always happened in the dark. Most are simply never brought into the light. I wonder how many bodies are to be found strewn in the footnotes to the stories of great men?

Enough: I am waxing philosophical. Mrs Lamb, when we spoke last, you asked me if it is possible for a person to see into the future, or to glimpse echoes of the past, in the form of apparitions that seem entirely real in the moment. I do not believe that it is. Such tales are as old as time, of course. But I have never heard of a single serious, scientific study that could lend credence to the notion. You asked me whether spectres of the past or future could change or influence the present – appear as warnings or prophecies of what is yet to come, or even intervening more directly. Such as by causing a gun to misfire. Again I say that they cannot: this would defy natural law. But, the more I have thought over our conversation – I do not believe that you really intended these notions to be proposed as questions, did you, Mrs Lamb?

I fear that this letter must close before I lose my credibility as a man of science. I sincerely hope you will reply to me very soon, Mrs Lamb. And perhaps you would permit me to visit you soon after that. In a professional capacity, of course.

Yours sincerely, as ever,
Doctor Clement Mayberry

Her eyes linger upon the name, printed in a careful and precise hand at the bottom of the page, for a moment longer, and then she looks up. She continues to hold the trembling leaf of paper in her fingertips, letting it flap and flutter in the blustering ocean breeze. She listens to the doctor's words repeating in her head without needing to see them on the page. She has read the letter over and over again, and she supposes that she will probably remember what is written there for the rest of her life.

She loosens her fingers by the smallest degree and the sheet is snatched in an instant by the wind, carried spinning up, up into the air, turning and tumbling like an acrobat, first this way and then that, carried out across the crystal waves until it drops silently down into the water and vanishes forever into the rolls of frothing surf.

Close at hand a bell is tolling. A voice is calling out, summoning passengers aboard. She blinks, and loses herself for a moment in the rhythm of the waves, white peaks rising and falling like tiny birds that flap their wings once and then are gone. She lifts her gaze to the ship before her; on its deck there is a cat with sea-green eyes. It looks back at her, winks, and looks away. She inhales a deep lungful of the bracing salt air, and then she begins to walk towards the gangplank.

Acknowledgements

Thank you to everyone at my publisher, HarperNorth, for their hard work and dedication in bringing both *The Water Child* and *The House of Footsteps* to readers. Thanks to my agent, Doug, for taking a chance on my writing and opening the door for me when I didn't have a clue what I was doing.

Most of all I would like to thank my editor, Gen, who didn't bat an eyelid when I turned in a messy first draft of *The Water Child* that bore only a passing resemblance to the original idea that had been pitched. Your wise and patient advice were invaluable in helping me come to understand the story I was trying to tell.

Thanks also to my brothers and sisters-in-law for being my first proof readers, and for putting up with me while I endlessly discuss plot points, character motivation, edits and revisions. I really couldn't do it without you.

* * *

The Water Child is not intended to be a historical novel – the vision of Portugal described in its pages almost certainly never existed, and owes as much to fantasy as to reality. That said, it took a considerable amount of research to get certain details right.

I would particularly like to acknowledge the thesis written by Amy Lynn Smallwood for Wright State University and published on their website, titled *'The Lives Of British Naval Officers' Wives And Widows, 1750–1815'*, which was one of the few historical sources I could find that provided invaluable insight into how Cecilia and her friends might have lived. There are endless books written about the lives of men who have gone to sea, but remarkably few about the women they left behind on land; which only made me all the more determined to tell my story and do my characters justice.

Content warning

Contains themes and instances of violence, animal cruelty and death, pregnancy, child loss, domestic abuse, alcoholism, racism and slavery.

Harper North

Book Credits

HarperNorth would like to thank the following staff and contributors for their involvement in making this book a reality:

Fionnuala Barrett
Samuel Birkett
Peter Borcsok
Ciara Briggs
Sarah Burke
Alan Cracknell
Jonathan de Peyer
Anna Derkacz
Sarah Dronfield
Tom Dunstan
Kate Elton
Simon Gerratt
Monica Green
Natassa Hadjinicolaou
CJ Harter
Megan Jones

Jean-Marie Kelly
Taslima Khatun
Sammy Luton
Rachel McCarron
Molly McNevin
Alice Murphy-Pyle
Adam Murray
Genevieve Pegg
Agnes Rigou
Florence Shepherd
Eleanor Slater
Emma Sullivan
Katrina Troy
Daisy Watt
Sarah Whittaker

For more unmissable reads,
sign up to the HarperNorth newsletter at
www.harpernorth.co.uk

or find us on Twitter at
@HarperNorthUK

Harper
North